The
WRECK

Meg Keneally worked as a public affairs officer, sub-editor, freelance feature writer, reporter and talkback radio producer, before co-founding a financial service public relations company, which she then sold after having her first child. For more than ten years, Meg has worked in corporate affairs for listed financial services companies, and doubles as a part-time SCUBA diving instructor.

She is co-author with Tom Keneally of *The Soldier's Curse* and *The Unmourned*, the first two books in *The Monsarrat* series. Her first solo novel was *Fled*, and *The Wreck* is her second. She lives in Sydney with her husband and two children.

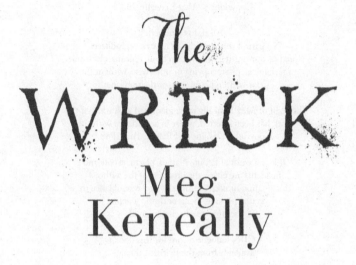

The

WRECK

Meg
Keneally

ZAFFRE

First published in the UK in 2020 by
ZAFFRE
An imprint of Bonnier Books UK
80–81 Wimpole St, London W1G 9RE
Owned by Bonnier Books
Sveavägen 56, Stockholm, Sweden

A CIP catalogue record for this book is
available from the British Library.

ISBN: 978–1–83877–139–3

Also available as an ebook

1 3 5 7 9 10 8 6 4 2

Typeset by IDSUK (Data Connection) Ltd
Printed and bound in Great Britain by Clays Ltd, Elcograf S.p.A.

Zaffre is an imprint of Bonnier Books UK
www.bonnierbooks.co.uk

For Judy, with love and thanks.

Part of this story unfolds on the country of the Gadigal people of the Eora Nation. The author acknowledges them and Traditional Owners of Country throughout Australia, and recognises their continuing connection to land, waters and culture. She pays her respects to their Elders past, present and emerging.

PART ONE

'Rise like lions after slumber
In unvanquishable number!
Shake your chains to earth, like dew
Which in sleep had fall'n on you:
Ye are many – they are few.'

The Mask of Anarchy, Percy Bysshe Shelley

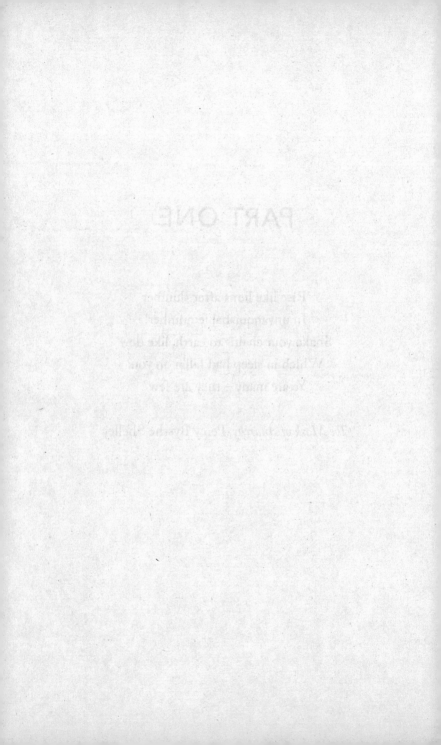

CHAPTER 1
Manchester, August 1819

Some called out to them on the way. Told them to go home. Said they were a rabble. If that was true, they were the merriest rabble anyone had ever seen, and none of them had any intention of going home.

Sarah glanced at the other Female Reform Society members marching with her. They had been easy enough to spot, walking with arms linked and dressed in white, wearing green rosettes or ribbons. Those like Sarah and her mother, who could not afford a white dress and wore their everyday brown or grey, looked like pigeons mixing among swans. Sarah and Emily had their dark hair stuffed beneath white cloth caps.

Whenever Sarah glanced at her mother, she fancied she saw the future of her own face. The skin sagged a little, emptied of any fat that had once resided in its cheeks, while Emily's smile revealed two black voids in the middle of her lower row of teeth. She was, though, still a handsome woman; she stood straight, when others her age were so used to rounding their shoulders they had forgotten there was any other posture, and her grey eyes still constantly searched for objects of interest on which to focus.

They had marched six abreast from home, the crowd swelling as they went, and it took some time for the narrower passageways to disgorge the choking stream of people onto the broader streets.

Sarah hoisted the flag she held a little higher. Today, she had the proud job of being the Society's standard-bearer. The shining white banner depicted a woman modestly dressed in blue, holding up the scales of justice and treading on a serpent over which Sarah had embroidered the word 'corruption'.

As they marched, the cramped cottages and tenements gave way to grander stone buildings, some two storeys high, many with shuttered windows as schools had sent their scholars home and shops had closed for fear of looting.

The crowd was jovial enough. Streams of chattering, laughing people who waved banners, draped arms around shoulders or linked arms, shouting and singing. Among them, though, were those who marched with set jaws and squared shoulders, and others whose heads were lowered, more suited to a mourning procession.

There had been talk, for a long time. Despair behind the single-brick walls of cottages and tenements. Men in the beer houses dropping their mumbled stories into cups. Wails as children were taken by the encroaching dark, discovered still and cold.

The discontent had leaked from the cottages and beer houses into open fields where speakers would call down condemnation on a government that seemed only interested in protecting merchants, with laws to keep out foreign grain that would have made sustenance more than a remote possibility. Then the anger propelled people from motley local gatherings into larger organised assemblies, where shouts and jeers accompanied the calls for annual parliaments and votes for all men.

The assemblies exposed the anger to air, and the smouldering became flame. The magistrates and the government looked fearfully across the Channel, worried the echoes of the bloody uprising in France were making their way across the water.

Now, one of the most famous speakers in all of England would give shape to the people's rage, and he would do it in a Manchester square.

Sarah was walking so fast, she nearly missed the notice. Bills proliferated on the sides of buildings throughout the town, so it could be difficult to pick out notices of interest. This one, though, was pasted over others, aggressive black letters making its intent clear. Some words were larger and darker than others: *ILLEGAL. ABSTAIN. PERIL.*

Sarah tapped her mother's arm, and Emily stopped to read the notice alongside her, as the crowd surged past them, occasionally pushing Sarah flat against the wall.

New Bailey Court-House, 31 July 1819

Whereas it appears by an advertisement in the Manchester Observer *paper of this day that a public and illegal meeting to be addressed by Harold Hartford be convened for Monday, the sixteenth day of August, to be held in the area near St Peter's Church in Manchester, we, the undersigned magistrates, do hereby caution all persons to abstain at their peril from attending such illegal meeting.*

Emily pursed her lips and glared at the notice as though it could feel ashamed. 'It's illegal because they say it is, because they fear it.'

'Why, though?' asked Sarah. 'It's just a talk!'

'Talk is where everything starts. And they know it.'

Sarah had not expected so many, nor had she expected she and Emily would be marching alongside the barouche ferrying the great orator Harold Hartford to the place where he would silence thousands simply by raising a finger, then hold everyone's trembling breath in his hand between that gesture and his first word.

Sarah was unable to resist glancing up at the open carriage from time to time. She had thought the famous man would be tall, severe, perhaps with a hawkish nose down which he could glare at his intellectual inferiors. If she had not seen him riding in the barouche, being borne on a wave of goodwill that seemed to propel the carriage every bit as much as the horse did, she would have thought him unremarkable. His face was clean-shaven, and his mouth neither sneered nor smiled but simply waited to be called upon. Light hair was brushed forward from the crown of his head. He looked, if anything, like a worker she might see at the mill.

The orator, though, was not the only reason she kept glancing at the carriage. Sitting next to the driver, in the white dress she always wore on such occasions, high-necked and demure, was a beaming Delia Burns. The founder of the local Female Reform Society, whose members she referred to as her 'Sisters of the Earth', was clearly having the most marvellous time. She waved a handkerchief at people as they passed, and some waved back at her, though far more at Hartford.

While the Sisters acknowledged Delia with nods and smiles, some in the crowd were less than entranced with the woman in white. The men must have understood they would be ill-advised to insult the woman riding beside Hartford; some women, though, had no such scruples. Sarah heard 'whore' hissing and slithering out of the crowd. One woman yelled, 'What right have you to be there? Leave it to the men who know their business!'

Delia simply wafted her handkerchief in the air and continued beaming.

The banner Sarah carried was one of many, and she could not guess at where people had found the fabrics into which they had stitched their desires: bright blue and green and black, words picked out in white or gold. The female reformers of Royton flew a flag bearing the words, Let Us Die Like Men, and Not Be Sold Like Slaves. Others called for liberty and fraternity, annual parliaments, universal suffrage. One, stark white on black, showed two clasped hands beneath Equal Representation Or Death – Unite and Be Free. Rising above them all was a scarlet cap of liberty on a thin wooden pole, the Latin word *Libertas* inscribed on it in gold.

The crowd moved onto the field in a jostling, chattering river, trailed by pamphleteers and peddlers who saw an easy audience, and an easy profit.

All of the glutted streets fed into a broad square, surrounded by buildings – a Quaker meeting house, a cooper's cottage and some three-storey slab-like structures, and at one end the church that gave the square its name.

Sarah had not been to a carnival, but she imagined this meeting would top any such festivity. Some people were singing and dancing. A group of Irishmen, marching under a green banner, began to dance as a band of musicians struck up a jig.

In the back of the barouche, Hartford stood waving the white hat for which he was famous while grinning at the cheers his gesture brought forth. The adulation seemed to transform him, broadening his shoulders and bringing forth an air of divinity about him. Sarah was unsure if he could survive too long without it.

The crowd became denser and louder as they approached the makeshift stage: two carts tied together and topped with planks. A few men were standing there already, waiting to greet Hartford. He clambered from the carriage onto the hustings and thrust his hat into the air. The noise of the crowd vibrated through the earth and up through Sarah's feet to her stomach. She wouldn't have been surprised to see buildings laid waste.

While Hartford was thrusting his hat and waving, a gentleman already on the stage walked to the side and solicitously offered his hand to Delia, who clambered up and waved as though the shouts and stamping feet were meant for her.

Sarah and Emily jostled closer to the stage and handed up the banner, which Delia waved from side to side, narrowly missing one of the worthies standing next to her. She glanced down, acknowledging Sarah with a smile and inclining her head towards the barouche. After returning the smile, Sarah scrambled into the carriage and stood on the seat that Hartford had vacated; she bent over and dragged her mother up too. The two of them gazed around at the crowd, taking in the colourful banners and excited people, and smiled.

Sarah tried to pick out the faces of her father, Jack, and older brother, Sam, but it was impossible. The field was so packed that anyone who stepped to the side would find their shoe on someone else's toe.

There were some faces that caught her attention, though. In a building across the field, three or four men stared out from the second-storey window of a well-built stone house. She could not see their expressions, but their white bibs – mere dots at this distance – marked them out as magistrates. Their presence indicated that they expected trouble, but Sarah knew they often saw what they expected to see, whether it was there or not.

The sound of the crowd was dying down now; Sarah looked to the stage and saw Hartford waiting for quiet. When the noise had reduced to a faint murmur, he took a deep breath before he cried, 'Friends!'

The crowd roared again, as though the endearment was a finely crafted argument.

Hartford put out his hands, one of which still grasped his hat, palms down until there was silence. 'It seems, fellow countrymen, that the delay in the proceedings has worked in our favour, as far more are now in attendance than anyone expected!'

Again there came a cheering and stamping and shaking of banners.

Sarah glanced over at the magistrates and saw one of them looking down on a piece of paper that he held forward so that his arms stretched out the window. She could not tell from this distance, but it seemed as if he was speaking.

'Friends, we are asking for the freedom that is ours by right,' Hartford said. 'But with that freedom comes responsibility. You may know that I refused to address this gathering unless there were to be no arms borne.'

The cheers gave way to a mutter.

'Looking out now, I see a peaceable people driven to desperation by their oppressors. Let us confound those oppressors with our good behaviour. I ask for your help in keeping the peace here – I ask you to keep order and restrain anyone who seems unwilling to do so. With our exemplary behaviour, we will shame our enemies!'

This was surely the start of what the crowd had been waiting for: a soaring Hartford rant laying out where they had been wronged and how it would be redressed.

When the cheering died down, though, it was not replaced with expectant silence; instead, a susurration passed from one person to the other from the corner of the field. Sarah stared across the heads of the crowd from her vantage point in the carriage. When she saw the cause of the disquiet, her chest tightened until she felt her heart might be stilled. She gripped her mother's arm and pointed to the edge of the field. The yeomen were advancing in their blue uniforms, mounted on the kind of horses only those from the wealthier families could afford.

The Manchester and Salford Yeomanry had only been running for a few years, and it attracted young men who felt anyone with radical leanings was a threat to their very existence. They also felt that violence was the first and best answer to any perceived threat.

The yeomen were sedate at first, almost as though they were trying to nudge the crowd out of the way with the chests of their horses. A few of them were swaying in the saddle, very possibly drunk – they were known for imbibing before an exercise. The one she assumed to be their leader was gripping his horse's neck for balance.

Emily squinted and drew in a breath, then squeezed Sarah's hand. 'They're not a threat, love. They are just here to show off.' Her eyes, though, were frantically sweeping the crowd for Jack and Sam.

Hartford, too, had seen the yeomen. 'Hold tight to your ideals, friends! Give them no provocation!'

The barouche rocked under Sarah's feet. She looked over to the hustings and saw that men in the surrounding crowd were linking arms to form a protective circle around the two carts on which Hartford and Delia were standing. When Sarah glanced at Delia, she gazed back calmly, without a trace of the joy she had shown earlier in the day. Her hands whitened as she gripped the banner.

Sarah's eyes flickered back to the advancing yeomen. She would never know what had set them off – it usually didn't take much. It could have been an insult called from the crowd. The shaking of a banner. Or perhaps nothing at all. Seemingly without warning or provocation, their leader brought the butt of his sword down on someone's head.

It was all the permission the rest of them needed. With a clang of metal, the blades were drawn. The yeomen raised them aloft like a forest of profane Excaliburs.

There was a held breath, a moment of stillness, before the swords arced into the crowd. When a hand rose up to protect its owner, the slash of a blade separated the fingers from the palm. Others were brought down with such force and at such an angle that Sarah wondered if she was watching a life being taken. The violence spread as the yeomen moved further into the field. Thousands of people screamed and began to run.

Then the shots started. From the other end of the field, Hussars were emerging around the corner of the building where the magistrates perched. Mounted like the yeomen, they were less wantonly violent but their presence was far more ominous. Why, Sarah wondered, did the authorities feel the need to deploy trained cavalry against women and children? She had seen them in increasing numbers over the past few weeks, riding as visibly as possible through the streets. She knew their presence was a threat, but she had not allowed herself to believe it would be acted upon.

In front of the Hussars, she could see bayonets and the occasional glimpse of red, as soldiers discharged their weapons into the air above the crowd before lowering them.

Sarah shook her head to clear the fog of disbelief. By sending in both Hussars and the Yeomanry, the magistrates were treating this peaceful crowd as a murderous rabble.

She gripped her mother's arm. 'We need to get away. They are coming, look!'

People ran in all directions, some from the Hussars but right into the path of the yeomen. Sarah saw one brute rein in his horse next to a man who was leaning against a wall and gaping at the carnage. The yeoman plunged his sword into the fellow's chest, then galloped away before he had slid to the ground.

Forcing their way through, dodging the fleeing spectators and stepping over prone forms, a group of constables made their way towards the stage while slashing as indiscriminately with their truncheons as the yeomen did with their swords.

'We are not leaving,' said Emily. Her lower jaw was jutting out a little, and she trembled slightly, but her eyes did not leave the crowd. 'Not without Sam and your pa.'

As Sarah craned her neck, she saw a mother lose her grip on her baby, the infant falling to the ground, trampled by fleeing feet and plunging hooves; the mother dropping to her knees, picking up the small broken bundle, lifting her chin and wailing at the sky. Sarah turned to her mother, grabbing her by the shoulders and bringing her face close to Emily's so she could be heard above the screams and hoofbeats and the ring of clashing metal. 'Ma, we have to go! Pa and Sam will have made it to safety, and those constables might arrest us!' They had seen neighbours arrested for sedition – neighbours who had not returned.

But Emily frowned as though she was struggling to understand her daughter's words.

The constables had reached the hustings, driving their truncheons down on the heads of the men with linked arms. Hartford screamed, 'These people have done nothing wrong! This is murder!' Delia was stabbing the banner staff at the constables trying to storm the stage.

Sarah jumped down from the carriage and tugged at her mother's arm. 'We have to go now! We're no good to them dead, Ma.'

Emily's face grew pale as she looked around at the bloodied and the wounded and those who would never feel pain again. She climbed down and grabbed Sarah's hand, and they began to push their way through the panicking crowd towards the edge of the field.

Sarah looked back at the hustings. Delia was still fending off truncheon blows when a constable grabbed her banner staff, pulled her off balance and sent her to the ground. Defiantly she tried to get up, but wobbled and landed in the dirt again. The constable laughed.

Many of the men who had closed ranks protectively were now insensible or nursing their wounds, and the constables scrambled over them to seize Hartford and the other men on the stage as horses foamed and plunged around them.

Delia was struggling to her feet, seeming as groggy as some of the drunken yeomen. She did not notice the horse rearing above her.

Sarah let go of her mother's hand. In a few steps, she reached Delia and pushed her to the side just as the horse's hooves plunged towards them, striking Sarah in the shoulder. Her teeth came down on her tongue as she hit the ground, and a trickle of blood ran down her chin as she gripped her throbbing arm. Now she and Delia were both in the dust; if they stayed there, they would not live long. Sarah dragged the woman to her feet and asked, 'Can you walk?' Delia, bleeding from a gash on her cheek, gave a slow nod, then unsteadily plunged into the stream of fleeing people.

It was only when Sarah had turned three times, in increasingly desperate circles, that she realised her mother was no longer nearby.

CHAPTER 2

Under a lightening sky that morning, Sarah and her mother had said goodbye to her father and brother outside their cottage. It was smaller than the one in which Sarah had been born, a half-remembered place where nothing was plentiful but where hunger pangs had not awoken her. The four of them had worked in that home, her mother spinning and her father weaving, taking pride in the snippets of fabric they produced. When Sarah was not peeling potatoes or sweeping out the cottage, she had watched her parents closely, trying to see what magic they were using to transform cotton into thread and thread into cloth. They built a reputation for fine, close-woven work and commanded a decent price for it. But when power looms appeared in greater numbers in Manchester's cotton mills – great steam-powered gnashers doing the work of many men – the demand dried up, and the McCaffrey family had to trudge every day to attend to the beasts that had reduced their livelihood.

They now lived in Angel Meadow, a part of Manchester where, it was said, only the insane, stupid or desperate went. Sarah supposed they were among the latter.

Their cottage, its walls a single brick thick, at least had a fireplace, but there was precious little wood to burn. They slept and ate in one room on sheaves of straw – although more often than not they ate at the mill, biscuits soaked in milk that had to be consumed quickly before they became tainted with cotton dust.

Angel Meadow was noisy with a certain type of life. Scuttlers spilled out of the beer houses, shaping up to each other on the street as others laid bets. Pigs wandered in and out of tenement doors, snuffling up piles of refuse. Prostitutes barely glanced at the rare man who could afford to lie with them as he handed over coins.

There was also more death than they had been accustomed to in their old home.

Emily was angered that her children frequently stepped over the bodies of the starved and diseased. They should, she often said, be spared that in the tenderness of their youth. There was a shrillness to her as she lectured Jack on what her children were being denied, what they were forced to endure. Sometimes, if she was particularly tired, she could not hide her fear that one day she would encounter Sarah or Sam lifeless in the street.

When Sarah and Emily had left for the assembly that morning, Sarah had thought it might be the first time since the cotton mill was built that no one had been there on a Monday to feed steam and thread to the spinning mules. Was it the first Monday on which the smokestacks had not injected their fumes into the air? Certainly it was the first she could remember since the gates of Hodgkins & Sons in Ancoats had opened to her and swallowed an eight-year-old girl.

Sam, a few years older than Sarah, had moved from foot to foot, impatient. He had his father's height and fairness, and those passing them would not have known he and Sarah were from the same family had they not been huddled so closely together. Jack was also eager to get moving; these past few years he had seen his family eat food not fit for dogs, and watched his children gradually waste, becoming creatures of sharp angles rather than gentle curves.

'You'll be all right, the both of you?' he asked his wife.

'Sarah and I? We're marching with the Sisters – couldn't be safer. It's you two little flowers I worry about.'

Sam chuckled, and even Jack managed a small smile.

✦

There had been, Sarah would learn later, upwards of sixty thousand people in St Peter's Field. But now, less than half an hour after the Yeomanry had started its assault, only a few hundred remained. Some were wandering in a haze; others were bending over insensible or lifeless forms, turning them onto their backs, exhaling with relief or gasping in despair.

Sarah walked around the field, yelling at the top of her lungs, 'Ma! Sam! Pa!' Inwardly she cursed everyone she saw for not being her family.

She was so engrossed that she jumped when a hand clasped her shoulder.

'Thank God,' said Sam, hugging her. Sarah's cheek was on his chest, but she could tell by the thickness in his voice that he was crying. 'Where's Ma?'

She shook her head. 'We got separated.'

'Pa and I too,' said Sam. 'They'll have made it to safety, of course.' He nodded, obviously trying to convince himself of this.

Keeping in sight of each other, Sarah and Sam went from one form to the next. Men who had poured out the last of their blood into the earth, some unrecognisable thanks to the horses' hooves. A woman, pregnant, lying on her side; another with her abdomen sliced open at an angle, probably the result of a wild flail. Here and there a child – perhaps they had started the morning aloft on their fathers' shoulders, brought to see the great Mr Hartford so that one day they could tell their grandchildren.

Jack must have been intent on getting as close to Hartford as possible. He had been like that at the other assemblies the family had attended, angling his body sideways, worming his way eagerly through a crowd, dragging a protesting Emily by the hand. There was no other way to explain his location, not fifty feet from the cart where Hartford had started to rail against oppression just before it made itself manifest.

Across Jack's chest there was a scarlet line, punctuated by the wound that had killed him: a deliberate stab, not a thoughtless slash. In the dim light from the cottage hearth, Sarah had watched that chest rise and fall in sleep. She had heard it fill with air and eject songs or jokes, endearments, shouts of anger. There was an ominous, disjointed quality to the world she had entered, one in which no more sounds would be carried out of her father's slack mouth. But she found herself watching his chest for a tiny lift she knew would not come. Eventually the stillness became unbearable, and she balled her fists and roughly rubbed her eyes.

When she opened them, she saw her mother.

After Sarah had dashed back to save Delia, Emily had not gotten far. Sarah must have walked right past her, desperate to find the living, not wanting to see the dead.

Emily was around ten yards from the hustings, her chest caved in from a hoof-strike. Perhaps the same hoof from which Sarah had saved Delia.

Sarah looked up, opened her mouth, tried to call her brother's name.

Her legs lost all intention, and she was on her knees, Sam drawn to her by a sound she had not intended to make, a keen she did not recognise. He knelt beside her but made no attempt to embrace her, to comfort her.

Swaying a little, he seemed not to notice the tears dripping from his chin and the end of his nose into the grass.

'This is their answer to our requests,' Sarah said, taking great draughts of air into her lungs to steady herself. 'This is the answer of the Prince Regent, the prime minister, the Cabinet.' She curled beside her mother, laid her head on the ruined chest. 'This is what they do when we ask for food, for rights,' she whispered. 'What we are worth.'

'It cannot go unanswered in return,' Sam said after a while, his voice rasping. 'It cannot.'

'It will not,' said a man who had come to stand beside them without Sarah noticing. He put his hand on Sam's shoulder and helped him up. The hand, half hidden by a lace cuff, was then extended to Sarah; she took it and was raised to her feet. She looked along the arm until her gaze reached a long nose that came down almost to his top lip. Her eyes lifted to his high brow and swept-back, greying hair. 'My name is Aidan Briardown. I will make sure your dear ones are seen to. And I promise you, those in power will have our answer soon enough.'

∗

Sam and Sarah stood by two jagged holes cut into the earth while the wooden boxes were lowered in.

Briardown had paid for a rough cloth pall and some bearers. Father Denny dispassionately said the rites; Sarah had seen him display far more emotion at other funerals, but he had spoken the words so many times over the past few days, it seemed as though he had forgotten their meaning.

Most who might have come to pay their respects were back at the mill. Some had been docked for missing a Monday's work, and there were many burials to attend.

But Delia came. Staring at her, Sarah felt a ripple of shock. She had never noticed before quite how short, how pale, how sandy Delia was. And now she seemed to have shrunk into one of the hollow-eyed creatures Sarah saw daily on the mill floor.

It was Delia who had started the reform society. Delia who had appeared in her white gown at assembly after assembly, leading a phalanx of women to the hustings, presenting the speaker with a green cap of liberty to bind him to her cause, and talking to people who had never heard a woman speak in public before.

'Dear Sisters of the Earth,' Delia would begin in her high, clear voice. Then she would talk of ragged elderly parents dying with the stink of corruption in their nostrils. Of near-naked, wretched children, their hungry cries decreasing in force until the day when the sun rose to silence. Of the corruption that slid into parliament through the rotten boroughs, which sent to Westminster men with loud voices but few constituents.

Towards the end of her speeches, when she was about to reveal her true purpose, the woman in white would pause, drawing back her shoulders. 'Dear Sisters, I speak now to the wives, mothers and daughters of the upper and middling classes of society. Our fate will soon be yours. When we are mixed with the silent dust, you will become the next victims to be chased to misery and death!'

Delia and the other female reformers would proceed back to the Union Rooms, the sparse meeting place of the society, and wait, often for hours. It was rarely in vain.

Women would trickle in, dressed in finer fabrics than those that touched Sarah's skin. They would form a queue in front of the table where Delia sat, smiling, and give their names in voices ranging from haughty brays to apologetic whispers. Many of them seemed uncertain, anxious, perhaps fearful of discovering they had joined a den of radicals rather than a group of like-minded women. All were drawn to the Sisters of the Earth by fears of their children's faces transformed into stretch-skinned masks and of their parents dropping from life in lice-infested rags.

Sarah had seen Delia command audiences, silence catcallers with a calm gaze, answer any challenge with determined conviction. Some of the challengers, after Delia had sweetly rebuffed their objections, simply sat and fumed. The fumers were no trouble, though – it was the underminers who were the problem.

'Female suffrage?' Mrs Bell, a newer member, had scoffed at one of their meetings. 'How ridiculous. It would never be allowed, and most women are sheep anyway and would vote as their husbands told them.'

'In Westminster they care not for us,' Delia answered. 'They care not whether we are starving. They simply care that the merchants are happy to have no competition from imported grain. Why do they care what the merchants think? Because they fear that a united effort from the merchant class will unseat them! And what can we do? Can *we* unseat them? Make them fear us? Only if we have the vote!'

'Fear you?' Mrs Bell retorted. 'They are laughing at you!' She waved a sheet of newsprint in the air, then strode to the front of the room and placed it on a small table for all the Sisters to see.

The caricature showed three women on stage, all with scandalously revealing dresses. One woman was straddling a stick with an elongated, phallic cap of liberty dangling from the end. Another had her arms in the air so that her breasts were almost fully visible. The third was pointing at the cap on its stick, declaiming: 'Dear Sisters of the Earth, I feel great pleasure in holding this thing, as our sweethearts and husbands are such fumblers at the main thing, we must of course take things into our own hands.'

Sarah glanced at Delia, who kept her head down, gazing at the parody as her cheeks reddened. When she looked up, Sarah realised they were coloured not from shame but from anger. 'I welcome this,' Delia said, 'for a wounded animal attacks.' She had drawn herself up to her full height.

She looks fearsome, Sarah realised.

'Well, Sisters, it appears there is a certain kind of man who is diverted by the sight of a woman on a stage. Most of Manchester will be at that meeting in St Peter's Field – including, most likely, whomever this fellow is. We must ensure that we give him what he wants!'

Now, standing next to her parents' graves, Sarah could not reconcile the woman who had led them to the assembly with this shadow who occupied only the space her stature allowed. As she began to walk over to them, Sam gave Sarah a brief nod and went towards the battered gate, its timbers lined with deep troughs from exposure to the weather, set in the low, moss-stained stone wall. Sarah knew he did not trust himself around Delia. He was, she feared, sliding away from her.

Only two heartbeats now, in their small cottage. No sudden snores from Jack or quiet remonstrations from Emily. But even with only the two of them, the cottage was too small to contain Sam's anger. He had taken, these past few nights, to stalking out, slamming the door so hard she feared it would splinter, then returning late with a split lip and a bruised cheek.

This was, Delia told Sarah, the third burial she had attended since the massacre. 'We lost, Sister,' she said. 'I am sorry. Nothing will change.'

Sarah shook her head and took Delia's cold hands in hers. She looked down at the dainty fingers that had wafted a handkerchief in the air, now bleeding around the nails where Delia had clearly been picking at them.

'No, this will not end. It is not over,' she cried out. Her cheeks were wet but she made no move to dry them. The holes in which her parents lay were now being filled in by a man who could have been digging in a garden for all the care he was showing. 'My parents will not have died for nothing. They're martyrs!'

Delia smiled weakly. 'They are, of course.' It was the kind of empty comfort usually offered to the bereaved, but under the circumstances its insincerity was insulting.

Sarah's jaw clenched, and she snatched her hands away. 'It would be you they're putting in the earth now, if I hadn't come for you!'

Delia, whose eyes were welling up, looked to the graves.

'My ma hated the damp and the cold, and now she will lie in it forever! And you mewl about how we've lost. You dishonour her, her sacrifice, and my pa's, by giving up.'

'No! I'm sorry, Sister!'

'I am not your sister.'

Delia's mouth dropped open. She reached out for Sarah's hands again, but Sarah turned her back and walked towards the churchyard gate where Sam was waiting. On the other side of the low stone wall, Briardown was standing near a cart harnessed to a low-bellied horse that was cropping the weeds. He had not attended the burial, despite having paid for it. She wondered if he was here to offer condolences, or to collect on the debt.

She nodded to him. 'I am grateful for your generosity in letting us see our parents decently buried. We both are,' she said, glancing towards Sam who was kicking at the dirt of the tree-canopied lane.

'You are most welcome,' Briardown said. 'They are martyrs. They deserved a far grander burial, but I did what I could.'

Sarah nodded towards the cart. 'You are leaving?'

'Yes. And I am very much hoping you will come with me. Both of you.'

Sam raised his head quickly. 'Come where? You're not suggesting we should leave Manchester?'

'Honestly, I don't think you have a choice,' Briardown said. 'You were prominent during the assembly, Miss McCaffrey. I was in the middle of the crowd and could see you quite clearly – which means others did as well. Standing in that carriage, you were very near to Orator Hartford. And I am sure you have heard what happened to him.'

Sarah hadn't, but was not going to admit it. She folded her arms and stared at him.

Briardown sighed. 'You know, some of us tried to talk him out of his short-sighted insistence on banning arms. Now he's in prison.'

'And you believe I might be arrested too,' said Sarah, an edge of scepticism to her voice. But she knew it was possible. Neither she nor Sam had gone back to the mill since the massacre. There had been her parents' funeral to arrange – and there had been a nagging fear of being greeted by a constable.

'Miss McCaffrey, an excess of caution has saved my life on numerous occasions,' Briardown said. 'I do not believe you can take your continued freedom for granted.'

Sarah's eyes were on Briardown – the man reeked of superiority – but she felt Sam's arm around her shoulder. He leaned down to whisper in her ear. 'He is right. You know he is.'

She did not respond. But she knew Sam's night-time forays into the streets, which had earned him some scuttler-inflicted wounds, might put him in prison even if she stayed free.

Briardown cleared his throat, reached into his breast pocket and drew out a small volume. 'May I ask, have either of you heard of the writings of Thomas Spence?'

When Sam shook his head – Sarah was not familiar with the name but did not want to give Briardown a reason to sneer – she perceived the hint of a smirk on the older man's lips.

He opened the book, then cleared his throat again. 'Mr Spence says that revolution would be "more exhilarating and reviving to the hunger-bitten and despairing children of oppression, than a benign and sudden spring to the frost-bitten earth, after a long and severe winter". No talk of asking nicely. No talk of avoiding provocation.

I heard what you said to your friend, Miss McCaffrey, and you are right – it is not over. Not as long as men of good heart are willing to join us.' He beamed at Sam.

Her brother would, Sarah thought, be extremely useful to someone like Briardown. A young man made malleable by rage. And she had noticed, through her grief, Briardown's approaches to other mourners on the field that day: they had all been men.

'And women of good heart?' she asked.

Briardown inclined his head and gave her a smaller smile. 'Naturally.'

Sarah knew the man was not there for her. There was, though, a debt she owed to the woman and man lying nearby, now completely covered by earth they should still be walking on. She leaned against Sam and whispered, 'Do you want to go?'

'I do not know. But I can tell you this – I do not want to stay. I do not think I would see out the year. And if I am to die . . . well, why not in the service of bringing pain to them who put our parents in the churchyard?'

Sarah nodded. She turned to Briardown. 'Where?'

'Well, as close to the heart of the serpent as we can get,' said Briardown. 'Which means, of course, London.'

CHAPTER 3
Marylebone, London, May 1820

No one noticed Sarah in her grey laundress's skirts. She wandered the streets of Marylebone, seemingly aimless, as the sky drew low around her.

She was not supposed to attract attention, and it wasn't hard to follow that command as she made her way through the crowd, turning side-on to make way for a woman carrying buckets of water from the nearby pump, ducking to avoid a ball kicked by one of a group of boys playing nearby. She couldn't resist the occasional greeting, though: a nod to another servant, a smile at the woman who sold cabbages here, her wares piled on a rickety table in front of her.

The message had been waiting for her that morning when she had opened the kitchen door of the grand house in which she now served, in order to accept a delivery from the baker's boy. No one noticed that he only ever came on days she was there, and that he only knocked at precisely eleven in the morning. The basket he handed her gave off the distracting waft of freshly baked bread,

31

but her interest lay in what was under the loaves. That morning it was scratched into the fibres at the bottom of the basket, faint but visible to someone who knew to look. One word: *Tonight.*

There was also a folded note where there had never been one before. Sarah quickly stuffed it down her shirt; she did not want to confuse it with the four slips of paper that were already in her pocket.

Now she stopped in front of a terrace and glanced around briefly before descending the steps and knocking three times at the door. She extracted one of the slips from her pocket, slid it under the door and moved along without awaiting an answer. A few streets later she took out another note and bent to slide it into a slightly opened window.

If anyone had been watching her, they might have wondered what was on the little missives. But when she stopped outside a tavern and languidly started drawing in the hoof-churned dirt with a stick, they probably would have decided the papers contained witless ramblings. It was like that with servants, sometimes.

Each note was crudely inked with a black circle, nothing more. It represented an alchemical symbol known as an ouroboros: a serpent eating its own tail in a cycle of destruction and renewal.

Sarah had only seen it herself for the first time after she and Sam moved to London. Briardown had told her its name. This symbol was unknown by most, and the message it carried was intended for only a few, who understood its import well enough.

In Sarah's wake, hands were unfolding the papers, then cloaks were being drawn tight around shoulders. For some it would be a long walk in the chilly evening, and no man among them could afford a coach.

✦

Sarah always kept watch during the meetings, crouched by the opening in the loft wall, having exchanged her dress for boys' breeches and one of Sam's shirts. She had a good view of the street and of the Horse & Coach tavern opposite. At the sight of a soldier or a Bow Street Runner, she would signal to the others with a nod. Candles would be snuffed with licked fingers, seats abandoned, and Sam would position himself at the top of the loft's narrow, steep stairs, ready to play a confused tenant should anyone hammer at the door below. They would wait, then, in silence, for half an hour or more, until Briardown nodded to Sarah, who would rekindle the candles with a taper lit in the low fire at one end of the loft.

The stable off Edgware Road, flat-roofed and grimy, had once housed cows on the ground floor. The upper floor, which hosted the gatherings organised by Briardown, had been a storage space for hay bales hoisted through a large opening in its wall, now covered in canvas. The smell of the cows remained, ancient excrement ground into the timbers, mocking those who met here with a reminder of the meat they rarely tasted.

This was more than a gathering place, though. After the men eventually left, Sarah and Sam would move the rough wooden table and chairs aside, spread out their bed-rolls, douse the candles and the lantern, and whisper to each other until they fell asleep.

With his own rough brand of love, Sam had coaxed her along these past six months. He would hold her after she gasped awake from a dream of their parents, shaking to find herself in a London loft rather than a Manchester cottage, gulping down sobs at the renewed knowledge that the world no longer included her mother and father. The dragging grief had gradually begun to subside. It still waited for her around corners, but there were moments now, sometimes whole minutes, when she forgot about the last time she had seen her parents.

She supposed this little collection of radicals was the closest she had to a family, now. Sam certainly felt so. Briardown had shown him some of Thomas Spence's works, and Thomas Paine's *Rights of Man*, and he read them until the candle flickered into darkness each night, occasionally waking her to share a passage he loved.

Briardown had lured his men with food and promises, collected them, and placed them precisely. This group – five men and Sarah, although Briardown did not include her in his calculations – was, he claimed, just one of a number of thickets of brave, visionary citizens sprouting across London. They probably passed their brothers in the street or sat near them in coffee houses and taverns, but Briardown said it was best for everyone that most of them could not identify one another if captured and questioned.

Sarah, still crouched, wiped her hand on the greasy floor beside her, then rubbed it against her cheek. She wanted her face to be less visible as she peered out of the loft. But she had another reason: if the government saw her as refuse, she would let them – after all, why should they fear her – right up until they felt the bite of metal against their necks.

'I'd keep two of the heads, for Westminster Bridge,' one of Briardown's earliest recruits, Tully, was saying. 'The others . . . I don't know, find a hill to roll them down most probably.' He chuckled and rubbed the big mound of his belly. It had already shrunk since their last meeting. In his job as a butcher's apprentice, he had supplied meat to some of the finest London families, including Cabinet members, and had taken the occasional choice cut for himself. Now, though, the butcher had no more need of an apprentice, particularly one with such a liberal approach to inventory.

'And this is why you're unwed,' said Sarah, looking over at him with a smile. 'Most girls don't like talk of beheadings.'

Tully jovially blew her a mocking kiss. He had decided that she was just as much his younger sister as Sam's – and she didn't mind, as it allowed her to wreath criticisms in affectionate sisterly scorn.

'Honestly, Tully,' she said, 'you seem far more in love with this enterprise than you could ever be with a woman. Mind your lust for it doesn't lead you to the gallows.'

Sam, next to Tully, reached over to pat the butcher's belly. Sam's whole body probably contained less fat than one of Tully's legs. He turned in his chair towards his sister. 'You'd marry him, wouldn't you, Sare? If he wasn't so bloodthirsty.'

A gust through the makeshift window blew her long dark hair over her face. She tied it in a knot at her neck, wrinkling her nose at her brother. 'Do we not have more pressing matters? Can we find Tully a bride, well . . . after?'

Sam might have responded, but Sarah didn't hear it – her ears had identified the footsteps she had been waiting for. They were light and quick, the soles of worn shoes barely troubling the loft stairs, their owner hungry but still strong.

'Who are we finding a bride for?' His voice was still stretching to reach into the corners of its final manly shape, but it and its owner had matured greatly since Sarah had first met him. A young man possessing a strong jaw dusted with ginger stubble was rapidly replacing the boy who had not known how to manage his long limbs. His brows were drawn together more often than they had been, but the blue eyes beneath still darted with curiosity. She had yet to see them reflect the deadened acceptance in some other men's gazes.

Henry Landers: the only one here who treated her as a young lady, not a sister or a resource or an annoyance; the only one who made the effort to acknowledge her each time he arrived.

She returned his smile. She had seen too much, lost too much, to play the coquette and cast shy glances. At the cotton mill, workers had filed past the gaffer each morning with their heads down as though they did not deserve the sight of his blotchy, whiskered face, but Sarah had always looked directly at him – she would never, she had vowed, let anyone tell her where to aim her eyes. Henry, though, presented a far more pleasant sight than the gaffer had.

She and Sam had met Henry shortly after arriving in London half a year earlier. Briardown had taken them straight to the stable, where Henry had been waiting to greet them. As the youngest of the men, he had been given the task of sweeping out all the unnameable substances that had gathered in corners during the place's long vacancy.

Henry had stared at Sarah then, too, although she hadn't noticed at first. After the long journey to London, four days past a blur of hedges and fields and trees, it had taken her a moment to realise the cart, with Briardown at the reins, was no longer moving. She certainly had no attention left to spare for the young man leaning on a broom, until he threw it aside and strode towards her, taking off his brown coat and settling it around her shoulders.

She looked at him and smothered a gasp. The lad had appeared like summer lightning in a world she had thought leached of kindness. Her gaze had followed his chin past the planes of his cheek, roughened with stubble and bearing the shallow indentations that told of a childhood marked by the pox. The eyes set in such a head were often dull, but his were the blue of slate after rain, beneath ginger eyebrows drawn together in concern.

As he helped her down from the cart, the cramps in her legs made her stumble against him. He chuckled, and she looked up, ready to rebuke him for the mockery. There was none, though – only a man who had given away his coat on a cool evening. Sturdy, if the firmness of his chest was anything to go by.

She soon discovered Henry was around her age, but he had been alone in the world since he was just fifteen. His mother, he told Sarah, had died because the government found this preferable to allowing her to eat imported grain. Sarah had seen many motherless boys in Manchester: blank eyed and shambling, or taking out their grievances in drunken brawls. Henry, though, had managed to cling to a sense of purpose. His mother had taught him to read – not a common skill among poor young men, and enough to get him work as a printer's apprentice. Now he was useful to a group that relied on anonymous pamphlets.

'We're looking for a bloodthirsty girl to marry Tully,' Sam told Henry.

Henry, though, was not paying attention to Sam, his gaze lingering on Sarah. He pressed his lips together and took off his rough wool jacket, the colour of oatmeal. He strode over and settled it around Sarah's shoulders. 'Still cold, these nights,' he said quietly.

She shrugged it off and tried to return it. 'Won't you need it?'

'I will be bathed in the fiery breath of Briardown,' he said, then went over to the table. When his back was turned to her, Sarah buried her face in the cloth and inhaled deeply.

At the table, Henry began fidgeting with a little leaden man that he must have taken out of his pocket before surrendering his jacket. He had made several such figurines from worn-out letter blocks, hammering them together, shaping them, colouring them with ink when he could get it, scratching features into them. Sometimes he worked on them in the loft while waiting for Briardown to arrive, frowning in concentration, unaware Sarah was watching him from the shadows near the window. People might pretend to be all sorts of things, she thought, but the pretence disintegrated when they did not know they were being observed. In all the time she had watched Henry, she had never seen his face contort into a sneer. Now he was just a man smiling down at a toy he had crafted, his red hair almost gold in the lamplight.

She had once asked to see the figurines, so he had laid four of them out on the table. After she settled on the chair beside him, he pointed to the one with a red splash on its torso and a sharp protrusion she assumed to be a bayonet. '*Soldat* – soldier.' To Henry, French was the language of freedom, and he picked up whatever words he could. '*Boulanger* – baker,' gesturing to one that held a misshapen lump of lead pastry. '*Voleur* – thief,' tapping a stooped, skulking figure. And last, one with white trousers and a blue splash of a shirt: '*Marin* – sailor.'

She had smiled. 'But where's the woman?'

'I haven't the skill,' he had said. 'I wouldn't insult you.' He had cleared the pieces off the table quickly, then proceeded to stare at her for the rest of the evening as though sizing her up as a model. She resisted the temptation to look away whenever his eyes caught her examining him just as closely. Instead, she gave him a smile that spoke of a confidence she did not feel.

Paper was scarce, but Henry brought her offcuts from the printers, and in the evenings when the candles were low and no men had gathered, she would take out her pencil stub to sketch the little figurines and inscribe their French names. She would always clear them away when he was expected – he didn't need to see her imprecise pen strokes.

'Anyway, enough about wives,' Henry said now. 'Most of us can't afford one. And where will you find a woman who can't smell, Sam?'

People did marry without being able to afford it, Sarah thought. Perhaps this was a fact with which she needed to acquaint Henry.

Briardown had arranged work for Sam as a tanner's apprentice, and now he always smelled of piss, a tool of his trade, and looked as though he had not washed his stained hands. But he was insistent that he would never again work at a mill.

Sarah heard more steps on the loft stairs, heavy ones unconcerned with concealing their approach: Briardown.

CHAPTER 4

This was not a regular meeting – there was no such thing, as it would have been far too dangerous for them to converge at the same time each week.

Sarah had read the note already; of course she had. She did not recognise the hand, but that was not unusual – Briardown seemed to have a broad network of informers, and information arrived tucked into the heads of cabbages like those sold by the woman she had seen earlier, or in a scuttle of coal, or a basket of bread. She remembered her mother's voice when Sarah or Sam had fidgeted while practising their letters: 'No matter what they take, they can't take what you know. Not unless they take your life along with it.' Emily had been alone among the women of their acquaintance in demanding her daughter be taught to read.

The note told of preparations for an event at the home of a senior member of the government – no source, no date, no time, simply that the event was to take place.

Briardown marched over to the table, scraping back a chair and throwing himself into it. Another man, who had followed him in, positioned himself behind Briardown's right shoulder.

Albert Tourville was the only one among them who had experienced a real revolution. He had told them his parents had sent their young son to England in the arms of a fleeing cousin, fearful that the tide of rebellion in Paris would not discriminate between insurgents and oppressors. He had never seen or heard from his mother and father again.

Tourville glanced at Sarah over his bulbous nose, and when she nodded a greeting he contorted his mouth into an approximation of a smile.

The others had gone silent, waiting for Briardown to speak. He said nothing, staring at each of his men in turn from beneath his extravagantly bushy eyebrows.

Tully hated silence. 'We've been talking—

'I come here every week,' Briardown said, as though no one else had spoken. 'I hear you all talk – and talk and talk – about the starved, about the lack of recourse for them or any of us, about lack of suffrage as though we are less worthy of the vote than those who happened to be born into land. I hear of your grievances with the King and his ministers, your desire for revolution, your willingness to hurl your lives and souls into the mangle to achieve such an end.'

Sarah was no good at keeping questions to herself. As a child she had been beaten by the parish priest for asking how he knew the wine had turned to blood when it still tasted like wine. This had seemed to her a reasonable question, and ever since she had wondered if those who objected to questions did not have reasonable answers.

'And why shouldn't we talk?' she said now.

Briardown raised an eyebrow at her as though a chair had started speaking.

'You've seen them, Mr Briardown. Likely stepped over a few on the way here. Those who can't pay even for scraps. The Prince Regent – well, the King now – and the prime minister might view them as human waste, but we do not. And you've been given no reason to doubt our sincerity.'

'Whether we have, or have not, is immaterial,' Tour-ville said, assuming a right to speak for Briardown that the leader did not correct. 'The point is, though, your chance has arrived. Your chance to prove that all that rum-soaked talk has done more than foul the air.' He took a scrunched newspaper cutting from his jacket pocket. Slowly, as though enjoying the process, he unfolded it and set it on the table.

Tully picked it up, squinting. His eyes, daily focused on the slicing of meat and splintering of bone, did not do well with small print and low light.

Henry reached out to snatch it. He cleared his throat. 'A dinner to accommodate secretaries of state from His Majesty's British Cabinet is to be held at the home of the president of the council, Lord Hargreaves, in Grosvenor Square.'

Briardown smiled. 'You see? Now I will be damned if I do not believe there is a God. I have often prayed that those thieves may be collected all together, in order to give us a good opportunity to destroy them, and now God has answered my prayer.'

The table, suddenly, was engulfed in the murmurings of the men.

Such events were not unheard of, nor was their public announcement. This dinner was, in fact, the kind of event Briardown had been waiting for: a gathering away from Westminster of those who had created the miasma of hunger and suffering that now hung in the air for so many of the governed.

Sarah had transferred the note from the baker's boy into her breeches. She extracted it now, stood up and cleared her throat. 'I received this today.' She opened it and was about to read it aloud when Briardown snatched it from her hand.

He glanced at it briefly and looked up. 'I had been expecting this. Preparations are being made. Orders are being placed.'

'Is this intelligence any better than the announcement in the newspaper?' asked Sarah.

Her question quieted the men. Briardown glanced at her, then away. She knew she was an annoyance to him, only here because of Sam – so she might as well be as annoying as possible.

Tourville aimed another kind of smile at her. He had a collection of them, none of which was called forth by genuine joy or amusement. This one was probably intended to be indulgent, as a parent would smile at a child using a stick as a musket.

'One generally finds,' said Briardown, 'that receiving the same information from two distinct sources tends to make it reliable.'

'Oh, does one?' Sarah asked. 'Does this information not seem a little too . . . fortuitous?' She had selected the type of word that Briardown would use – half in mockery, half in hope it would soften him to the message delivered in a female voice. 'It's unusual to have such luck, Mr Briardown.'

Sam smiled at her and nodded upwards. Their mother would have approved.

'Perhaps someone is sympathetic to our cause,' Tully said. 'And highly placed – high enough, at any rate, to know things others don't. Of course, they're not going to introduce themselves. They'd be no good to us if they did.'

'Well, it does seem rather a confirmation, I must say,' said Tourville.

'Confirmation? It's a clarion trumpet!' said Tully. 'Begging for us, they are, all of those exposed necks, red from baths drawn by their servants, waiting for the caress of my knife.' He slapped Henry on the back and laughed, then withdrew a sharpened blade from his jacket and fiddled with it, deliberately pricking his thumb so a bead of scarlet emerged.

Sam laughed and said, 'We can't just send Tully in to swing his chopper around.'

Sarah closed her eyes against the sudden wave of pain she knew would break over her. She had seen men swinging blades above their heads before, and their shadows came galloping back far too easily.

'We have a week,' said Briardown, 'and we should use every second of it in planning. Both the attack, and what comes after.'

'But the people will take care of what comes after,' said Henry.

'The people,' said Sarah. 'You all seem to believe they will rise up as easily as they exhale. But if they haven't done so by now—'

'They will,' said Tully. 'They haven't heard the rallying cry till now, is all. They've shown themselves willing, though. They have rioted for food. They have emptied storehouses.' He looked at Sam. 'They have broken frames in cotton mills up North. When they see those heads they'll know it's time, and they will break over Westminster until it is rubble.'

CHAPTER 5

After the others had left, Sarah and Sam sat side by side in the loft, their legs dangling over the edge.

'To hear them talk,' said Sarah, 'every fishmonger and cooper and cobbler is sitting around with half an ear cocked for a signal to grab a cosh or a pitchfork and take to the streets. But do people know they're supposed to rise up?'

'They know things cannot be borne as they are,' said Sam. 'Nothing has changed. It's grown worse. When did you last taste meat?'

Sarah frowned. They were better off than many; Sam brought in enough money for oatmeal, occasionally flour for bread. They were poorer than they had been in Manchester, but free use of the loft meant they were able to survive.

Meat, though. She could smell it sometimes as she walked past some of the finer houses, tendrils of cold from the cobbles reaching up to envelop her foot through a hole in her shoe. Her mouth would fill with moisture that trickled down her throat in cruel mimicry of the juices from a roasted lamb leg. Every so often she worked as a laundress in the bowels of one of those houses, where she sometimes scrubbed gravy out of tablecloths. She chose to believe it was gravy she was scraping off the bedsheets, too, and distracted herself by pretending her mother had spun the threads and her father had woven the cloth.

'Meat,' she said longingly. 'Not since long before Ma and Pa . . .'

Sam squeezed her shoulder. She squeezed his, and he winced. She grimaced; sometimes she forgot that he had been beaten at the cotton mill when he was barely ten years old, for the supposed crime of dropping a handful of bobbins. His shoulder had never fully healed. 'I'm sorry,' she said. 'I keep forgetting. So much has happened.'

Sam shook his head. 'Don't worry, it doesn't hurt so much anymore.'

She knew he was lying, had heard him grunt when he rolled over in his sleep, clutching as he always did a now-grimy ribbon that had belonged to Emily.

Running towards a spinning mule, Sam had tripped, and spilled the armful of bobbins he had been carrying, which rolled towards the skirting boards and under the machines. When Mr Harris, the gaffer, discovered the mule was no longer spinning, Sam stammered out an apology. Harris listened until the boy stopped speaking. Then he raised his cane. When it connected with Sam's shoulder, the boy let out a yelp and tears sprang from his eyes.

As soon as Sarah heard the *thunk* of the cane, she darted forward. But she wasn't quick enough; the gaffer brought the cane down on Sam's other shoulder, the strength of the blow forcing him to his knees.

Sarah knelt and put her arms around her brother. 'Please, Mr Harris, he didn't mean it.'

Emily, who had been out of the room, hurried in. She marched over to stand between her children and Harris. 'What are you doing? They are only children!'

'They are here to work, like everyone else,' Harris said. 'If they can't do it – or if they make it harder for others – they will be punished.'

Sarah, peering around Emily's skirt, heard her mother take in a shaky breath. 'Punish me, then.'

Harris shrugged. He pulled back the hand that held the cane, then paused. Instead of bringing it down, he moved it forwards and used it to push down the top of Emily's dress. Not by much, certainly nowhere near enough to reveal her breasts, but enough to make his intent clear. And enough, he must have believed, to remind this woman that she was under his control. 'See that your children aren't so stupid, in future,' he said, lowering the cane. As he walked away, he hit one of the bobbins so that it rolled beneath a machine.

'You should stay away,' Sam said now. 'When we go to His Lordship's and mount the attack.'

51

'Why?' Sarah asked. 'Am I somehow less hungry, less wronged?'

'Of course not. But ... well, *you* must live, at least. As long as they haven't caught all of us, they cannot be victorious. Nothing can happen to you, Sare. You must promise.'

'How can I? How can any of us? But you all seem to see the success of this attack as a certainty.'

'No, just as the only path left to us.' Sam squeezed her shoulder again, then gave her a playful cuff.

She laughed, grateful for the rough brotherly gesture; it helped her ignore, briefly, the relentless churn of her stomach. She had decided, while the men were talking, that if her brother went to the gallows, he would not be going alone.

✳

It had never happened before: two meetings in as many nights, increasing their chances of discovery. But if the plan worked, discovery would be inevitable, and glorious.

'I will go to the door with a note to present to the lord,' said Briardown, his voice louder than necessary in the cramped loft. 'You, my friends, are the advance guard. When the door is opened, you will rush in directly, seize the servants who are in the way, aim a pistol at them, and directly threaten them with death if they offer the least resistance or noise.'

Tully scoffed. 'If they are disgusted at having to clean up after their betters for so long, they will no doubt greet us as liberators.'

'Perhaps,' said Briardown, 'but it can't be relied on. There are other sympathisers in Lord Hargreaves's employ – you have not met them yet, nor will you until afterwards, either as fellow members of the new provisional government or in the hereafter. They will rush forward to take command of the stairs. One will have a pistol, and he will be protected by another holding a grenade. A couple of men will take the head of the stairs leading to the lower part of the house. Once the house is secured, a group of us will go in for the assassination. I know precisely what I shall say.' He stretched his neck and cleared his throat. 'Well, my lords, I have as good men here as any in England. Enter citizens and do your duty.' Briardown looked around as though expecting applause.

'Others?' said Tully. 'I thought I—'

Briardown shot him a look of annoyance, then raised his eyebrows at Tourville, who said, 'The importance of your part in this cannot be understated. The final act, the swing that will bring freedom, will not happen unless you pave the way.'

'But you haven't stationed a lookout,' said Sarah. 'That's my job. Always has been.'

The men glanced at one another.

'She has a point, actually,' said Tully.

'She also has ears,' said Sarah.

Henry smiled at her. 'You have, and I know they function perfectly well. Everyone is just distracted.' He looked at Briardown. 'Isn't that correct, sir?'

'Nothing distracts me from the crucial task ahead of us. Or at least it didn't, until you made your suggestion – which, by the way, is preposterous. What if you swoon in the excitement? We would endanger ourselves rescuing you.'

'Swoon?' Sarah scoffed. 'Was I swooning when you met me in the aftermath of a massacre?'

'I don't doubt your fortitude,' Tully said with gruff kindness. 'But a lookout? What if a soldier comes, a runner? Won't your presence at the front of the house confirm to them that something is amiss?'

'They do have women in Grosvenor Square, Tully,' said Sarah.

'Not normally loitering outside His Lordship's house.'

'I'll dress as a stableboy, then,' said Sarah. 'There are lads years younger than me who are taller, so I could pass very easily. I'll grime my face. No one pays any attention to the dirty, unless they're threatening to soil fine cloth.'

Briardown had stopped scowling, and he looked at Sam. 'Would you permit this?'

'It is not his decision!' said Sarah.

'His is the only word on the matter I will accept,' said Briardown.

When Sarah looked at her brother, all her right-eous indignation, all her excitement, all her annoyance at Briardown and Tully vanished. Sam was the colour of spent coals in a dead fireplace. His mouth was open, his eyes fixed on her. She suddenly felt mean, selfish and disloyal for making him endure this when he was about to embark on an endeavour that could potentially take his life.

But, she reminded herself, she had just as much right to participate as he did.

She walked up to him, took his hand, looked down at his stained skin and her own cracked nails, and said, 'I am as wronged as you.'

He gazed at her for a minute, and she had the uncomfortable feeling he was trying to commit her face to memory. Then he nodded.

CHAPTER 6

Sarah stood in the loft, staring at the gun barrels poking out from under the hessian, afraid to look away in case they somehow vanished. She had checked the weapons hidden in the loft twice, three times. They were all still there; they had not moved of their own accord.

The weapons had been smuggled in over the past couple of days. Always by a different man, always only one or two firearms.

Henry had been the last to come, early that morning after Sam had gone to Grosvenor Square. Briardown had told her brother he would be one of many men, from other groups like theirs, to pass by the Square that day: not to stop, not to stare, just to see if it looked as though preparations really were being made for a dinner, or if anything seemed amiss.

'You're not a toy soldier,' Sarah had said to Henry when he arrived. 'Not anymore.'

He was nervous, moving from foot to foot, his eyes darting around the loft as if he expected to see a half-concealed Bow Street Runner. He had probably seen as much death as Sarah, but she doubted he had seen as much blood spilt in violence. He might see his own by the end of the day.

She wanted to cup his face, stroke his hair, murmur half-formed words of reassurance. Fall against his chest, this time deliberately. Breathe in the faint odour of sweat with which everyone but Briardown and Tourville was wreathed; a scent that, on Henry, was far from unpleasant.

He smiled, something he did even more often than Tourville although far less artfully. Then he dipped his hand into a pocket that was coming away from his coat – it must have seen some heavy wear, as she had rarely seen him take it off since the night he had put it around her shoulders – and extracted the little lead soldier. 'I carry it for luck,' he said, straightening the tiny bayonet before putting it back. He rummaged again and took out the sailor. 'Hold this,' he said, closing her hand around it. 'We will all need luck today.'

He looked, somehow, straighter. He had lost the natural hunch of a boy who needed to protect his food from theft and his belly from a boot.

'Henry,' she said, 'do you believe in what we are doing? Is there really a chance?'

'When I was a child,' Henry said slowly, 'I was taught to believe that there is a God, and He is loving, but that belief died with my mother. I was then supposed to believe I was intended for my poor station in life, and I refused to accept that. So I have to believe in Briardown.' His smile was lopsided, and quickly gone.

'I hope he's worth your faith,' she said.

'So do I, for I am not fighting only for Briardown.' He stepped forward, inhaled deeply as though gathering courage, and kissed her cheek, resting his lips there for an instant.

When he straightened, she raised her hand to her face, felt the growing heat.

He frowned. 'I'm sorry, I shouldn't—'

She shook her head, unable to supress a grin. 'Don't be. And don't die.'

He smiled again, more broadly this time. 'As you command,' he said. 'But you must make me the same promise.'

'Very well, I promise not to die.'

He had given her an apprentice's interpretation of a courtly bow before leaving the stable.

Now Sarah restrained herself from checking the weapons again, and reminded herself that Henry and the others would be back shortly. One way or another, this would be their final meeting in the loft. Right at this minute, though, they were probably saying good-bye to parents, sisters, sweethearts – Sarah tried not to imagine Henry farewelling another girl. Perhaps some of the men were writing letters, explaining actions that might seem inexplicable. Others might simply be staring at the walls of their homes, committing each crack to memory in case they spent the remainder of their days in a prison cell.

She didn't hear Sam when he came in, didn't know he was there until he clattered some guns on top of the arsenal. She started. He walked over and gently put an arm around her shoulder, led her away from the stockpile, sat her down at the table.

'I'll have the worst of it, you know,' she said.

'How's that?'

'I'll be waiting around outside. Fretting. You won't have time to worry. You will be too busy carrying it all out. By the time you've leisure to let any fear in, you will either be victorious or . . .'

'Or in a position never to be afraid again. Or, well, to exist in eternal fear – that's where many will think I'm bound.'

'I didn't think of it! I'm so stupid, I should have arranged a priest. You should have absolution. We both should.'

'And what would I say? Bless me, Father, for I am about to sin?'

'If it's sin, it's for the good of all.'

'Sare, we're about to take part in one of the most seditious acts committed in this realm. I'm not sure what the ledger of the Almighty looks like, but I'm certain that if you seek absolution for a sin, and then die in the commission of that same sin . . . well, it probably doesn't count. Oh, and the priest would very possibly be off to the Runners in about five seconds flat, sanctity of the confessional be damned.'

'But what if you . . . ?'

Sam put a finger to her lips, a gesture he'd used since they were children whenever he wanted her to stop squealing or squawking at him. He had pressed hard then, hard enough to hurt. Now the pressure was barely discernible pressure.

'I'm hoping not to be able to answer that question for some decades yet,' he said. 'But I fancy God is fairer than the government. I can speak to Him directly, and He knows my heart, so He knows I believe that what I am doing is right.'

'I do hope intention is enough.'

'It's all I have – apart from you, of course. And you must survive this. Go at the first sign of trouble. Don't stop to warn us, not if there's no time. Just go, and don't come back here.' He took her hands in his. 'Promise me that if something goes wrong, you will flee.'

'I will not.'

These past months, Sarah had noticed a certain set to Sam's face. He still laughed – he joked all the time with the other men, without meaning to exclude her from their banter – but he was careful never to show fear or sadness, as though expressing those emotions would cause them to arrive in greater number.

Now, though, he looked frightened. 'You must!' he said. 'I cannot draw myself up for what's to come, good or bad, without having your promise.'

'Where would I go, anyway?'

'Well, as to that . . .' Sam reached into his shirt pocket and extracted a token: smooth ivory etched with the ouroboros. 'It could mean death to be caught with this. But in the right company, it might save your life.'

'Have you met any of the others outside our group?' she asked.

'No. Briardown told me of one, though – a man who captains a ship that will be at the docks. Before he weighs anchor, if anyone boards and gives him this token he'll stand them passage. But I don't know where he's going, or even the name of the ship. According to Briardown, we shall know it when we see it.'

She held up the token. 'Do the others have one?'

'Yes.'

'Henry?'

'Yes, I believe so. Briardown pressed this one into my hand a few weeks ago and whispered the instructions. Took all of a minute, and I saw him do the same with Henry a few days later, and Tully.'

She frowned. That Henry had carried this possible salvation in his pocket with his figurines, yet hadn't told her – well, it stung.

Of course, Sam hadn't told her either. When she asked him why, he looked down. 'I should have, I know. But

I hoped it wouldn't be needed. I've barely been able to look at it, honestly, because I wish it didn't have to exist. As for Henry, he probably assumed you have your own, the mooning idiot. I don't think he's interested in a world that doesn't contain you. No more than I am.'

'But Briardown . . . he didn't think I was worth saving.'

The sting came, then; the hurt at being excluded. She always tried to deny it entry into the front of her mind. It was a feeling worthy of a child excluded from a game, and it weakened her.

'I suppose he didn't think you'd need it, as you weren't to be involved,' said Sam. 'You should take it, though.'

'But you might need it!'

'Sare, you know I won't. I will be in a new world tomorrow, however things go.'

CHAPTER 7

Sarah was breathing in the dung-infused air as she watched the lowering light eat away at the corners of the loft. Running her finger over the token, she felt the smooth ivory riven by the grooves of the snake. Sam had gone to wash himself before the sun set and the pump water grew even more uncomfortably cold. For now, this room in which a new world may have been conceived was hers.

She had changed into breeches and a loose shirt under a jerkin. Tied her hair up in rags and shoved it into a cap, praying it wouldn't betray her by tumbling out. Smeared some dirt onto her face in the hopes it would mimic the shadow of emerging whiskers.

She was alone, at the edge of everything.

She wondered whether she could kill someone if she had to. Could she slice a person's skin with a piece of metal? Perhaps she would not emerge any better than the yeomen of St Peter's Field. But when she pictured her mother and father, their blood leaking into the dirt, her fist clenched as if around an imaginary hilt.

Sarah went to the wall of the loft and removed a loose section of wooden board, revealing a small hollow. It was home to a scrap of oilcloth that she used to store her offcut paper from the printer's shop, together with her pencil stub. *To the finder of this letter*, she wrote.

I do not know whether I will return here. If I do not, it may be that I am too occupied with the formation of the provisional government. It may be that we have failed, and I am in prison. It may be that I have flown.

It is my intention to burn this letter if I ever return here. If it remains long enough for a stranger's eyes to fall on it, I wish it to stand as my testimony.

My mother and father were slain by men on horseback who cut into their own countrymen for no greater crime than listening. It should not have been so. My brother has gone hungry many times these past years so that I can eat. It should not have been so.

I pass bodies sitting with their backs propped against walls, having died where they begged. I see small bundles placed on the dead carts. Those left alive are in mortal danger if they gather to raise their voices against the injustice. There is food, I am told. It sits just across the seas. It could relieve our hunger, if the government was pleased to let it in. But the English merchants object, and the government has more fear of their displeasure than of the poor, and so the dead increase. It should not be so. It should never be so.

It is why I will go with the men when they rise, though most do not want me to do so. Women hunger, and women die, so women must also fight.

It is my hope that we will have entered a better world by tomorrow. If we have not, we may well have entered the next world.

We are not lawless. We are not savage or evil. We do not seek charity. But honest work – when it can be had – is no longer a path to survival. The government is deaf to us. We have tried to make them listen, and they have stuffed their ears. Revolution is the only remaining course.

She signed the letter, folded it, and wondered if anyone would ever read it, ever know a woman had been involved.

Her jaw clenched as she thought of Briardown's belief that she should be excluded. He had used the fiction of feminine frailty like a cage, when it suited him. She was sure some of the yeomen on St Peter's Field had held similar views, which hadn't stopped them riding women down and inserting steel into their hearts.

✦

Sarah was still fuming about Briardown when she heard Tully plodding up the narrow stairs. He emerged into the loft, florid and coughing, and thrust a cloth bundle at her, which she nearly dropped. When she unwrapped it, she was amazed that the cloth was not shredded: inside lay five cleavers of varying sizes, all polished.

Sam came in then, negotiating the stairs more easily than Tully had. He looked at the cleavers on the table, then at the butcher.

'The right tools for the right job,' Tully said.

The others arrived over the next half-hour or so. Henry, hands jammed into his pockets, walked over to her and bent to whisper, 'After . . . well, everything. Would you accompany me on a walk?'

The suggestion seemed almost obscene: strolls in the gardens were for the free and fed.

Before she could answer, Tully walked over to them.

'I want you to see this,' he said, bringing out a small, well-made wooden box that was banded with iron. 'My mother's,' he said. 'She kept her precious things in it. A ribbon from my father. My milk teeth. We all have something precious, and I think she'd like it if I used it again.' He opened the box and handed it to Henry, who placed his little baker and thief figurines inside. Sam put Emily's old ribbon next to them.

Sarah wrapped her letter back in its oilcloth and handed it to Tully. 'I know a place to keep the box,' she said. 'Just until we're back later.'

They heard the door opening, and Tourville climbed the steps into the loft. He pressed his back against the wall, standing to one side like a sentry to signal the imminent appearance of their leader.

'I have written a declaration,' Briardown said when he entered the loft, holding a scroll. He paused when he saw Sarah, perhaps not recognising her in her urchin disguise. 'Our lookout?' he asked.

She nodded.

'So do your duty.' He inclined his head imperiously towards the opening in the loft wall, and she turned away before he could register her annoyance and upbraid her.

She walked to the wall, crouched and pulled back the canvas.

'As to this declaration,' he said, unfurling the scroll and holding it like a crier with one hand on top and one on the bottom.

Sarah listened with half an ear as she stared out at the darkening street. Across the road, men were going into the Horse & Coach tavern. Some in small knots, some alone; well dressed, mostly, with a few labourers mixed in.

'Your tyrants are destroyed,' Briardown began.

She was surprised to observe a few men emerging from the inn. Wasn't it a little early for anyone to be leaving? Perhaps they had been in their cups all day, yet they were not staggering as men usually did after many hours in the tavern.

'The friends of liberty are called upon to come forward!'

More were emerging now, none obviously the worse for drink. There were, suddenly, ten, fifteen of them.

'The provisional government is now in session!'

One of the men began striding across the road towards the stable. The others followed, reaching into their coats.

'They are coming!' Sarah cried. 'They've been waiting at the Horse & Coach, and now they're coming! A dozen, more!'

There was a silence, then an intake of breath. Tully picked up a cleaver. Sam, who wore a dagger in his belt, reached for a rifle and positioned himself between Sarah and the top of the stairs. Henry reached over to snuff out a candle, but Briardown shook his head. He drew his pistol and gestured for Tourville to station himself at the other side of the door.

Tourville either ignored or misunderstood his leader. He drew his pistol then dashed down the narrow stairs as fast as he could without breaking his neck.

'What in God's name . . .?' Briardown yelled after him.

Sarah glanced out around the canvas again. Downstairs, the leader of the men from the tavern – constables and Bow Street Runners – pounded on the stable door, the sound reverberating throughout the loft. Some of his followers were holding pistols.

In the next instant, after only a few strikes of his balled fist, the stable door yielded, gaping open. Two of the constables grabbed Tourville and dragged him outside as he struggled and shouted, while footsteps pounded up the loft stairs.

'They will only be able to come up one at a time,' Briardown hissed at his men. 'So that's how we will take them.' He whirled, pointing his pistol at the stairs.

But the leader of the constables was already at the top. He whacked his staff against Briardown's arms, forcing him to drop the pistol, before hitting the back of Briardown's head until he buckled.

Their leader, who seconds earlier had been preparing to declare a new government for the whole of England, was now slumped on the ground like a rag doll.

The Bow Street Runner moved aside to make way for his fellows and the constables. In seconds, the small loft was a mayhem of shouts and shots and the scrape of metal.

Sarah pressed herself beside the opening in the wall and tried to see Sam among the knots of men now struggling with each other around the room. None of the intruders had noticed her yet. She didn't know what she could do for Sam, but she intended to try. She tensed, ready to spring as soon as she saw him.

Tully held his cleaver in front of him as though he was about to chop into an animal carcass. A constable kicked him in the stomach, then two of them dragged him by the hair and under his arms to the door.

When Henry reached for one of Tully's knives, the butt of a pistol was brought down hard on his wrist. He cried out, bending and grasping it with his other hand.

Beyond Henry, Sarah glimpsed Sam in the far corner of the room. One of the constables was approaching him. His shoulders tensed as he raised the rifle. Aimed. Fired.

The ball caught the top of the constable's hat, carrying it halfway across the room before it flopped onto the floor. The man ruffled his own hair, as though grateful that the hat was gone, smiled, and started moving towards Sam.

Sam did not turn to her, so she startled when he yelled shakily, 'Go! Get out of here!'

'Not without you!' she called back.

Why was the constable being so slow in his approach? She saw that Sam's rifle was slung over his shoulder, and he had drawn his long dagger from its sheath.

'We've been asked to take you all alive,' the constable said, inching closer. 'Is that possible? You going to put down your knife, lad? You were talked into this, weren't you, by the older ones. Put that thing down now, and we'll see what's to be done.'

Without lowering the dagger, Sam shouted, 'Go! Now!'

Sarah glanced outside to the slick cobbles below. She looked back at her brother, willing him to struggle and break free. 'You too! Run!'

The constable had nearly closed the distance when Sam thrust out his arm, keeping the man at dagger point. Suddenly he turned to face Sarah and darted towards her. She allowed herself a small sliver of hope as she braced for the impact when they both jumped.

The constable caught Sam by the back of his coat.

He struggled as he kept his eyes on Sarah, who was frozen, waiting for him, unable to believe they would not make this journey together.

The constable now had his hands around Sam's upper arms. Sam inhaled, lifted his legs, and kicked her. Not enough to hurt, not badly, but enough to send her toppling out of the opening in the wall.

CHAPTER 8

Sarah lay on the stones for a moment or two. Breathed. Tensed, rolled onto her stomach, winced, saw rivulets of what was probably her blood between the cobbles.

The noises around her came back gradually at first – muffled shouts, clangs, stamping feet – then in a rush, slicing at her ears.

She looked up to see Sam being dragged out of the stable. She must only have been dazed for a few moments. Now she was on her knees, staring at her brother. Sam, still struggling, widened his eyes at the sight of her.

One of the Bow Street Runners turned in her direction and saw what he no doubt thought was a boy. He started towards her and moved past Sam, who violently lurched to one side and sent the man sprawling.

The constables tightened their hold on Sam and shoved him into the back of an enclosed cart, which started to drive away. Sarah went to run after it.

Several seconds passed before she realised her legs were carrying her not after the cart, but towards the docks.

✦

Sarah could not hear footsteps thundering behind her, though that did not mean she was safe; she could only hear the drag of chains at anchor as the tide scraped them against the rims of their hawses. All ships scheduled to depart on the evening tide were making ready to do so.

She kept looking around for Runners and constables as she tried to convince herself to run back, put on women's clothes, and plead for mercy at the gates of the gaol that held her brother. But she knew there would be no mercy for him. And she would be swallowed alongside him, picked clean, digested.

At that thought, she wanted to sit down, close her eyes and clamp her hands over her ears to keep out the noise of the docks – she did not want clanking and lapping and sloshing. With those sounds muffled, she could perhaps convince herself that she was part of a victorious mass streaming through the streets.

It was an indulgence she could not allow herself. As she walked, she tried to imagine dashing back up the loft stairs, taking her letter from Tully's box and burning it. Then she would give the sailor figurine back to Henry, closing his hand around it as he had hers, telling him she did not need luck anymore, that she had all she wanted.

Her breathing slowed, but then it caught on the image of Henry's face, her terror that his quick smile might be ruined by a fist or a boot, the lips and cheeks bruised and sunken without the teeth.

Henry and Sam were young, but their youth would not inspire kindness in those who extended none to thousands of ragged, hungry children.

There was some hope that if Sarah remained at liberty she could do something for them. Perhaps with the help of other radicals – this ship captain might have connections.

She understood Briardown's need for secrecy, but she wished he had told Sam the ship's name. In the low light, she was finding it harder to read them. And as she weaved between the sailors, the longshoremen and the passengers, she knew that she would soon attract attention. She appeared to be a slight lad with a dirty face, so she might be taken for a pickpocket. But she had to keep trying.

Briardown had told Sam that they would know the ship when they saw it.

She passed one called *Hanover* – not a place Briardown had ever mentioned, as far as she could remember. *Lady Adelaide* – did one of the Cabinet ministers have a wife of that name? She might need to come back to it. *Mermaid* – Pa had told them stories of such creatures, but Sam had never really listened.

Manchester. She paused. The ship was bustling, all right, as people and cargo were being loaded. She was about to approach the gang-board, to take a chance, when she noticed that some passengers were not of the paying kind. About twenty of the men were dressed in filthy canvas, probably given to them when they were sentenced to transportation. They had clearly been on road gangs while awaiting exile; their legs were ironed, their hands manacled. They kept their heads bent as they shuffled up the gang-board, an overseer screeching orders behind them.

Surely this wasn't the right ship. Maybe there was just enough time to press on further.

Her determination was rewarded. A few moments later, she saw the hull of a ship with its name painted in gold: *Serpent*. Beside it, unadorned but visible, was a drawing of a snake eating its own tail.

The hull swept down in a graceful curve, above hatches that were closed. No light could be seen leaking out from any of them. The three masts, without sails for now, looked like dead trees in what was left of the daylight.

The gang-board was down but so was the anchor. Perhaps the captain was not planning to depart tonight.

A few sailors were scurrying about the deck. 'Oi!' she yelled to them in her best approximation of male aggression, delivered in a higher pitch than she would have liked.

The sailors stopped, staring at her.

'I want to see the captain!'

'Well, he doesn't want to see you,' one of them called back.

'He will! I've a message for him – from some friends.'

The sailors looked at each other, then one of them shrugged and called towards the bridge. 'Lad here to see you! We'll send him on his way, shall we?'

'Not just yet,' a deep voice called back. 'I am expecting a message. I'll see what he has to say for himself.'

The sailor jerked his head at her to come up, and she was at the top of the gang-board within seconds.

The man who now approached her wore the standard uniform of a merchant captain: a high-necked blue jacket with gilded buttons at intervals, stitched in gold. It was either new or meticulously maintained, the buttons shining and spotless to match the gold buckles on his shoes. She observed that the jackets of the other crew were already speckled with salt or soot.

The captain had not, though, taken nearly as much care with his hair. The wearer of such a jacket would normally have a black satin bow at the nape of his neck, his hair straggling down his back in a constrained tail, whereas this man's black mop was unbound and unruly, being whipped into an untameable state by the wind. He ran a hand through it as he narrowed his eyes at her. 'A lad, you say. Come on then . . . boy.' He raked his eyes up and down Sarah's body, a small smirk on his face. 'You may deliver your message in my cabin.'

The last thing she wanted to do was follow such a man. Everything about him, from the way he stood to the way he looked at her, screamed of arrogance. Still, there was no one else to help her, so she followed him through a low doorway into a room half the height but otherwise nearly the size of her family home in Manchester. In the centre was a green baize table littered with charts and nautical instruments that would surely find themselves on the floor at the first nudge of a wave.

The captain sat down at one end of the table, then gestured for her to do likewise at the other. 'So ... you're someone's daughter? Wife?'

'Sister.'

'I see. When no one arrived, I had hoped ...'

'You had hoped?' she asked when he didn't continue. How could she be certain of his sympathies, or his intentions?

He seemed to be having similar reservations. 'I had hoped to get on with my work without the intrusion of a girl dressed as a boy. The least you can do is tell me who you are.'

'Sarah McCaffrey. Sister to Samuel.'

'Not a name I have heard. And do you have a message for me?'

'Not exactly.'

'What, then?'

'I was told to come to you. For passage.'

'Well, you will have to wait, as we are not sailing for a week or so. And when we do, all of our cabins will be full. But even if they were not, it doesn't look as though you have adequate funds to pay the passage between here and the estuary, let alone the vast distance we will be travelling.'

'I am hoping that the unique currency I carry will change your mind.' She took the ivory token from her pocket and held it out between her fingers, feeling the engraved snake; hesitant, almost, to hand it over. It had carried her here, bringing her to what might be her only chance to survive and rescue the others, so perhaps she owed it protection. Still, she laid it on the table.

The captain gave her a shrewd look.

She tried to stop herself squirming in her seat like a young girl who hadn't finished her darning. He was surely aware of the symbol's significance, but she did not find that comforting. Was he assessing her, trying to decide whether she had come by the token honestly? Or he might be considering whether to turn her in.

'Do you know its import?' he asked.

'I was told it might be worth something, on the right ship.'

'An ouroboros,' he said, as though she had asked him to explain it. He stood and began to pace around the cabin. 'A serpent eating its own tail. Destruction, leading to renewal.' He put both of his hands on the table, looming over her. 'The fact that you brought it here leads me to believe that there has been destruction but precious little renewal.' When she stayed silent, he sighed and went to the cabin door. 'Stay here,' he said as he went through it. After he closed it behind him, she heard the click of the lock.

✦

There had been no lamps burning in the cabin when she entered. As night fell, the corners of the room disappeared. Were it not for the full moon, she doubted she could have seen anything at all; as it was, she feared tripping over an unseen obstacle as she paced the room.

Sam was surely still alive. They would want a show trial, no doubt, to ram home the cost of rebellion. She had no illusions about what would happen to him after that – after the judge had made disapproving noises, had told him that he was a traitor to a king whose people were left to starve while he fed leftover venison to his dogs.

She had not prayed since her parents' deaths. Prayer seemed worse than useless to her now, because it tricked her, despite herself, into believing a splinter of hope existed. Still, she breathed out a benediction, hoping the wind would carry it to the cell where Henry and Sam now rested. She tried not to cry – the captain could be back at any moment, and she did not want to show weakness. But tears flowed onto her cheeks anyway, so she pressed her hands against her eyes until exhaustion overtook her and she laid her head on her arms.

Then someone was shaking her, dragging her into consciousness. She sat up and looked around, disoriented, expecting to see the chinks in the stable roof that let moonlight through.

Lamps had been lit, and their low light brought the cabin back into existence for her.

She stared at the captain, open mouthed, feeling saliva pool behind her teeth and knowing it would dribble out if she didn't swallow.

'Well?' he said.

'Well ...' She stood and walked around the table to clear the fog of sleep, and the shock of waking to a world she didn't recognise. 'I don't know. I do not even know your name. Perhaps if you felt able to answer some questions, I'd be able to leave you in peace.'

The captain sighed. 'I'll answer the first question for you, at least. Captain Alistair Watkins.' He made a bow so perfunctory it was almost insulting. 'And now I have a question for you. Do you know why I locked you in here? Government spies are breeding like lice at the moment – London is crawling with them. I did not know who would come to me bearing such a token, but I had expected it to be a man.'

'I am sorry to disappoint you.'

'Are you, though? Or are you looking forward to disappointing me very much, perhaps by ensuring my arrest? I have just been to meet some friends, you see. The city is buzzing with rumours. Your – brother, was it? – and the others, it is said, were the victims of a police informant.'

Sarah's queasiness had nothing to do with the gentle rocking of the ship on its anchor. And it wasn't disbelief. It was a chime within her, the instinct he was telling the truth – and that he was right. 'Are there ... Were any names mentioned?'

'No. Everyone is always very discreet, although your friends were not discreet enough. If they were your friends.'

'What, you think it was *me*?'

'If it was, I can simply nudge you overboard and deny any knowledge.' His smile was friendly enough, although the smell from some of his more decayed teeth made her wish he would close his mouth. He patted her hand, for all the world as though he hadn't just threatened to murder her. 'Still, you may be who you claim to be. Why don't you tell me exactly what happened?'

She informed him of almost everything; she stopped short of mentioning the planned beheadings in case his concern about her credentials was a mask for his own duplicity. And she did not tell him of the deaths that had propelled her from Manchester to London – that information needed to be earned.

After she had finished he was silent, scratching at the stubble on his chin.

'Do you not believe me?' she said.

'If it is a lie,' he said, 'it's one of the more imaginative ones I've ever heard. Have you any idea who betrayed you?'

She would not look the possibility of treachery in the face. She couldn't, not now. 'Perhaps it wasn't a betrayal – perhaps it was just a mistake. Maybe we weren't careful enough.'

'Oh, it was a betrayal. Not that they are likely to make the man's name public. They will guard it closely, for his protection and to preserve his usefulness.' Watkins clapped his hands together. 'Very well. I choose to believe you – for now. You know what will happen if you give me cause to change my mind. You may hide here until we're ready to set sail, then we'll see what's to be done. We will have to sort out some clothes for you. Oh, and your surname – you share it with your brother?'

Sarah nodded.

'It will have to be changed then. What shall we call you?'

There was something else in her pocket; she reached in and felt the little lead figure Henry had given her, the sailor who might soon be going to sea for the first time.

'Marin,' she said. 'Sarah Marin.'

Watkins bowed to her again, this one formal and polite. 'A pleasure to meet you, Miss Marin.'

CHAPTER 9

Watkins had sloshed some rum into a battered tin cup, sat and tipped his head back, pouring most of the liquid into his mouth, then held the cup out to her, an offer she declined.

'If they're looking for a boy tonight,' said Watkins, 'you'd best dress as a woman as soon as you can.' He rummaged around in his cabin and extracted an old dress from a sea chest. God knew what it was doing in there. Faded blue flowers were printed on the kind of fine cotton her pa used to weave. When Sarah pulled it on over her breeches and shirt, she found it had been made for a woman blessed with more abundant food than she had been. 'I will send for the first mate, Mr Coombes,' Watkins said. 'He will go ashore for needle and thread.' The captain then handed her a yellowed lace cap from the bottom of the chest. 'Tuck your hair into this. They might already be looking for a woman of your description, if their informant told them of your involvement, and your hair is your most memorable feature.'

He brought her out of his cabin and down a ladder, past a low-ceilinged room in which hammocks were strung, and then down again through the hold, empty but barred – maybe, she thought, to stop the crew helping themselves to the cargo – and through a small door nearby to a storeroom. The musty space was half filled with barrels and crates, some of which emitted the pleasant scent of tea while others oozed the odour of pork that had not been on the trotter for some time.

'This won't do for long,' Watkins said, 'as we'll be loading more. But it'll do for now. Mr Coombes will bring you down a hammock to rig up. He is, shall we say, sympathetic.'

'Very well, I will stay here until you depart,' she said. 'Before you set sail – my brother, the others – isn't there something we can do for them? There must be some way . . .'

Watkins was shaking his head. 'They're not in a country house, I can assure you.' He sighed. 'All right. I'll go ashore tomorrow to see what I can find out. But I fear your brother is as lost to you now as he would be on the other side of the world.'

'The other side of the world?'

'That's where we are sailing. New South Wales.'

⁂

She paced around the hold after he left, looking at the words on the crates and barrels without seeing them.

The hatch opened again, but the man who came down the ladder was smaller and thinner than Watkins. There was a stoop to him that hadn't been caused by age, as the hair on his head was more blond than grey. His posture was that of somebody engaged in daily manual labour since their early years.

This sailor lacked the opulent flourishes of his captain. His shoes did not have buckles, and his breeches and stockings were darned, as was the waistcoat over his shirt with its neckerchief. Still, everything looked clean; he was surely a fastidious sort. Slung over his shoulder was a large bundle of canvas, which he toppled so it landed with a thud on the floor between them. Then he turned to leave.

'Wait!' said Sarah. 'You are Mr Coombes, the mate? I am Sarah Mc ... Sarah Marin.'

'I know who you are. And whatever Watkins says, you make a fairly convincing boy.'

'I'll look less like one when I'm able to take in the dress the captain gave me. He said you would fetch a needle and thread?'

'Ah, the captain said that, did he? And, of course, I've nothing else to do, what with getting the ship ready to sail – not long now. Of course, milady, I'd be delighted to run into town for you. Would milady fancy anything else? Ostrich feathers, perhaps?'

Her face burned. 'Captain Watkins said you knew ... you understood ...'

'Well, I know why you are here. And you expect me to thank you, perhaps, for your sacrifice, or your bravery? Little girls playing at soldiers get people killed. But you'll have your bloody thread.' He started towards the door, then stopped and put a finger to his lips.

She could hear many footsteps up on the deck, the footfalls vibrating down through the timbers, each thump louder and closer than the one before. Abruptly they all went still, before muffled male voices floated down through the timbers.

Coombes nodded towards the dress lying on top of a crate. Sarah nodded, picked it up, and drew a circle in the air to ask Coombes to turn his back. He rolled his eyes but did so. She took off Sam's shirt and threw the dress on over her breeches. It was ridiculously large, billowing from the shoulders down to the hem. Then she tucked her hair into the musty lace cap.

'That's thief-takers up there,' Coombes said. 'The Bow Street Runners. Too many of them to be anything else.'

The footsteps were audible again, coming closer. Coombes stepped through the small door connecting the storeroom to the hold, positioning himself in the middle of the empty space. Sarah glimpsed her shirt on the ground, picked it up and flicked it behind a barrel.

Watkins came down the stairs into the hold, followed by five men in tall hats and long black jackets with silver buttons down the front and on their cuffs.

Her best hope was that they were still looking for a boy.

Watkins glared at Sarah and pulled back his shoulders in what was perhaps a slightly overdone gesture of frustration. 'That's the second time I've found you down here disporting yourself with the crew, you strumpet!' he snapped. 'Back to the galley, now!' He looked at Coombes. 'I'd have expected more of you, Mr Coombes. See it does not occur again.'

'Yes, captain, although the temptation is difficult to resist.'

Watkins gave a small, almost imperceptible quirk of his mouth. 'Back to it, both of you.'

'Yes, captain,' Sarah said and scrambled up the ladder, hoping she looked as though she was going straight to the galley, although she didn't have any idea where it was.

As soon as she and Coombes were out of sight of the open hatch, Sarah whacked him on the arm. 'Difficult to resist, am I?'

'I did just save your life.'

She chuckled. 'You did, and I thank you.'

To her surprise, he smiled back, the creaking movement of a mouth out of practice. 'I hope you're worth all of this trouble.'

✦

In the following week, Sarah fell into a routine of sorts. She would mend and wash clothes, patch sails, peel potatoes, and do whatever other chores were asked of her.

As she worked, she found herself picking at the corners of the idea of Sam's death as though poking a loose tooth with her tongue. She was desperate to see him – and she would not let herself presume that this could only take place at his execution.

Each afternoon, as soon as she had a spare moment and was unobserved, she would sidle off the ship and walk to Newgate Prison. Watkins had told her that her brother and the others were being held there, charged with high treason. She would pace around the walls, looking for vulnerabilities that she knew, deep down, did not exist.

The walls were angular and unadorned, with sparsely placed blank windows except in the peaked central section that had several arched apertures, none of which admitted any light. Some of the windows seemed almost as large as the doors set into the central edifice. Occasionally there were constables in front of those doors, although the walls seemed thick enough to withstand a cannon blast. She tried not to walk past them too often, moving in step with one of the many others who paced outside the prison, or behind a slow-moving cart. She was hoping to overhear snatches of conversation about the conspirators, or to catch a glimpse of Sam or Henry – even the faces of Briardown, Tully and Tourville would have been welcome.

But perhaps one of them was not in a cell. One of them might be having his hand shaken, receiving a purse of money. Told it was a job well done, the capture of these depraved insurgents.

She could not quieten her mind on the subject of who it might be. Not Sam, of course. Briardown was unlikely . . . or perhaps not – he may have gone to Manchester to set a trap for radicals, and seen Sarah and Sam's bereavement as the ideal opportunity. Or was that too far-fetched? Tully – well, he didn't have it in him, did he? Perhaps she had underestimated him.

That left Tourville and Henry, and it could not be Henry. She would not believe it, as there didn't seem to be any guile in him at all. But of course, a talent for hiding his true nature would make him valuable as an informer, and she had to admit she may have let her feelings scramble her judgement.

It maddened her that Watkins would not show her newspapers or give her the means to purchase them. And he absolutely refused to give her any information on the trial at the Old Bailey. 'You will find out more in good time,' he had said. 'What does it matter, anyway? There's nothing you can do.' He was obviously trying to keep her calm and under control, so that she would not cause any trouble for him. How did he not realise that he was instead forcing her to steal away from the ship?

She would stalk around the prison for half an hour or so, never seeing anyone go in or out save guards and officials. Then she would return to the ship and try to distract herself with the menial tasks Watkins and

Coombes demanded of her. But she could not escape the grasping fear of what would happen to her brother. Or her thoughts about the spy, if he existed. She could only presume that he did, based on Watkins's behaviour. And a spy would surely have told the magistrates and their constables by now not to look for a boy but for a woman named Sarah McCaffrey. Then again, it would not take a spy to convey that information; even Henry might have informed on her for the chance at a lenient sentence.

One afternoon she was walking around Newgate when a heavy hand clamped down on her shoulder. She wheeled around, raising her elbow to strike at her assailant, and pulled it back just soon enough to avoid connecting with Coombes's jaw. 'What are you playing at?' she hissed. 'You scared the life out of me!'

'You'll find your life leaving you sooner than you want, if you keep doing this.'

'I won't. I'm careful, I just want to see him. Just once.' Her voice was quavering – she hated the sound; knew her apparent strength was her best chance of maintaining a level of friendliness with Coombes, and Watkins for that matter.

The first mate, though, was not angry. 'I know, lass. I know. Do you think, though, that he wants you to put yourself in danger?'

'I am not in danger!'

'Are you not? I noticed certain things when I followed you here. And if I can follow you, so can others. We'll be going back to the ship now, yes? And then we'll try to decide exactly how much danger you are in.'

* ☀ *

Watkins glared at Sarah as he chewed his stew. She tried, for the sake of keeping the peace, to look contrite. But she didn't seem to be managing it too well, and she would be damned if she apologised for trying to get a last glimpse of Sam.

'Every afternoon?' Watkins asked. 'I've given you one of the safest places in London to hide, and you walk straight into the dragon's mouth.'

'No one has noticed me,' she said. 'The guards don't pay attention to the girls and ladies parading up and down outside the gaol – they just assume we're all wives, mothers and sweethearts.'

'Or the sister of a brother who tried to overthrow the government,' said Coombes. 'While you do occasionally see women pining outside Newgate, it seems you are more noticeable than most.' To his captain, he said, 'The constables were looking at her and nodding. They've noticed her before, I'd wager my life on it.'

'So what if they have?' said Sarah. 'I wear my lace cap every day and keep my head bowed.'

'Perhaps they would ask their spy to watch you from inside the prison,' suggested Watkins. He spat the gristle onto his plate and wiped his mouth with the back of his hand.

Sarah knew it was pointless to request more information; if he had confirmed the existence and name of the spy, he certainly would not share it with her now. 'Are you going to lock me in the hull?'

'It had occurred to me,' he said, and paused as though seriously considering the idea. 'But we'll keep the irons in abeyance for now. You must promise me, though, on all you hold dear, that you will not go to Newgate again.'

'I would,' she said, 'if anything I held dear was left.'

CHAPTER 10

One week into her stay on the *Serpent*, Sarah had been moved to a tiny cabin. She tried not to think of it as a coffin, but her bunk was so narrow that she had fallen onto the floor a few times when she was rolling over in her sleep. Not that sleep was a frequent visitor. At night her mind conjured grotesque phantasms: Sam, purple-faced with his tongue lolling; Henry, having a furtive conversation with a Bow Street Runner at the Horse & Coach.

This morning her nightly visions had propelled her to the deck, where she hoped the salt air would dull them.

Coombes walked over to her. 'You'll find it easier once we set off.'

'But I won't be here.'

He shrugged and said nothing further on the matter, as parsimonious with words as he was with money while he checked cargo, inspected the sails, and yelled at the increasing number of young sailors. 'Captain wants to see you,' he said, looking over the rail. 'Ah. Cargo's here.'

But there were no barrels or crates. Instead, about fifty men were lined up along the ship's side, encumbered by irons and by the red-jacketed soldiers guarding them. They walked one by one up the plank, across the main deck below Sarah and down through the hatch. Most kept their heads lowered, but some looked up and around. One, short and scrawny, seemed little older than the baker's boy who had given her the note about the cabinet dinner.

She turned to Coombes. 'That – that is the cargo?'

'Navy Board pays six shillings a man,' Coombes said.

'Did you know about this?' she asked, then shook her head. 'Of course you did. The captain can go to the devil, as can you.'

'We no doubt will. But you will want to hear what he has to say first.'

As they walked towards Watkins's cabin, they passed knots of men loading provisions and calling to each other in voices made hoarse by wind and salt.

'Why were you and Watkins both aboard so early?' she asked.

'Can only speak for myself,' said Coombes. 'I came aboard to watch the captain.'

'Why would he need watching?'

Coombes stopped walking. She thought he was going to reveal something, but he seemed to think better of it. 'My reasons are my own,' he said, and kept going.

The cabin was in its usual chaotic state – Watkins kept it locked when he wasn't there, so Sarah had never had a chance to tidy it up.

Had Watkins not been there, she would have had no shortage of newspapers to read. They were strewn all over the green baize chart table, some slipping off its edge onto the floor. A plate of half-eaten mutton was by the captain's elbow, and a smear of grease led from it to one of the documents spread out before him. The curtain that concealed his sleeping alcove was open, the bedclothes twisted and jumbled, a frayed shirt lying across it.

Watkins had his head in his hands as he looked down at a sheet of newspaper. 'Shut the door,' he said without glancing up. 'Mr Coombes, stay if you please.' He slid the paper over to Sarah. 'I am sorry.'

She waited a moment before she looked at it.

The dreadful sentence of the law has been passed on three of the conspirators who had intended to carry out the most atrocious conspiracy to murder ministers of the Crown. Aidan Briardown, Harold Tully and Samuel McCaffrey have been convicted of high treason and will be executed tomorrow morning outside Newgate Prison.

There was more, but Sarah could not read it, her vision blurring. She tried to swallow, then put her hand over her mouth as her stomach contracted and spasmed.

The author of this article and the publisher of this newspaper, who invited her brother's extinction with such fervour, and those in the court who had sat in judgement on him – they had not been there when the gaffer's cane had come down on him. They had not been there whenever he gave a quiet sob of hunger at night, or when he had found his mother trodden into the earth. To them he was simply another gaping mouth that hoped to inhale as much of their treasure as possible.

Watkins looked at Coombes then nodded towards a stand near his sleeping alcove. 'Get the basin,' he said flatly.

Sarah, still with one hand over her mouth, waved the other. 'Don't bother,' she said. 'Don't bother with anything. There is no longer anything worth bothering with.'

Coombes squeezed her shoulder, while Watkins just stared; his dark eyes contained nothing.

'They pardon people, sometimes,' she said.

Watkins shook his head. 'Not people who wanted to assassinate the Cabinet.'

Why, then, were only three to be hanged?

'Henry – one of us – he's not mentioned, nor Tourville. Do you know what happened to them?'

Watkins shrugged. 'I know you do not want to believe there was an informer, but perhaps there were two.'

Had Henry been a fiction? She tried to be glad he was not listed to be hanged, but if he had put the other men on the gallows, he was not *her* Henry, and she could not be glad for the salvation of a phantom. Had Henry been secretly laughing at her and Sam, all this time? Had he sneered at the naive girl who seemed to believe he harboured some affection for her?

She could hear Coombes shuffling from foot to foot just behind her chair. Watkins kept staring at her, to the point where she wondered if her appearance had suddenly changed, if the skin on her face had shrunk so that she looked like the corpse she felt herself to be. That her brother would soon be.

'I have to go there,' she said. 'Tomorrow. I want to . . . I want to see him. Give him the chance to see me.'

Watkins shook his head again. 'That is an extraordinarily bad idea.'

'What will I do instead? Peel vegetables in the galley, wondering if my brother's neck is already being broken?'

'I'll go with her,' Coombes said.

'Oh, you will?' said Watkins, an eyebrow raised. 'You do not have other duties?' To Sarah, he said, 'We sail Monday night. I cannot be without a first mate while we are preparing, you understand.'

'My duties will be attended to,' Coombes said, a touch peevishly as though insulted the captain would think anything else. 'But unless you accompany the lass, I will. She'll go anyway, we both know that. She should not be alone.'

'And then . . .' Sarah said. 'Then, after – you'll be rid of me.'

'What on earth would you do in London, alone?' said Watkins.

'I would find a way to continue,' she said, drawing her shoulders back to convince both him and herself of her fortitude. 'It is not over. It is never over.'

CHAPTER 11

The last time she had put on the clothes of a stableboy, Sam had been free. Now, by the time she took them off, he would be dead.

She had wanted to look like herself, to give Sam the best chance of noticing her in the crowd. 'Yes,' Coombes had said, 'but others might notice you as well, and if there was an informer they know they're looking for a woman. I won't go with you if you dress as one.' So she had laced up the shirt, tied back her hair and jammed the boy's cap on her head.

The area outside Newgate was already thronged when Sarah and Coombes arrived just after dawn. The street was blocked, and barriers had been erected to stop the crowd pressing in. But the seats facing the scaffold – those with the best view – all seemed to be empty.

'Why do they do this?' asked Sarah, as she and the first mate made their way to the central area. 'Why do they insist on having spectators to someone's last breath?'

'So those in power don't draw their last breaths with knives to their throats. And because there would be a public outcry – no one forced these spectators here.' He wormed his way through the crowd near the barriers to the side, dragging Sarah with him.

They passed peddlers setting up their stalls, preparing to sell chestnuts or potatoes or meats on sticks to a crowd made peckish by carnage. Sarah had not thought to bring food, and she did not know when or how she would ever eat again.

As she and Coombes made their way closer to the scaffold, a squat man in a grimy waistcoat, wearing an incongruously clean, satin-banded hat, jumped in front of Sarah and thrust a pamphlet under her nose; it had a picture of several men lined up on the scaffold, below the heading *Last Words and Confessions of the Malefactors.* Coombes roughly shoved him out of the way.

'But what if something useful is in there?' asked Sarah. 'Something from Sam, some sort of message to me?'

'There won't be,' the first mate said. 'That weasel will have made it all up, and he will charge me a shilling or two for the privilege.'

As the sky lightened, Sarah saw well-dressed couples lining up at the stands, handing over their shillings, taking their seats. Men leant on their canes and inclined their heads to their female companions, making observations at which the women trilled with laughter.

'Collar day! Collar day mementos!' the man with the filthy waistcoat and fancy hat shouted. One hand held the pamphlets in the air; the other accepted payments.

Sarah narrowed her eyes at the food sellers, the man taking money for seats, the broadside peddler, and the fiddler standing near a wall, playing jauntily. They would all earn some pennies from her brother's death; they all deserved a curse.

By the time the sun had cleared the roofs of the buildings all around, there seemed to be almost as many gathered as there had been at St Peter's Field. Most seemed as cheerful as those who had walked through Manchester's streets, unaware some of them were on their final march.

But today some stood sombrely and were dressed respectfully in black. As Sarah looked around, she saw several men gazing towards the gallows, their hats off, their jaws set. Perhaps they were fellow Spencean Philanthropists, or some other stripe of radical. Perhaps they had known Briardown; maybe they had taken part in planning the attack. They might even be feeling a measure of guilt that it was not their 'collar day' as well.

Such men were far outnumbered, though, by chattering and laughing people. Sarah wanted to kneel on the ground, put her forehead on her knees and throw her arms over her ears. The fact that so much merriment was called forth by the anticipation of Sam's death made it unbearable.

Some of those in the crowd behind the barricades with Sarah and Coombes had clearly emptied their cupboards of every brightly coloured scarf or cravat or hat or shawl. Among them were women in silks with garishly painted mouths who would, after a brief conversation, disappear around a corner with certain gentlemen.

Of course, those who had paid for their seats were more reserved, the men in plain waistcoats and carrying canes with ornate silver tops, the women in muted blues, greens and yellows, their faces shaded by broad-brimmed hats sprouting feathers and swagged with lace. They sat in front of a platform with three nooses dangling from a crossbeam. In front of the nooses was a large wooden block, indented at the top. Three coffins had then been laid out in front of the gallows.

'Why is that block there?' Sarah asked Coombes.

He did not answer.

'Tell me!' she said, angry at him for trying to spare her horror on this day, which was saturated with it already.

'They are going to take off their heads,' said Coombes quietly. 'Afterwards.'

She swayed, and he put a hand out to steady her.

It seemed the ultimate act of vindictiveness. If all the government truly wanted to do was remove wrong doers, they would have no need of these blocks. But this posthumous humiliation spoke of the barbaric spite of which she well knew they were capable.

A moment later, a hush fell across the crowd. There was a murmur from those in the seats, but Sarah couldn't see anything beyond craning necks.

'What's happening?' she asked Coombes.

'I think they're being . . . yes, there, see?' He pointed, and Sarah positioned herself between the two people in front of her so she could watch three figures being led towards the gallows. They were wearing the clothes in which they had been arrested. Briardown's lace cuffs were caught in his manacles. Tully wore a plain waistcoat, slightly less strained than it had been, but no jacket.

Sam would surely come into view next, but she grasped this last moment of hope: perhaps there had been some reprieve. Then he appeared, wearing his rough worsted coat and a familiar cap that was now dirty.

The three men lined up quietly, politely, to have their irons struck off. Briardown's hands were freed first, and someone in the crowd yelled, 'How are you feeling?'

He looked pale, but smiled. 'I have never been in better spirits in the course of my life.'

Tully was almost dancing when he walked up, smiling to the crowd as he presented himself to have his irons removed. Someone yelled, 'God bless you!' and he bowed.

No one yelled for Sam. Sarah was desperate to say she loved him, to wish him a joyful reunion with their parents. She did not, though, and chided herself for her cowardice.

The freedom was momentary; the men's hands were immediately bound with rope in front of them. They mounted the scaffold one by one, each standing in front of a noose. As soon as Sam took his position, a great roar erupted from the crowd, louder than the one that had greeted Orator Hartford on the hustings. It vibrated in Sarah's chest so violently that she thought her heart might stop, and she did not know if she would mind.

When the noise died down, Sam stepped forward. 'I die an enemy to all tyrants!' he yelled, his voice a little shaky.

The crowd roared again, mingling shouts of outrage with those of elation. Did people actually believe they were about to watch three men be killed and decapitated – or did they feel, somehow, that they were watching a play?

The executioner was approaching, black hoods in his hand.

'Sam won't see me,' Sarah said to Coombes. This, suddenly, felt like the most important thing in the world, blotting out any caution she might have felt at being too visible herself. 'But he has to see me – he has to know that I'm alive! And that I'm with him at the end.'

'Do not draw attention to yourself,' said Coombes urgently.

'He won't be in a position to pay attention for much longer – please!'

The first mate sighed and shook his head, then knelt to grab her around the waist so she could sit on his shoulder. He stood up with a groan of complaint. As she looked around, she saw others borne aloft, children and small women, avidly staring at the gallows.

The crowd grew very quiet as the executioner approached. Sarah knew that if she called out to Sam, she might soon find herself standing before a noose. But she had to do something, anything, to draw his attention. She realised there was one phrase she could use; it might be uttered in either sympathy or condemnation. She took off her cap, letting her hair spill down her back. After drawing in a deep breath, she paused, then yelled at the top of her lungs, 'May God have mercy on your souls!'

The condemned men turned in unison, as did the executioner and some of the nearby officials. She fancied there was surprise on Briardown's face, and a slight grin on Tully's. When Sam saw her, his eyes widened, and he let out a low moan of hopelessness. In a gesture she hoped most would miss, she swiftly held her hand to her heart and then out to him.

The executioner began to lower the hood over Sam's face, and he kept his eyes on her until the moment the fabric descended. Then Briardown's long nose disappeared beneath the cloth. The last words from Tully's mouth were, 'Finish us tidily!'

The executioner went from one man to the next, draping the nooses over their shoulders. He moved to the lever that would make the platform drop from under their feet. On a nod from the governor of the prison, and amid a silence Sarah had not thought so many people capable of, he pulled it.

The ropes snapped taut as the men dropped. Sarah braced herself, knowing that hanging was an uncertain fate. Briardown jerked, his legs flailing, his body moving from side to side as a dark stain spread on his trousers, before he became still. Sam and Tully were luckier: they jerked briefly, then went limp.

Amid loud cheers from the crowd, Sarah howled and began to sob. Coombes dipped his shoulder, and she slid to the ground, sinking onto her hands and knees. He helped her to her feet and held her, making the kind of shushing noises she had only ever heard from her mother's lips.

When she looked back to the scaffold, the executioner was behind Briardown's body, cutting the rope; when the body fell, he and an assistant dragged it out in front of the scaffold, then he roughly pulled off the hood. Briardown's neck was placed on the block. A surgeon began to cut through the muscle and tendon and bones. Sarah didn't want to witness this, but she could not avoid the sight of the executioner holding up Briardown's head, blood still dripping from the stump of his neck, one eye a little more open than the other, his tongue swollen and slightly protruding from his mouth.

There were cheers at this as well, but they were somewhat less enthusiastic. *Perhaps more of them finally understand*, thought Sarah. *Perhaps they know, now, that this is no play. Perhaps they are ashamed of coming here for entertainment. If they are, they deserve to be.*

She bent over and retched, ejecting a small dribble of bile. Nearby, she heard the sound of others doing the same.

'You don't need to see that happen to your brother,' said Coombes. 'Come on, now.'

She certainly did not want to. But wouldn't it be cowardice to leave before the lid of his coffin was nailed shut? 'I should stay,' she said, wiping her mouth.

Coombes glanced at the scaffold and frowned. 'No, you shouldn't,' he said. 'Look.'

One of the officials at the edge of the gallows was talking to a man in a long black coat – a Bow Street Runner? – and pointing towards Coombes and Sarah.

'Ready?' asked Coombes. She nodded. He grasped her hand and dragged her through the crowd. When they got clear of the main press of people, they ran all the way to the docks.

✳

They found the *Serpent* at the centre of frantic activity. Baggage was being loaded, while passengers, in fine dress and plain, were walking up the gang-board.

'I shouldn't be here,' Sarah said to Coombes as they boarded. 'I can't leave England, Mr Coombes, I just can't. I owe it to him, to all of them, to find our fellow radicals. To try again.'

'There will be time for all that,' said Coombes. 'But wait a while until we talk to the captain. Don't go to your cabin – hide yourself in the hold. If that was a Runner we saw, he may well have followed us here.'

She did as he said, squeezing herself between two wooden crates. She could hear feet running above, backwards and forwards, no doubt those of crew loading last-minute provisions and seeing to passengers – the *Serpent* was to sail that night, and it was already early afternoon. Occasionally she heard sailors shout to each other, but none were alarmed. She was surprised not to hear the captain's low bellow, as surely he would have returned to the ship by now.

Then she heard him giving a command that she couldn't quite understand. She understood what was happening well enough, though, when the ship lurched and swayed. The wooden crates rocked towards her, and she had to hold them apart, her arms straining, to keep them from crushing her. When the ship steadied, she crawled out from between them, went over to the ladder and pushed at the hatch. It was locked.

She pounded on it, yelling. No one came.

She went back to the shelter of the crates, put her head on her knees, and sobbed.

Another half-hour or so dragged by before Watkins and Coombes stared down into the dimness of the hold.

'I wanted to stay in London!' she screamed at them. Her throat felt raw, and her eyes ached and itched. 'Mr Coombes, I told you, I have to do something! Please take me back – you will never hear from me again, I promise you.'

'I understand it has been an upsetting day for you,' Watkins said, 'so I'll forgive the insolence. But I cannot take you back.'

'Why? You are the captain, surely you have some authority here!'

Watkins handed her a page of newsprint.

We are informed that a woman is being looked for in connection with the terrible plot to murder members of the Cabinet. It is believed the woman is Sarah McCaffrey, sister of conspirator Samuel McCaffrey who is to be executed today at Newgate. No further particulars have been provided. It is understood the lady in question has been sought for some time, however the government now wishes for any individual who may be of assistance to come forward.

'Still,' she said after a moment, 'they do not know I am on this ship.'

'Perhaps they didn't know, then,' said Watkins. 'I will wager you that they suspect it now. Mr Coombes tells me

113

you attracted some attention at the execution. Not many boys call out in a woman's voice.'

'I am willing to take the risk!' she said. 'It is not up to you to decide.'

'That is all very well,' said Watkins. 'And are you willing to risk your friend here?' He inclined his head towards Coombes. 'I assure you, the Runners will be at the docks by now. If they had found you on board, not only would you have followed your brother, but Coombes and I might also have taken the same route into the afterlife. If they were certain we were harbouring you – and they are not, or they would already have been here – we may well find a welcoming party when we reach our destination.'

'I will simply disembark in Portsmouth, then.'

'You cannot,' said the captain, 'as we're not stopping there.'

'So where are we to stop? I can find a route back to London from there.'

'You can try to find your way back. From Cape Town.'

She looked at Coombes, who was staring at the ground. Although she felt remorse over having put him in danger, an odd mixture of grief and petulance was rising in her, threatening to sweep everyone away.

Glancing between the two men, she said, 'I do believe I require some time on deck, with your permission, captain. The air in here is quite stifling.'

As soon as Watkins nodded, she pounded up the steps and hurried to the rail of the ship. Watching London recede into the distance, she hoped none of the crew came close enough to see that she was quietly replenishing the ocean, drop by drop.

CHAPTER 12
Cape Town, July 1820

These docks, like others she had seen, had streets choked with people, clanking metal and creaking wood, and spires in the distance from which bells rang out every hour. The wooden piers and platforms were all gummed up with shouting men, backs bent under crates or barrels or bolts of cloth, alongside women weeping in the arms of soldiers, seamen or emigrants about to depart. Other women who had provided a less chaste farewell were scanning the crowd for their next customers: disgorged sailors heading for taverns.

But unlike the English docks, these ones nudged the flank of a large, flat mountain, the tallest object Sarah had ever seen. In the few days she had been here, she had spent hours gazing at its cloudy peak.

Sarah still clung to her hope of return, of revenge, but the vision was threatening to soften and fade away. Alone in her cabin, she would call forth images of Sam hanging limp on the end of a rope. She would trace a line across her chest where the Hussar's blade had slashed her father's. She would embed her nails into her bare thigh, digging for proof that she still possessed the ability to feel.

She would possibly have ample proof, soon enough – that was partly why she had sent James McDonald ashore. She was now watching his broad back as he tried to thread and angle his way through the dockside crowd.

'Lucky, aren't you, to have such a handsome errand boy.' The words came with a gentle nudge in the ribs, before freckled forearms settled on the rail next to Sarah's. Maisie Cavanagh craned her neck, her eyes on the tall young man as he strode through the chaos.

Sarah closed her eyes at the words. James was a little older than Henry. On his return to the ship, he would likely make much of his bravery in battling the crowds, while Sarah nodded and thought of a lad who had never drawn attention to his natural courage.

She was struggling to resist the urge to run ashore herself. She still had the boys' clothes in which she had watched her brother die; they were wrapped in a bundle under her pillow. Apart from the ivory token, imprisoned in Watkins's seachest in his cabin, they were all she had of Sam, as the little leaden sailor was all she had left of Henry, although she did not know whether it was a clever distraction or a token of affection. They tethered her to England and the accounts to be settled there.

She had considered putting them on. She could smear some of the ship's plentiful grime on her face, keep her head down, shoulder her way through the dockside crowd. Find a ship that would carry her in its belly as it slid back across the seas the *Serpent* had just navigated. It was a tempting course of action. Futile, though. The little disc was the only currency she had. She would have to stow away or disguise herself as a cabin boy for the entire journey, and arrive destitute in a friendless city.

This course of action was unlikely to succeed, but at times it seemed that any action would be better than standing at the rail day after day. She could feel impatience stretching within her, along with a panicked urgency. Today she had realised she could at least seek out some information with help from James.

She took a breath and smiled at Maisie. 'Don't let James hear you call him handsome,' she said, 'or we'll have to submit to another lecture on what's wrong with the old world and how he will make it right in the new one.'

'I wouldn't mind. I'd just watch those lips moving – wouldn't listen to a word, of course.' Maisie was a great admirer of the male form, although she never let her enthusiasm off its leash in mixed company. She was being exported as governess to a family of seven rambunctious children, and she was careful to present the aspect of an austere, decorous woman.

'I'm sure he'd be happy to have such an attentive audience,' said Sarah. 'You had best truss him up before the girls in Sydney get their chance.'

'It's a chance I'll never have, as you well know. His eyes wander, certainly, but not in my direction.' There was no malice or jealousy in Maisie's expression. She had a broad, open face, anchored by a little snub of a nose. Her skin was the smoothest Sarah could remember seeing. The girl rarely frowned, and Sarah had never heard her utter a harsh word towards a sailor who clumsily bumped her on the deck, or another of the passengers who trod on her foot when the ship lurched. Such events caused other women – particularly the older ones – to draw themselves up and reprimand the miscreants; Maisie simply smiled and walked on.

'James's eyes can wander right off again,' Sarah said, earning a snort and another sharp nudge from Maisie's elbow.

It was Maisie, actually, whom Sarah had to thank for the clothes she was wearing. Some quiet enquiries by the captain among the officers' wives and the few unaccompanied female passengers had revealed only one woman willing to sell a dress to the young lady whose luggage had mysteriously fallen overboard.

Sarah had played with other girls as a child and been friendly enough with them as she grew. But since she and Sam had moved to London, she had barely seen a girl or a woman. Well, there had been fellow servants, pinch-faced and silent; the bowels of a great house were not an ideal place for jovial conversation and the forming of friendships.

In Maisie's company, some of the tightness that banded Sarah's chest had begun to ease. The frivolity of the girl's conversation – the store she set by such things as pleasing manners in a man and soft fabric in a shawl – would have clenched Sarah's teeth, had it not been cut with a sly wit. Maisie allowed Sarah to sink into a world where such inconveniences as a missing button or a bout of seasickness were the worst that could befall a person.

But would Maisie have been as willing to lend her clothes had she known the truth? Sarah had told her friend what she told everyone who enquired: she was seeking work in Sydney where she had heard domestics who lacked a convict stain were prized.

The ship was not so large that Sarah could avoid some of the more dour and judgemental among the passengers. On this wooden colony with close to two hundred people bumping up against each other, they could even hear each other's moans of sickness or desire through the cabin bulkheads. She knew well that there were whispers about her: a girl no one had seen boarding, one whose luggage had somehow found its way into the ocean when everyone else's trunks were stored below. She seemed, too, to be a favourite of the captain, people said; perhaps she was paying for her passage in something other than coin.

'She speaks in that Northern manner, of course,' Mrs Simkin had murmured to her husband last Sunday as the two of them walked past Sarah on the deck.

Reverend Simkin usually stalked the decks in sepulchral silence but grew animated each Sunday when the ship's bell was rung. Most of the *Serpent*'s free population would make for the poop deck, safe behind a line of soldiers clutching bayoneted rifles. Below them, in leg irons, the convicts would be brought up to the main deck. Twice a day, while at sea, they were allowed up in groups to breathe the same air as their guards, before being reclaimed by the dimness below. Usually they were allowed to amble around unfettered, but on Sundays, when they were asked to absorb the lessons of a loving God, they were ironed – they couldn't be trusted, apparently, not to mutiny when everyone else was distracted by devotion.

The boy who reminded Sarah of the baker's lad was among those to emerge from the hatch each Sunday. On occasion he looked up to the passengers in their reserved paradise of the poop deck, and Sarah sometimes caught his eye and smiled. He would quickly grin at her, then look down. He was learning, already, that there was safety in not attracting notice.

As the weeks had passed, Reverend Simkin had been called on a number of occasions to intone over a shrouded figure brought up from the cell and slid into the ocean. He would stand at a flag-draped table and exhort the men before him to have a care for their immortal souls, in tones that suggested he wasn't at all sure they possessed such things. Then the main deck would be left to the free, and Mrs Simkin would promenade on the arm of her husband while shooting spiteful little darts out of the corner of her mouth: 'The Northerners, they are a bit, well, common. And as for him – nothing would surprise me.'

Sarah assumed the *him* referred to Captain Watkins, and on this she agreed wholeheartedly with Mrs Simkin. Many on board did, including James. 'He is irregular,' the young man would say as he watched Watkins clip the ear of one sailor for leering at a female passenger, while another of his crew lay passed out on a pile of rope. For James McDonald, irregularity was the worst of all crimes.

An Irishman, James called himself, and it was true his voice had something of the lilt, although he worshipped in a Protestant church. He was the ninth son of a merchant from County Antrim. Mr McDonald senior already had more than enough successors to his drapery, so it was as well that James had found a position as factotum to a surgeon seeing to the health of those on board the *Serpent*. The young man had hopes of obtaining work in Australia; he had heard that land grants were doled out to those looked on favourably by the administration. 'It is so wonderful to be the only McDonald for once,' he had said to Sarah. 'No one in Sydney will ever call me the draper's youngest.'

Whenever Sarah was on deck, with or without Maisie, James would hover off to the side, waiting for an opportunity to be of service, prove himself in a field less crowded than that in which he had spent his youth. He had been delighted when Sarah, feigning homesickness, had asked him to go into Cape Town and fetch the most recent English newspaper. She wanted to know if those in power were still looking for her – and, if they were, how far they were gazing.

James was not the only man from the ship disappearing into the crowd; she had spied Watkins's spotless blue jacket among the rough clothes of the longshoremen. He walked with a purposeful stride, anxious to get to wherever he was going.

She heard a grunt and saw that Coombes was standing a few feet from her along the rail, his eyes narrowed as he watched the departing captain.

CHAPTER 13

The first mate had, on occasion, said hello to Sarah on the deck. If Maisie was with her, or if she was within proximity of another passenger, he would pass without acknowledgement; when she was alone, though, he would nod to her and exchange pleasantries. He seemed to be longing for their old banter, diminished by what Sarah thought of as her kidnapping. 'Too good for me, I suppose, now you're a passenger,' he had said once, smiling to let her know the intention behind the words.

Despite her anger at her forced departure from England, she had not forgotten sobbing against his shoulder as her brother died. 'Never too good for you,' she'd said, and smiled just as Reverend and Mrs Simkin passed by, heads together and muttering.

Now, though, Coombes seemed to be in an irritable mood. He spat on the deck, an action that would have seen any other sailor deprived of rations. Then he noticed her approaching him and nodded politely. 'Beg your pardon.'

'Are you upset, Mr Coombes?' Sarah asked, as Maisie wrinkled her nose at the gesture – she deplored rudeness – and walked off a short distance to gaze at the dock.

'By them that get money where they shouldn't, yes. And by them that spend it where they shouldn't, too.'

'Is that what the captain is doing?'

'You asked, in London, why I was aboard so early,' he said quietly. 'Our man's not averse to making a profit in ways not to my liking. He picks off whatever parts of a ship he thinks he can sell – it's why he's often on board a couple of weeks before anyone else. Not many ships will take him anymore, but I suppose the owner of this one was desperate or hadn't heard the rumours.'

Sarah looked down at the timbers of the deck, wondering if they were as solid as they seemed. 'Is the ship safe?' she asked.

'I had thought so. He's been crafty. But sometimes it's what you don't see that you have to worry about. He went ashore yesterday, too, carrying a sack. And I know what was inside, for it was in his cabin when I brought him some ale, and he'd left it open. I saw enough to recognise a gudgeon.'

'What's that?'

'It keeps the rudder on the back of the ship. The pintles were surely in there as well.'

'So . . . the ship has no rudder?' she asked, resisting the urge to bolt for the dock rather than stay on a maimed ship that might be blown anywhere.

Coombes shook his head and chuckled joylessly. 'I keep forgetting you're not born to this – of course it has a rudder. We've managed to steer this far, haven't we. But what's keeping the rudder on the stern? Probably not what the shipwright put there. Rusty, maybe. Flimsy. There's a wound on the back of this vessel, and part of it has disappeared into a shipyard here.' The deck creaked, and Coombes looked around belatedly for anyone close enough to hear them. He suddenly seemed agitated, as though worrying he had spent his words unwisely. 'Beg pardon, I have duties,' he said, and scuttled off.

Sarah stayed at the rail until she saw James striding back, newspapers under his arm, walking with the confidence of a man who had completed an important mission. She felt a surge of irritation, as he would expect an inordinate amount of praise.

'Your knight has completed his quest, I see,' said Maisie, who had rejoined her when Coombes left.

'And I will need to swoon when I hear about the dragons he battled,' said Sarah.

She would have gone straight to her cabin if Watkins's jacket had not caught her eye again. He was carrying a long, unwieldy canvas-wrapped bundle back to the *Serpent*.

In the life she should have had, she would not have been on board this ship. She would have been in Manchester with her parents. She might have attended Sam's wedding by now, or even greeted a niece or nephew. And she would have had no idea what a package shaped like that could possibly contain.

In the life she had been given, though, she had seen more than enough swaddled rifles to recognise them, even from a distance.

✦

James seemed gratified by his reception when he returned with every edition of *The Times of London* he had been able to find, some stretching back almost to her departure. He bowed, made to present them to her, then seemed to change his mind and tucked them back under his arm. 'I went to stores and coffee houses and every tavern I could, begging anyone who had an old paper to give it to me. It's so alive here. Isn't it wonderful?' He gently took her arm with his free hand, as though they were about to walk into a ball. 'Of course I had a devil of a time getting them for you – some of the alleyways behind the docks, well, I could have been pulled in and never heard from again.' His shoulders straightened, his chin lifted; maybe he was waiting for her praise. 'I would ask if there is any particular area of interest in these papers,' he said, when it became clear she would not faint over his bravery. 'I know you won't tell me, though.'

She was unable to resist sliding a hand into her pocket and closing her fingers around the little leaden sailor. 'Why does it matter? When we arrive in Sydney, I'll be into someone's household, and you'll be off to make food from some unruly scrap of land.'

'You can always come with me,' he said softly. 'If you're going to fetch and carry, you might as well be in your own household.'

It was not the first time he had suggested this, nor the first time she needed to find a way to politely deflect the question.

Had she been what she claimed to be, she would have considered it. They got along well enough, had some lively conversations, and he was handsome. He did not disturb her thoughts the way Henry still did, walking into her dreams to jeer at her or reproach her for doubting him – but that was of no consequence, she told herself. People were rarely able to marry those who invaded their minds unbidden, whose presence or absence could change the complexion of an entire day. Such unions were for the fairy stories her ma had told her.

If she could know for certain that she was no longer a fugitive, she might consider marrying a man like James. 'We shall have to see if you are as you appear,' she said to him. 'Perhaps you're really an escaping footpad who bails up carriages and leaves the passengers without their jewellery.'

James usually laughed at such deflections; this afternoon, though, he frowned. 'I am not the worst of all possibilities, you know. Your refusal to discuss the matter with any degree of seriousness is beginning to insult me.'

She bit the inside of her lower lip to keep from saying that his refusal to accept her answer was the true insult. It was vital that she not appear unladylike. 'I mean nothing by it,' she said demurely. 'I am new to this, that is all.'

'As you will be to Sydney. You have no experience of danger, Sarah. No experience of want. There are opportunities in the colony, yes, but also peril and deprivation. I am offering myself as a shield against them, but will not do so for much longer.' He released her arm, bowed stiffly, handed her the newspapers and stalked off.

She was astonished he could not read it in her face: the violence she'd witnessed, the loading of rifles and hiding of arms, the fall onto the cobbles. The roar of the crowd at the sight of a man waving a white hat or of a rope tightening around a man's throat.

But it wasn't fair of her to blame James for his ignorance – all he knew of her was what she had chosen to tell him.

In any case, it was convenient that he had taken himself off. Now she could bring the newspapers to her tiny cabin, spread them out on the floor, and hunt through them for any mention of the names Sarah McCaffrey, Henry Landers and Albert Tourville.

✦

She had almost reached her cabin door when she heard a man's voice: 'You will find nothing in those to help you, and plenty to harm you.'

She had been so intent on the bundle of papers that she had not seen Captain Watkins approaching. He inclined his head to her, and she bobbed in greeting just as the ship gave a lurch and sent her stumbling against the bulkhead.

'I trust your own excursion today did not involve anything harmful.' Embarrassed by her stumble, she spoke more harshly than she had intended. She expected him to be mildly irritated, maybe to walk off.

Instead, he narrowed his eyes and pursed his lips. 'Captains do go ashore. And their reasons are their own.'

She felt the trickling heat of an emerging bruise on her shin. 'Well, I'm grateful for your warning about the perils of these newspapers. But I think I will survive time alone with them.' With that, she opened her door and ducked into her cabin.

When she reached the third page of one of the papers, she regretted those last words to Watkins. She was not at all sure she would survive this.

The final member of the Horse & Coach conspirators to remain at large is believed to be the sister of conspirator Samuel McCaffrey, who was hanged at the Newgate.

Like her brother, if apprehended Miss Sarah McCaffrey will stand trial for high treason. She will then almost certainly hang for her part in the evil plot that saw her brother so justly executed.

It seems the McCaffrey family is steeped in villainy. Our correspondent in Manchester writes that the parents of these ruffians brought about their own deaths by resisting lawful direction from yeomen at the infamous public meeting in St Peter's Field last year.

While some have reported seeing a woman with a resemblance to Miss McCaffrey in Scotland, there are others who believe she has left these shores, although it is not known where she might have come by the resources to pay for her passage.

The government has a reasonable idea of Miss McCaffrey's appearance, as a description was furnished by one or more spies who had infiltrated the conspirators. His or their identities have been protected.

Familiar bands of fear encircled her chest. She had been hoping to learn that the search for her had been abandoned, or to find nothing in the papers and allow herself to assume that public interest had faded.

Closing her eyes, she tried to remember Sam's laugh, even his snore, but he was becoming indistinct like their parents. Surely this must be her deficiency, because a truly loving sister and daughter would carry such things with her to the end of her life.

She was desperate to wail, to shout – that, though, would bring the solicitous Maisie running, together with James who would sense an opportunity to prove himself a capable protector. She asked Coombes to tell James she was unwell and required uninterrupted solitude. He grunted, mumbling about his other tasks, but stalked off to carry out her request.

✳

Sarah almost welcomed the worst of the sea's anger. As the weather roughened and the *Serpent* pitched, water gushed down ladders and wet her stockings when she stepped out of her small bunk. The fear the ocean brought, the knowledge that she was prevented from sinking by nothing more than wooden planks and bolts, was the only force that could push thoughts of Sam, Henry and her parents away for a moment or two.

In the midst of a storm, she could howl and no one would come running; no one would ask what on earth that awful noise was, and what creature could possibly be making it.

Once she had screamed her grief and anger into the maelstrom, her head grew clearer for a time. England had transplanted part of itself to New South Wales, and the shadows of those who had killed her brother could surely be found in the colony, so she might yet be able to cause them some pain. If Watkins was bringing those rifles to fellow sympathisers, they must have a plan. And perhaps they would welcome some assistance.

CHAPTER 14

Something had exuded from that newspaper, curled around her, suffocated her without letting her die. The flare of fear when she thought of the constant threat of capture. The choking stress at having to maintain a fiction all her life. The faint hope of finding some vengeance, some redress in Sydney, followed by the renewed realisation that no one would care if she succeeded or failed, lived or died.

It was days before she emerged into full sunlight.

She could not stand the sound of male voices now. The educated ones all reminded her of Briardown's pompous speeches and Tourville's oily solicitousness. The sailors' shouts sounded like those of the Runners, the thuds of their feet on the deck like the hooves of a Hussar's horse.

She would walk on the deck at dawn, when the place belonged to her, the crew and an occasional soldier. At this hour the convicts would still be in their irons, attached to the ship. The water sloshed against the hull in the morning dark, the furthest reaches of the ship appearing as the sky lightened. She felt, at those times, as though some of the world was hers again.

Watkins was known for keeping late hours, so she was surprised to see him on deck at such a time. His face was speckled with overnight growth, his eyes perhaps a little less bright than usual, but judging by the commands he barked at his crew, he was no less capable of sailing the ship.

He was a man of movement and noise, so she started when she realised he was standing next to her by the rail. At her intake of breath, he shook his head. 'How is it possible for me to frighten a woman who has endured and risked so much? Are you truly so changed already?' It might have been a rebuke, but his voice was heavy with resignation.

'I am not changed at all, captain. I still believe as you do – fortunately for you. I saw that you carried a parcel back from Cape Town, and I suspect it was not rum.'

'Why would it not be? You have seen how I imbibe.'

'A captain does not go ashore merely to collect rum, not when he has an entire crew at his disposal.'

'Well, Miss Marin, I am not in the habit of justifying my actions to passengers, and nor do I intend to start now.' Watkins began to walk away.

'I am not asking you to justify anything,' she said. 'I am asking you for a promise.'

He stopped and looked back at her.

'I saw my pa's innards, you know.' She was surprised at the steadiness of her voice. 'They were bulging out of him, shiny. As though they couldn't wait to be free. My ma – her chest was no thicker than a book. And my brother, now. Strangled while people gossiped and bought trinkets from the peddlers.'

'All of this I know.'

'The hand that killed my brother – one of its fingers is in Sydney. I wish to lop it off, and you will give me the means to do that.'

Watkins scoffed. 'How on earth–?'

'You could spare some of your cargo from Cape Town.'

✦

They were less than a week out from New South Wales. If the winds were favourable, Watkins had told her, maybe a few days. She was almost as distant from the graves of her family as it was possible to be, and the strangeness of the colony – the tall tales she'd heard of bloodthirsty convicts and hopping monstrosities – seemed more ominous than intriguing. Particularly now, when she knew what lay beneath a board in the captain's quarters.

He had led her there that morning, after their conversation on the deck. On the way to his cabin she had noticed a couple of the older women whispering to each other, and she had felt like stopping and bowing.

Watkins had locked his door behind them before levering up the board, then pulling out and unwrapping the bundle of half a dozen rifles. 'You'll take these ashore with you.'

'And they should go to . . . ?'

'To a tavern near the docks – I will point it out when we arrive. Now don't flinch, it is empty during the day. Well, mostly. But if you knock at the right time, a man will answer, and you will recognise him.'

'How?'

'How did you recognise this ship? How did I know you for what you were?'

When she nodded, Watkins bowed, took her hand and moved it towards his mouth, but he stopped short of letting his lips touch her skin.

Afterwards she had returned to the deck, and she had not sought shelter when it started to rain. When the wind drew her hair over her mouth. When the light faded. She did not know whether the moisture on her face came from the sky or the sea, and she shivered as the shawl she had crossed over her chest and tied at the small of her back began to soak up water.

Maisie would have chided her for that, had she not already closed her cabin door against the rain and wind plucking the sea into little hillocks. She had given the shawl to Sarah shortly after they had met. 'You are not an inside woman,' Maisie had said. 'You will need something as you wander the deck, getting under the sailors' feet.'

How would Maisie react if she knew the truth? Sarah pictured a frown creasing her heart-shaped face. Maisie would care more about the existence of the lie than its substance.

James would be a different matter. It was one thing to be the brave rescuer of a dark-haired girl whom fate had cheated, another to conceal a revolutionary. He might rage, he might strike her, he might even have her arrested when they landed, an opening gambit in winning the good graces of those in power.

The weather was inclement enough to rouse the sailors from their evening torpor. They began scurrying around the deck, attending to the sails. Watkins strode out of his cabin and slammed the door flat against its frame, issuing orders that were taken by the wind before they reached her ears. She watched as he stopped a sailor, a hand on the man's shoulder, and gestured over at her.

The sailor approached her slowly, as though she might be dangerous. 'I don't know what you're doing up here, miss – some of the lads think you're touched,' he called above the howl of the wind. 'But you're to get below now. Captain's orders!'

She stared at him, and he stared back with his head to the side, perhaps wondering if she was indeed touched. Then she nodded to him and picked her way across the tilting, rain-slick deck to the ladder below.

CHAPTER 15

The rain kept thickening, and the winds kept building, while most passengers kept to their cabins. They were accompanied, in those last days of the journey, by vast grey creatures, monstrous in their appearance but not, apparently, in their nature. They made no move to attack the boat; in fact, at times they seemed to be sporting with it, keeping pace, sometimes lurking just under the surface, testing it occasionally with their tails and slapping the water for some imagined offence. Or they would miraculously propel their vast bulks all the way out of the water so that Sarah could see their white, grooved throats.

The route of the ship was hugging the land fairly closely now, a coastline of honeyed stone, crumbled like biscuit, under continual assault from the sea. Boulders had been shaved off the cliffs and deposited into the water, some forming platforms on which seals lazed. The cliffs seemed to suffer still from their wounds, sharp and jutting in places, the litter of stone spiky and ragged along their base.

The rain had not left, nor had the wind. Sarah had grown used to crouching and extending her legs to absorb the worst of the ship's bucking. She had even begun to enjoy it.

Earlier that day, Sarah had tempted Maisie on deck to see the whales. Maisie, never really comfortable on the sea, had given a stiff little smile and said of course she'd be delighted. Increasingly Sarah craved the girl's company, as Maisie could usually be relied on to share Sarah's amazement at the strange sights that greeted them on their journey. But if the whales were still accompanying them, the girls could not see through the pounding rain. 'Do you know,' said Maisie after a while, 'I do think I'd be better off below. I'm afraid my stomach is not enjoying the view.'

Sarah remained there, staring into the grey until the water had seeped into her clothes.

'They do think you're fey, you know,' said Coombes, coming up beside her.

'Good. Probably keeps them away.'

'Oh yes. Most of 'em wouldn't be up here if they had a choice. Why don't I take you below? If only to save the lads the embarrassment of the sight of a girl handling the ocean better than them.'

'In a minute, perhaps. I have to see the captain.'

Coombes snorted. 'He's sleeping off the lunchtime rum. Don't wake him, we'll need him if this storm gets any worse.'

'How long till we arrive?'

'Tomorrow. Later tonight if the weather clears, which would be a miracle.'

'Will you take me to him, then? I need to collect . . . some things he promised me.'

Coombes frowned. 'Which are?'

Sarah sighed. She had not told anyone, of course, about the rifles. The information sat within her, pulsing and stretching and pushing to get out. She knew, though, that if either of the men were honest with her, it was more likely to be Coombes.

'Rifles. I'm to deliver them where they'll be put to use. To those who know when to use them, to best effect, to deliver the loudest possible message.'

Coombes chuckled and shook his head.

'I wasn't trying to amuse you,' she snapped.

'And you haven't. Told you to call at the tavern, did he?'

Sarah stared at him. She was surprised that he knew, but it also showed her that she had been right to confide in him.

'I was afraid of this,' Coombes said. 'Can't help himself. He's not what he was, our captain. Got sick of looking at those he hated riding in fine carriages that splashed him with mud. Decided if they could find profit in tyranny, he should be able to find it in rebellion.' The first mate grasped her shoulder, his voice dropping to a whisper. 'I will not have this happen. I will not see you hanged to put coins in Watkins's pocket.'

'Hanged?'

'Well, the fellow at that tavern will take the arms from you and thank you kindly for them. And they will be distributed. Not to the children of freedom, though, but to landowners and smallholders and anyone else who doesn't feel like paying duty on them. These men will pay the fellow from the tavern, and he will find a way to get the money back to Watkins. And should the local constabulary find out, our captain runs very little risk of being caught.'

Sarah clenched her teeth, then bit into her tongue as she imagined Sam might have done on the gallows, the blood trickling down her throat. Her brother had died for ideals that to Watkins simply represented a chance to earn a profit.

'Take me to him,' she said, resisting the temptation to scream the words.

Coombes nodded and gestured for her to follow him. As they approached Watkins's cabin, she noticed the deck tilting a little more violently than she had ever seen before.

When Coombes rapped at the cabin door, Watkins roared, 'Go to blazes!'

'Would like to oblige, captain, but Miss Marin is here to see you. She seems agitated.'

There were a few thumps before the door was yanked open by Watkins, in his breeches and shod but with his white shirt loose and unlaced at the front. He looked over Combes's shoulder. 'Miss Marin. I do hope you understand, this is not a terribly convenient time.'

Sarah pushed past Coombes into the cabin, which was in even more disarray than usual. The small sleeping alcove off to the side, usually shielded from view by a curtain, showed signs that Watkins had only recently arisen from his bed, sheets strewn on the floor and soaking up some of the water that the rain and the movement of the ship forced in even here. Stacks of papers sat unsteadily on the green baize chart table, while others had fallen off and lay tumbled together, scrolls rolling backwards and forwards.

'Come now, Miss Marin,' Watkins said, 'I'm sure Mr Coombes can assist you with whatever it is you want.'

'I'm not sure that Coombes can,' said the first mate.

'He can't, unless he has guns,' said Sarah. 'The ones you want me to deliver? That are to be used for an uprising?'

'Ah, well, I rather thought that transfer might happen after we dock,' Watkins said. 'And really, there is quite a lot to do between now and then, so . . .'

'The ones that were going to be sold on,' she continued. 'The ones I could have been arrested for in your place.'

Watkins glared at Coombes, who shrugged.

'Someone has been making up stories, I see. Very bad for morale aboard ship. You know, Mr Coombes, how I deal with that.'

'The sea might deal with us all before you get a chance to,' said Coombes. 'New parts are generally not replaced with rusted ones, especially those that fix the rudder to the stern.'

Watkins drew himself up, his nostrils flaring. 'You, Mr Coombes, will be dealt with. You will be put ashore in Sydney, and you will not be making the return voyage with me or any other captain.'

'I'll be dealt with, eh? I have lied for you. Spent the coin of other people's trust on your behalf, so you remain unsullied but everyone looks sideways at the shifty first mate. I've put to sea with you, knowing the ship is not as sound as it could be. But now you want to send this lass – after what she has lost – into a tavern she may never come out of! Put me ashore if you must. I could tell quite an interesting story, with all that time to myself in Sydney.'

As Watkins stepped forward, he looked as though he would attack Coombes if the ship's movement let him.

Sarah put herself between the men. 'I will be taking the weapons, and I will be finding another home for them.'

'You will not, my dear,' said Watkins. 'I'm sorry but I cannot allow it.'

Sarah had, since girlhood, been told what others would or would not allow. Such words only lay comfortably in the mouths of tyrants.

'I, too, have an interesting story to tell,' she said.

'So interesting that it would end with your neck in a noose,' the captain retorted. 'And which of us will they believe – a mysterious girl no one saw until the voyage was underway, a girl of no family, a girl no one will miss, or a captain of good standing?'

'Quite poor standing, according to the Sydney harbourmaster,' said Coombes. 'He's always thought you were a bit of a loose one. Willing to take the risk?'

'Oh, and I want my token, too.' Sarah nodded to the seachest lying on its side on the floor, presumably flung from the table by the rocking of the ship.

Watkins barked a laugh. 'Been meaning to throw it overboard – wouldn't do to be caught with it. I'm sure that if you take it, you'll soon see your brother again.'

This man was willing to twist Sam's death into a threat. She inhaled a great gulp of air at the thought, expelling it as she lunged towards him.

Coombes drew in a sharp breath and reached out to stop her. She was quicker, though she had no thought of what she would do to Watkins. Some damage, hopefully – a punctured eye, a scratched cheek.

The ship gave a violent lurch, and she and Coombes barely kept their balance. Watkins was jolted onto his back, sliding across the floor and cracking his head against a leg of the chart table. He groaned, showing he was not completely insensible. Sarah could not quite decide whether this was good news or bad. Everyone's survival, after all, depended on a competent captain.

When Coombes gently shoved her out the door, she needed no further urging.

CHAPTER 16

Out on the deck, those who normally stayed below in foul weather were emerging. The cabins were claustrophobic enough, and when one was being rocked about and knocked into walls they felt a little too much like coffins.

Maisie, now in her nightdress, kept wiping the water from her eyes as the rain added more. White as an apparition, wide-eyed, her hair smeared across her face, she whipped her head from one side to the other. Sarah ran up to her, taking off her sodden shawl and draping it over Maisie's shoulders. Maisie's soaked nightdress was revealing more than the young woman would have tolerated had her terror not choked off any rational thought.

'Here,' Sarah said, moving towards the port rail, 'we'll be safe over here. We can see what the crew is doing, and we can hang on.'

She spied Watkins stepping out of the door that led to his cabin, pulling his blue jacket over his still untucked shirt, followed by Coombes. The captain was looking about, presumably for his crew, who were scrabbling across the deck in what did not seem a coordinated fashion. His eyes skidded over her, wide in the small ration of light that the clouds let through. Then he dashed to the wheel and screamed at the two sailors trying to control it. 'Keep your luff! Steer nearer the wind!' Then, in a screech that exceeded that of the gale: 'All hands square away!'

It was a language Sarah did not speak, had no hope of understanding. His howls were met, though, with immediate action from the crew.

More passengers were emerging, wrapped in cloaks or shawls or coats over their nightclothes, some men hiding their terror by demanding information from the crew.

'You mustn't worry,' Sarah said to Maisie. 'Storms are like children – they make a lot of fuss then quieten down. Don't be frightened.'

'I'm not frightened,' said Maisie, gripping the rail as the ship's prow suddenly pointed upwards, climbing a wave that disappeared underneath them and sent the vessel crashing into the water. A gout of ocean spread across the deck.

The lookouts fore and aft were yelling now – not to each other but to anyone within hearing range. 'South Head!' they cried. 'Can anyone see South Head?'

The dim afternoon light, whatever managed to penetrate the clouds, made it hard to see, but the shape of the cliff was still visible. Sarah had no idea what South

Head was, but she squinted and hoped she would know it when she saw it.

Was that a light? She stared at it until she was sure it was there, then turned to see if anyone was close by. Figures were moving behind the rain, but she could not see their faces. She inhaled, drawing in water vapour along with air, and screamed as loud as she could. 'A light! A light, there on the cliff!'

One of the shadows came closer, Watkins's face emerging through the rain. He peered in the direction she was pointing. Then he whipped around, stalking back to the wheel with Sarah scrambling after him. 'The light at South Head!' he called as he passed groups of sailors. 'We just have to keep off the rocks a little longer!'

'The prisoners,' Sarah said, 'have they been rail-ironed for the night? Tell the soldiers not to!'

'I have more immediate concerns!' the captain shouted.

Another shape appeared through the rain, white hands grasping at Watkins's sleeve. Mrs Simkin cried out, 'Are we doomed?'

He shook off her hand. 'Not if you allow me to attend to my duties, madam,' he said, turning again to the wheel. 'And I suggest you ask your husband to attend to his – a little divine assistance with the elements would be welcome.'

One of the lookouts called so loudly that he must have scalded his throat. 'Breakers! Breakers, there!'

'Starboard!' screamed Watkins. 'Breakers abeam, hard a-starboard!'

Sarah looked over the side of the ship. Lines of white foam were appearing and disappearing, keeling over onto themselves. These were not the whitecaps of the open ocean; these were the sentinels of the shore.

Another scream, broken by the wind, from the men at the wheel. 'Won't move . . . jammed . . . change course . . .'

Maisie gripped Sarah's arm. 'Can they . . . can they not steer the ship?'

'They've been able to so far, I don't see why they can't—'

Maisie's expression stopped her, and she turned to look.

The light she had seen was closer now, almost in front of them rather than off to the side. Then, rushing towards them, looming out of the dark, was the jagged, indifferent face of the cliff, almost close enough to touch.

The men at the wheel were trying to haul it while Watkins screamed at them as though they weren't putting in enough effort. Sarah could see no hopeful sign of the ship's prow thrusting towards the open ocean.

The cliff seemed to hover for an instant, perhaps deciding whether or not to take the ship. Then there came a rumbling and a screech and a *crack* like a cannon blast, and the mightiest of all jolts.

The impact knocked Sarah and Maisie off their feet, sending them on their backs to the starboard rail along with everyone on deck. Someone's foot hit Sarah's temple on the journey, and when she shook her head enough to clear it, she saw that some had travelled faster than others, nearly vaulting the rail. Maisie was lying next to her, moaning.

Sarah could hear a desperate shout, almost a screech. 'Help! Help!'

The ship had recoiled from the cliff, landing on submerged rocks and tilting so that the starboard rail was at an angle. Dangling from the wrong side of the rail, each hand grasping the opposite wrist so his arms made a loop around it, was Coombes. 'Help!' he yelled again, his hands slipping, his wrists emerging from his slick grip.

Sarah manoeuvred onto her haunches and dragged herself along the diagonal uprights towards him. Before she could get there, the ship was lifted again by the ocean. As its port hull had already been breached, it didn't float properly but pitched over, sending people hurtling towards the now-damaged rail.

Sarah was dimly aware of shapes sliding through the gap that had appeared in the rail. She whipped her head around to find that Maisie thankfully remained next to her, pale and wide-eyed and panting.

Watkins was still shouting commands at sailors who might already be dead, while he hauled on the wheel as though steering from the cliffs would make any difference now.

Coombes had somehow clambered back aboard during the last lurch and was pulling people to relative safety in the middle of the deck.

Sarah heard a low groan. At first she thought it might be from a passenger, but this sound, long and undulating, was loud enough to be heard well above the wind. It was followed by a *crack*, and the mainmast toppled across the deck towards the bow. One of the older sailors was pinned, unmoving. The sails came down too, the first shroud for a few other bodies that had not yet been washed over.

Sarah took Maisie by the shoulders. 'Can you swim?'

Maisie stared back with blank eyes.

'Maisie, can you swim?!'

'Yes, but . . . but we are safer here than in the ocean. Aren't we?'

'No, dear. In there, we might at least have a chance.'

Maisie looked over the rail into the churning water, then back at Sarah. Her eyes were not fixed on anything. Her mouth was slack.

Another wave hit the ship, and more people lost their footing, slipping towards the gap in the starboard rail, their hands scrabbling, using the last air in their lungs to scream, nails uselessly digging into the deck as they slid over the side.

There was, maybe, a minute until the next wave hit. Each one wrapped around more ankles, filled more mouths and noses, tugged more people into the sea.

'You must trust me,' Sarah told Maisie. 'We are going over here now.' She half helped, half dragged her friend towards the gap in the rail created by the first impact.

When Maisie saw where they were going, she began shaking her head, pulling backwards. 'No,' she said. 'No-no-no-no-*no*.' Each syllable was longer, more guttural than the one before, until the last came out in a moan.

It was a matter of seconds before the next wave hit. Sarah put her arms around Maisie, and Maisie put her head on Sarah's shoulder. 'Dear heart, I am sorry, but we will die if we stay here,' she said, and then stepped sideways into the air, taking Maisie with her.

The freezing water ripped them from each other. Sarah emerged into air so thick with vapour it hardly deserved the name. She whipped her head around looking for Maisie, wanting to tear her hair out as it slapped across her face, filling her mouth. She croaked out her friend's name, knowing she had no hope of being heard over the gale, the crash of the waves and the screams from the ship.

The current had taken her towards the stern. It had taken others too. A woman floated face down, her skirts billowing slightly with air trapped beneath them as they gradually took on water. A man with a badly grazed face – Reverend Simkin, it looked like – was face up, his eyes open towards the thick clouds that were becoming less visible as dusk began to draw in.

The bodies were surrounded by chunks of wood, and clothes that had burst from a passenger's trunk. In the middle of them was the convict boy she had seen on deck. His presence told her the hold had been ripped open, and that at least some of the prisoners had not been rail-ironed for the night. The lack of irons had not helped the lad, though. The ocean rolled him over and wrapped him in a stray skirt, the closest he would come to a shroud.

Another large wave was coming now – Sarah could just see its white ridge. She swam frantically against the current, making little headway but enough to keep her from being between the ship and the shore when the wave hit. It curled over her, cutting off the sound of the wind as it span her around, shoved her down, and finally let her go just as the burning in her chest was becoming unbearable.

Again, she wheeled around looking for Maisie. She grasped at a passing piece of wooden plank, hardly noticing when its splintered edge grazed her palm; she only realised she was bleeding at the sting of salt water.

She was dangerously close to the listing ship. Smaller waves, foot soldiers of the monsters taking the vessel apart, slapped her in the face as once more she swam against the current that was sweeping more detritus towards her. She refused to accept that some of the shapeless objects might be human. Might be Maisie.

A sliver of white peeked out from behind a barrel. She began kicking again, and while she didn't seem able to move forward she could at least hold her position until the barrel and its passenger reached her. Maisie was as pallid as the boy had been, but she had retained enough awareness to cling on to the barrel. As it passed by, Sarah let go of the plank and grabbed the barrel opposite Maisie, who gaped at her – this familiar face that had suddenly appeared from the ocean.

Sarah, in spite of everything, started to laugh, a dry, coughing sound. She reached across the barrel and squeezed Maisie's arm. 'We just need to hold on. We will hold on and stay above the water until we're rescued, yes?'

She did not know whether Maisie was capable of answering, but the young woman was clearly still capable of seeing, as her eyes fixed on a point above Sarah's shoulder. They were clear of the stern, and another wave lifted the barrel and sent the *Serpent* rolling towards the cliff again. The impact, this time, was too much for the mizzenmast, which fell, overbalanced across the stern and crashed into the water, creating a wave that swamped the barrel.

Sarah risked taking one hand off the wood to wipe her eyes. When she opened them, she was alone. She croaked out Maisie's name.

No light was coming from the crippled ship and precious little from the sky, so Sarah did not see the next wave until it was almost upon her, a shelf of black, angry water flinging her and the barrel towards the rocks.

PART TWO

For my ways are strange ways and new ways and old ways,
And deep ways and steep ways and high ways and low;
I'm at home and at ease on a track that I know not,
And restless and lost on a road that I know.

The Wander-Light, Henry Lawson

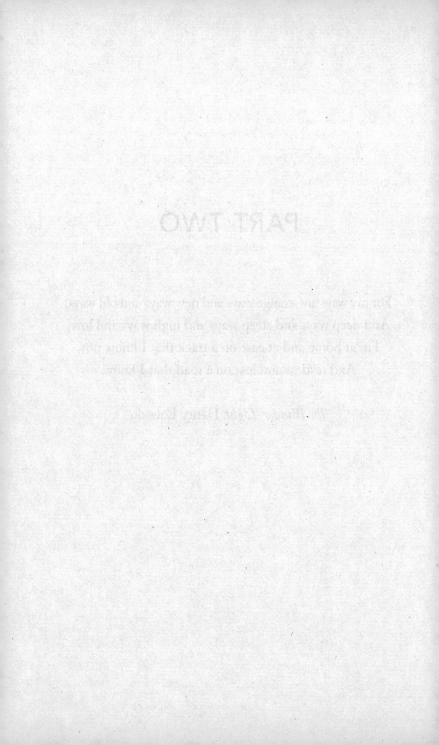

CHAPTER 17
Sydney, New South Wales, August 1820

For a minute after her eyes opened, Sarah lay there rolling snippets of memory around in her mind, trying to make them adhere to one another, to stick and tangle until they formed a coherent story.

Her hand moved down to her side, searching for a pocket that wasn't there.

She sat up, breathing heavily. Her head did not want to move thanks to the stiffness in her neck, but she forced herself to look from one side to the other, searching for her clothes.

There was a woman. Thin, grey clad. She was, perhaps, on the other side of her sixtieth birthday, although it was hard to be certain as her hair was tucked into a white cloth cap. Simply standing, watching, as Sarah sought to bring order to her jumbled thoughts. Perhaps she was dead, and the woman was an unadorned angel, or a demon disguised beneath drab veils.

When Sarah gasped and tried to sit up, the woman showed no surprise. 'There you are,' she said, as though

Sarah had just walked in from the street and started taking off her coat. 'You've been tossing and turning for a little while now. That cot told me you'd be waking up soon – I keep asking for beds that don't cry out so, but apparently the colony has more urgent plans for its money.' She was surely a nurse. She walked over, sat on a wooden stool next to the bed, and gave a tight smile. Placing a hand on Sarah's shoulder, she forced her firmly back onto the pillow.

Sarah winced, sucking in a breath through her teeth.

'I do not mean to hurt you, silly girl,' the nurse said. 'But you look as though you're about to faint. Might have fallen out of bed, banged your head on the floor. And I think your head has been through quite enough, along with the rest of you.'

Sarah reached up to her face. A gash ran from her temple to below her ear. She winced again.

'Well of course it's going to hurt if you go poking at it. It will scar, I'm afraid.'

'My clothes.' Sarah had never heard her voice sound like that before – like a chair being scraped across a stone floor. She did not want to own it. 'My things,' she said again. 'Are they . . . ?'

'At the bottom of the sea, I very much fear. As you nearly were yourself. A lot of care has been taken of you, so make sure it isn't wasted.' The nurse walked away so briskly that Sarah thought an expression on her face might have caused offence. But she soon returned with water in an earthenware cup, supporting Sarah's back while holding it to her mouth. 'Gently, now. A little sip at a time. Heaven alone knows how much seawater your stomach has in it. We don't want it to stage a rebellion and force everything out – not over these sheets, which have just been washed.'

Rebellion. Could the nurse know? Had Watkins raved in his sleep?

Sarah tried to sit up again. She needed to find Coombes, see if he would help her. He might know some of the local radicals; he could start her on the path of transforming Sam's death from a morning's spectacle to an outrage around which she would rally an army.

First, she needed to get her bearings. The room was long and narrow, as though someone had pinched each end of her childhood cottage and drawn it out. A young woman in the late stages of pregnancy occupied the bed across from her, one of several jutting from each wall so that their feet faced each other, interspersed with tall, thin windows. Another woman was a few beds away, sleeping. There was no one else.

The nurse noticed Sarah's distress. She sat on the stool and gently took Sarah's hand. 'Your shipmates . . .'

As Sarah tried to sit fully upright, she coughed. The nurse put the flat of her palm to Sarah's shoulder and again pushed her back to the pillows.

'Maisie,' Sarah said. 'My friend, I lost her . . .'

'She is not here. None of them are, it grieves me to say.'

'Where are they?'

'With God.'

As a child, Sarah had been told that God was everywhere. Watching, judging. Ready to catch out wicked little girls. So it took a second or two for her to grasp the nurse's meaning. When she did, she rejected the notion. 'They're not . . . not all of them. They can't be! If I lived – well, there were many on board stronger than me.'

The nurse took Sarah's hand once more, this time squeezing it a little too tightly. 'Their strength availed them nothing, I'm afraid.'

'I don't believe you.'

The nurse inhaled sharply and let go of Sarah's hand. 'I would suggest looking around you. If there were others, why are they not here?' She stood and walked over to the bed where the young woman with the distended abdomen lay propped on her elbows, watching the discussion without a hint of apology for her interest. The nurse placed a hand on the swollen stomach. 'Movement?'

'Yes, missus. Not half an hour ago.' The girl spoke like Tully, a Londoner. She had a sharp, foxy little face scattered with blotchy freckles, and a mouth that naturally quirked up on one side as though she was perpetually on the verge of a prank.

'And you'll remember to be respectful, when Mrs Thistle comes in. Her reputation is important to her, Nell. She knows your past, but she would not take you if you acted like—'

'Someone who takes money to pull up my skirts behind taverns? I'll be good, missus. But I won't say sorry. Those who disapprove can try to live on fresh air and see how far it gets them.'

The nurse pursed her lips. 'I do understand. But many don't.'

'People think I do it for fun,' Nell said. 'Or because I'm mad. Or a natural whore. Their charity doesn't extend to feeding the poor, but God help the poor if they try to feed themselves. Don't fret, though. I won't share any of this with Mrs Thistle.' She craned her head up between her sheet-covered knees and winked at Sarah.

'Stop staring at your wardmates, Nell,' the nurse said. 'It's impolite, and Mrs Thistle sets great store by good manners.' She looked back at Sarah, and left the room.

Sarah glanced at the unconscious woman, who was moving only to emit sodden coughs, and Nell followed Sarah's gaze. 'Been here a week, never seen her awake. Surprised she's still here. Haven't been near her, don't want that cough to jump into me.' She met Sarah's eyes. 'Nurse Haddon – the nurse, you see – she's all right, not the worst of them. And she's telling the truth, you *are* the only one left. Famous, you.'

'Me? I doubt it.'

'Don't. Nurse Haddon likes reading me the newspaper, thinks it will make me attend to improving my letters. Some say you're lucky. Some say God spared you because you're virtuous. Others say He did it to give hope.'

'Well, if He wanted to give hope, maybe He could have prevented the wreck in the first place – fiddled with the winds so they blew us to safety, perhaps.'

Nell snorted. 'Don't let Nurse Haddon hear you say that. A churchy sort, she is.'

'And you are not?'

'No more than you, and I've little patience for those who claim to know God's mind.'

'You seem to like Nurse Haddon well enough,' Sarah pointed out.

'Well, she's decided my body's worth saving even if she's not sure about my soul. She thinks my child deserves to be born. And she's in with Mrs Thistle.'

'Who is that?'

Nell was prevented from answering by Nurse Haddon's heavy-footed entry. She was carrying a newspaper under her arm. 'You have your letters?' she asked Sarah.

'Yes – enough, anyway.'

'Perhaps not enough for this,' said Nurse Haddon, sitting on the stool and unfolding the paper. 'We have collected further facts on the tragic wreck of the *Serpent*,' she read. 'The *Black Swan* brought to Sydney nineteen bodies on Saturday, besides a considerable quantity of mutilated remains; and yesterday the body of a seaman, with the letters HC over an anchor on the right arm. There were remains also taken from The Gap of two other bodies, supposed to be seamen. People, in vehicles and on horseback, and an immense number on foot, visited the Heads yesterday. Four or five boats proceeded outside the Heads, and went along in front of the cliffs. No living person was seen, and from the close proximity of the boats to the cliffs, it can scarcely be doubted that if any others had escaped from the wreck they would have been observed.

'A woman, then, remains the only survivor of the catastrophe. She is understood to be receiving care at the infirmary. Those who saw her, who put their own safety at risk to rescue her by means of rope and harness, say she is young. No one recalls seeing a wedding band, although seas so violent would surely be more than capable of claiming such an item for the depths. No one knows how she survived, or why, whether by design of the Almighty or through chance, although she seems to have climbed or been thrown onto a ledge. As the *Serpent*'s manifest is lost, no one knows so much as her name.' Nurse Haddon looked up at Sarah. 'What is your name, my dear?'

'Remember, missus,' said Nell, 'I told you she looked like an Emily.' Nell nodded enthusiastically towards Sarah, encouraging her to prove her right.

'Not an Emily, though I've always liked the name,' Sarah said, trying to keep the wobble out of her voice at the thought of her mother.

Sarah could not hear the word Nell muttered, but it earned the pregnant woman a sharp glance from Nurse Haddon.

'I'm Sarah,' she said.

Nell bobbed her head from side to side, clearly rolling the name around in her mind. 'Well, you look enough like a Sarah for me.'

'Many Sarahs in the world,' said Nurse Haddon. 'How do we distinguish you from the rest of them?'

Nell chuckled. 'Well, missus, she is the only one lying here, for a start.'

Nurse Haddon half lifted herself, turning her body towards Nell. 'You are getting far too brazen, young woman. The granting of a favour does not entitle you to such familiarity.'

Nell rearranged her features into an appropriately chastened expression but smiled at Sarah when Nurse Haddon glanced away.

'Miss Flaherty likes to pretend she has no wits,' the nurse said to Sarah, 'and is now pretending she does not understand the nature of my question. But you do, I'm sure. I ask, of course, about your surname.'

Sarah opened her mouth to say 'McCaffrey', and closed it again. What was being hailed as a miracle could just as easily be denounced as the work of Satan if her past became known. 'Marin,' she said. 'My name is Sarah Marin.'

Mrs Haddon nodded and folded the paper. 'Well, Miss Marin, I will be honest with you – you can rely on me to be that, if nothing else. I do not know what is to become of you.'

CHAPTER 18

Maisie's face was the colour of a fish's belly and covered in bloodless gashes. Her mouth was closed; perhaps someone had done that for her, or perhaps she had gritted her teeth in futile defiance, trying to deny the water entry. If someone had gently lifted her chin, made her lips meet, they had not extended the courtesy to her eyes: the lids were slightly open, a sliver of white under one and an absence under the other.

Her nightdress may have been taken by the sea or by the undertaker, and she was covered to the neck by a canvas sheet. Sarah pinched the fabric, rubbed it between her fingers, and silently began to cry. She did not believe Maisie would have survived had she stayed aboard the *Serpent*. But if Sarah had held on to her, perhaps the falling mizzenmast would not have swept her from the barrel. Two girls might have woken up in the infirmary.

'You recognise her, then,' Truman said. He was a surgeon, the first man she had met in the colony when he had come to examine her shortly after she regained consciousness. He had been three or four times in the past week. Had taken her pulse – which Nurse Haddon seemed perfectly capable of doing without him – and looked into her eyes and mouth, although she had no idea what he expected to see.

Now Sarah nodded, watching a tear that had skidded down her nose splash onto the canvas. 'Can you get Maisie a softer sheet? She hates rough cloth.'

Truman inhaled sharply. 'I am sorry, honestly, that this falls to you.'

Sarah looked up along the row of bodies in which Maisie lay. There were around a dozen in this line, one of several stretching out across the floor of the dead house that squatted near the docks of the town's main quay. The building had never seen such an influx. Some faces were purple, some blue, some white; most were abraded. There were also lumpen masses wholly concealed beneath canvases.

She had not seen James. Was part of him under one of these shrouds, or had he been wholly consumed by the ocean?

Coombes was there, though, still in his shirt and neckerchief. She put her hand on the shoulder she had cried into as her brother choked.

There were other faces she recognised, here and there. A bearded young sailor who had enjoyed leering at her then quickly looking away when she whipped her head around to challenge him. Mrs Simkin, the muscles around her mouth now slack. One of the soldiers who had guarded them from leg-ironed convicts during Sunday service. She could not see any of the convicts; perhaps many of them had been ironed for the night.

She stopped when she saw the blue jacket with the gold buttons, some of which had been picked off by the sea. Watkins was missing an arm. His face had been slashed by rock or splintered wood, and she could see his teeth behind an open cheek.

She paused beside the man who had steered the ship into a cliff. The man who had reduced the bravery of others to a handful of coins. She wanted to thump his chest or slap his open cheek, a punishment he would never feel. Instead she put a hand on his remaining arm and crossed herself.

'The captain,' said Truman.

Sarah nodded.

'I must ask, Miss Marin – what happened? You are the only soul breathing who knows.'

'But I know little of the ocean,' she said, 'or of how men move all that wood to heave people across the sea. There was a storm, and the ship was forced towards the rocks. There was noise, screaming. My friend and I were washed apart, and then ... well, then there was your infirmary.'

Truman pushed his spectacles up the bridge of his nose. It was a habit of his, she had noticed, one necessitated by his insistence on dressing as though he was in London – though even now, in the final days of winter, it was as warm as an early summer in England, and there was a continual slick of perspiration over his skin. He had clearly taken some trouble with his hair, pasted down by sweat and repeated combing. It did not seem to approve of such tyranny, as it insisted on springing up at random so that he looked like a spectacled hedgehog.

He seemed far too young to be weighed down by the grand title of surgeon. He did not look any older than Sam, but he must have been to have trained in doctoring and then found his way out here. Tall and as thin as a weaver, he moved through the dead house and the infirmary with an unwitting authority, the gait of a man who knew he would not have to run at a moment's notice. She recognised that walk from the idle sons of the houses for which she had done laundry. Truman, though, lacked their hauteur.

'There is to be an inquest,' he said. 'When you are strong enough.'

'An inquest will not help them,' she said, inclining her head towards Maisie.

'It may help others, Miss Marin. Ships do not routinely run into the rocks here. The captain may have been at fault, and if he was we need to understand its nature. If there was another cause, we may take steps to ensure the next ship reaches our harbour safely.'

'So a trial for a dead man, then,' she said.

Watkins had retained enough of his clothes for decency in death. She looked at the still legs and remembered them carrying him from one end of the deck to the other, darting, shouting. Throwing a command over each shoulder, not pausing to check if the words had been snatched by the wind. Racing towards her, intent on her destruction. And straight at the wheel, steering as though the ship could be steered, yelling instructions to the dead.

He must have been at least partly responsible for bringing his ship's passengers and crew together in the dead house. She knew he'd been a venal man who had abjured his belief in equity; she knew he had made changes to the ship in exchange for money. But the yeoman who had gutted her father, the rider of the horse that had trampled her mother, neither of them had been brought before an inquest, and there had been no attempt to cast blame over a field of bodies. If those who had put them there did not answer for it in life, why should Watkins answer in death?

But as she well knew, there were those who wanted answers and refused to accept that the *Serpent*'s only survivor didn't have them. Most of the colony had read the article that Nurse Haddon had shared with her, and most had an opinion on her survival, ranging from the assistance of God to that of the devil, to fate, and to some concealed unnatural strength. Whatever their view – whether she was a miracle or an abomination – they were all determined to see her.

The article had mentioned the infirmary, and it seemed everyone in town knew the building with a rickety veranda around the second floor, where Sarah slept. On her first afternoon there, she had asked Nurse Haddon if she could take some air on it, and been rebuffed. 'Quite unseemly to appear in your nightdress for anyone to see,' the nurse had said. 'And I would not be taking any chances on that balcony's ability to support you.'

When Nurse Haddon had opened the veranda doors to allow in the day's ration of fresh air, Sarah had heard the uninvited visitors. At first there were just a few muffled conversations, then as the days went on a generalised murmuring, and the occasional raucous shout that made her think some of the gawkers had brought their own refreshments, of which Nurse Haddon would certainly disapprove.

They had crowded around as she'd stepped outside the infirmary that morning, some of them pressing forward, hands grasping at her. A few evidently still clung to hope of their loved ones' survival. One yelled, 'Tom? Have you seen my Tom?' Another, 'Did you know Emma? She wore a yellow dress most of the time.' Sarah stared straight ahead, trying to breathe steadily, to ignore the tugs on her skirt and sleeves, while knowing these people would not be satisfied by any answer she could give them. She jammed her hands into new pockets provided by charity, which did not contain lost loved ones or little leaden sailors.

She wished she could help them by giving them hope. She remembered the temptation to descend into madness after her parents were killed, to pretend they still lived. And she had ample proof of the reality of their deaths – a year ago now, she realised with a shock. Most of these people would never have anything to bury.

On the outskirts of the throng stood a man plainly dressed in a brown coat and white cravat, all clean enough. He had not been as particular with his hair that sprang in crinkled greyish licks from under his hat. As Sarah and Truman were approaching the coach, he stepped closer to them.

Truman pursed his lips and said, 'Not now, Mobbs.'

'When, then? She's not your property,' he said in an accent that told Sarah he had not been born far from her. He took another step forward. 'Hello, lovely,' he said to Sarah. He thrust a thin booklet at her, and she took it without thinking. 'That is what happened while you were sleeping,' he said, nodding to the document. 'I have tried to contact you through several avenues, but your guard dogs are too vicious.'

'She's not talking to the *Colonial Flyer* or any other paper,' Truman said, bundling Sarah into the carriage and climbing in after her. 'I am sorry, Miss Marin,' he said when they sat down. 'Mobbs has been quite persistent, but you are under no obligation to speak to him.'

Sarah looked at the document the journalist had given her. It was a pamphlet, she realised. She had not been inclined to speak to Mobbs and now felt even less so; after all, the last man to thrust a pamphlet at her had been the barker at her brother's execution. Unlike that pamphlet, though, this one did not have a drawing that had been reused for printing after printing. Beneath large letters – which told her she was holding *The Melancholy Wreck of the 'Serpent'*, available for purchase for one shilling – was a pen-and-ink drawing of a figure being pulled up a cliff face on the end of a rope, above the curled waves of an angry ocean. The person looked like a shrouded corpse or a bat wrapped in its own wings, but the small caption left her in no doubt about what was being represented: *The Survivor Rescued.*

Had the ropes under her arms bruised her flesh? She had occasionally peeked down the neck of her nightgown when Nurse Haddon wasn't watching – the woman would never approve of such immodesty – and had seen a collection of colours from grey to purple to yellow on her skin. Her arms, when she rolled up her sleeves, were similarly festooned. But if any of those marks had been left by ropes, they were so subsumed in a wash of other bruises that it was impossible to tell.

She scrunched the pamphlet and considered throwing it out the window of the coach, but instead found her hand reaching for her pocket. She could feel its weight in there for some time afterwards. *Two pamphlets*, she thought. *Two McCaffreys. And each of us at the end of a rope.*

CHAPTER 19

'How many limbs? How many heads?'

Nell's questions were not ones Sarah felt like answering. When she had returned from the dead house, she must have looked pale, as she had been put straight to bed by Nurse Haddon. Sarah had secreted the pamphlet under her mattress. She felt insubstantial, as though the flesh in the dead house had absorbed a part of her soul. When she had been in that room she had seen only what was there, her eyes too full of actual horror for her mind to invent any. Now, though, she could only see Sam in her imagination, his head separated from his body, which was laid out before being tipped into the earth.

Nell was sitting as far forward in her bed as her stomach would allow, eyes wide.

This is what you have now, Sarah thought. *This is all you have.* The remembrance sickened her; she was impossibly far from a home where no one was left for her anyway.

'I did not count the limbs or the men,' she told Nell sharply. 'And I saw nothing that would make me blush.'

'Well, if it wouldn't make *you* blush, it would have no effect on me.'

Nell had decided that Sarah was a prissy woman of constrained morality, although she did not seem to resent Sarah for her imagined prudishness any more than she would resent rain for being wet. 'But you must have seen something,' she said. 'I'll not force you to yell it across the ward.' She swung her legs over the edge of the bed and braced herself with her hands, about to get up.

Sarah stood herself, and was nearly forced back onto her cot by dizziness. Nurse Haddon insisted young women who were ill enough for the infirmary needed to prove it by lying down as much as possible. But Sarah imagined Nell tripping and falling, the moving knot just under the skin of her belly suddenly still. The only way to dissuade Nell from coming to her was to go to Nell, so she crossed the short distance to Nell's bed and perched on the edge.

'I'm not half as sick as she'd have you think, you know,' said Nell. 'Nor you, I suspect. She's a collector of lost birds, is Nurse Haddon. So's Mrs Thistle, who owns half of Sydney. Warehouses. Ships. Houses. Inherited her husband's business, and now she can buy and sell most people here. She won't send us back out to the cats if she thinks we can't fly fast enough.'

✳

Sarah had flown without knowing it. She had skidded up along the cliff face, nothing between her and the rocks and waves except air, and perhaps the phantoms of those who had perished.

In sleep she dipped, as she did so often now, in and out of fragmented dreams in which screams gave way to the sound of water. So she was the only one in the infirmary awake the next morning to see the dawn seeping in through the windows. Enough light to read by.

She cursed the rattle and squeak of her cot as she got up. She gently reached under the mattress to extract the pamphlet, rolling onto her side and pulling up her sheet so she could pretend to be asleep if someone woke or came in. Then she straightened out and opened the pamphlet. Another drawing greeted her, this one of rescuers crowded at the base of the cliff, watching jagged timbers and masts being lashed by waves. Below it was dense text, with the heading *The Melancholy Wreck of the 'Serpent'*.

Grief lies heavily upon this town. A cataclysm has occurred of such proportions that it has reached into every home and every heart. And with the cataclysm, a mystery, for very little is known of the woman who was pulled from a sea that claimed her fellow travellers.

For most of us, the first intimation of the horrors to come arrived in the form of sundry articles floating in from the sea. Those who braved the rain that morning reported seeing cabin doors, their thick timbers shredded like paper, the bolts that had secured them twisted and deformed, along with casks of tripe and beer. There were also personal effects such as a lady's nightdress and a child's toy. A mailbag, its contents no doubt sodden to illegibility, was marked 'No. 2, per Serpent, Plymouth, May 1820'.

If any doubted that these artefacts presaged a calamity, they had only to wait by the waters. One report we received was of a man, his face wounded but white, washed of blood. Many others followed. Some were convicts who had been transported in the hold, but most of them were surely dragged below by their leg irons. Other witnesses spoke of limbs, of a torso in a midshipman's jacket, and of a boy, perhaps three or four years old.

The brig 'Vixen' followed these horrors into the harbour, making all haste to the shore, its captain running to the harbourmaster with tales of a sea full of the deceased. The harbourmaster, we are told, already knew about the wreck, as the lighthouse keeper had come to him at dawn. The keeper said he had been unable to see or hear anything through the gale, but had been alerted by his dog, running to the cliff and back, barking until hoarse.

A lad was sent, running against the easterly rain, to the place called The Gap. The ocean has paid special attention to that part of the cliff over the centuries,

*wearing it away to the point that those without inti-
mate knowledge of Sydney's edge might mistake it for
the entrance to the harbour. When the boy returned, he
would not speak.*

*By the time the harbourmaster set out for The Gap,
hundreds were doing the same. Those who arrived
with the dawn said there was little left of the vessel,
although the winds it had sailed through were still
present, hurling gouts of spray so high that the water
speckled the faces of those watching. The passengers
and crew were there too: thrown against the shore,
reclaimed by the waves, then thrown again. Some
had lost their clothes to the sea, while others were
in nightshirts or uniforms. There were some solitary
limbs being churned together with fragments of sail,
cases, clothes, and crates of pickles and pork.*

*Those present on the cliff declare themselves to have
been transfixed by horror, retching and wailing, unable
to look away.*

*Every vessel with a master willing to take to the seas
was sent up and down the coast. They did not expect to
find survivors, and they returned only with corpses to
the dead house at the quay.*

*When the seas began to shrink, the harbourmaster
ordered that men were to be lowered on ropes over the
cliff. He was perhaps moved by the impulse to ensure
a Christian burial for as many as could be retrieved.
Those that did come up were beyond any help but the*

Almighty's, and it seemed that the sea would yield only the dead.

The harbourmaster had counted over one hundred when a woman near him called in disbelief that she had seen a body twitching. The rescuers moved as fast as they could over the flat, smooth rocks, scrambling towards a small white figure that lay on a high rock, out of reach of the worst of the waves.

Many colonists have been nursing the hope that the survivor could be a loved one, but no one has claimed her as such. If the cause of the 'Serpent's misfortune is the most pressing question in Sydney at present, surely the identity of this woman cannot be far behind it in importance.

There was more – breathless accounts of the state of the bodies and the suffering of bereaved families – but Sarah had no desire to read it. She crumpled the pamphlet again and pushed it back under her mattress. She had wanted to sink into the river of the newly arrived, her true identity obliterated by the wreck of the *Serpent*, and set about finding those who held the beliefs her brother had died for, shaded by the anonymity of a brown dress and a white cloth cap. Instead, she was now one of the most famous women in Sydney.

✦

Truman was among those presiding over the inquest. He sat at a long table beside Nicholas Greenwich, the superintendent of police, who seemed to enjoy slapping his open palm onto the tabletop. Sarah sat in front of them, alone on a rickety chair, in the shadow of the empty magistrate's bench under the courtroom's vaulted ceiling.

Greenwich's face had been deeply engraved by the sun and wind, etched with channels that no doubt captured raindrops when the weather was bad.

Sarah did not tell them about the rudder, although she felt a corrosive anger at the knowledge that Watkins had put Maisie beneath that rough canvas cloth in the dead house. If he had lived she would have done anything to force him to pay for it, but he was beyond payment now, and she could not indict him without questions about why he had cannibalised the ship. She might set in train events leading to the arrest of those she did not yet know; those whose beliefs were closer to her own than Greenwich's would ever be. So she said that the captain had been imbibing, and that his men had seemed unable to steer the ship.

'Watkins was a rogue, in my experience,' Greenwich said. 'He has caused us to exert ourselves at various taverns over the years. I presume you found him somewhat irregular as well.' He peered at Sarah from beneath scraggly grey eyebrows, clearly expecting her agreement.

She shut her eyes; there was Watkins, hauling on a wheel that would not respond.

'Odd, maybe,' she said. 'Not mad.'

'Not the act of a sane man, though, is it?' said Greenwich, looking at Truman. 'Procedure dictated he should stand off until morning.'

'We should not be bringing snippets of rumour into these proceedings,' said Truman.

'Ah, but rumour can be quite illuminating,' Greenwich retorted. 'And it is, of course, one of the chief currencies of the sea.'

'So the man drank,' said Truman. 'He's hardly the first sea captain to do so.'

'Perhaps. But that is not the rumour that chiefly concerns me. It is said the captain had certain radical sympathies.' The superintendent looked at Sarah, one eyebrow raised in a question.

'It is also said that many shipwrecks are caused by sea monsters,' she said.

'I find that a rather interesting response,' said Greenwich. 'Perhaps you share his views?'

Sarah focused on keeping her body still, her face immobile, even as she wanted to leap from the chair and run from the room, then hide in the crowd outside the infirmary or in the wilderness that fringed the settlement.

'What the captain's beliefs were,' she said, 'I'm not to say.'

'There are rumours, too, of treasure,' Greenwich said as he dipped a pen into a wooden ink pot and began scratching at a piece of paper, his eyes cast down – perhaps wanting her to believe that the question was of little consequence.

Truman sighed. 'Superintendent, I have heard similar rumours about just about every wreck for the past five years.'

'Yes, well, I never claimed they were true. And they don't have to be, to cause trouble. Perhaps the men got wind of it. Perhaps there was an assault on the captain's cabin, a mutiny.' Greenwich stopped writing and met Sarah's gaze.

'I saw no treasure, nor heard any talk of it. Captain Watkins, he certainly didn't dress like a man with a chest of gold in his cabin.'

'Well, if it exists,' said Truman, 'it is at the bottom of the ocean now.'

'Yes, better prepare yourself, Mr Truman,' said Greenwich. 'There is always someone who hears of treasure and decides to go looking for it, even if it's in a dozen feet of water.'

✦

Sarah's bed was occupied when she returned to the infirmary.

Truman had escorted her back in the coach, which shielded her again from the shouted questions, the touches, the invocations and exhortations and curses. He had intended to check on Nell but was met with resistance from Nurse Haddon, waiting at the entrance. 'Really,' she said, 'I should not have to tell you that these young ladies need their rest. We look forward to seeing you for rounds tomorrow. I'm sure Miss Marin has had a very trying day, and I intend to ensure she gets undisturbed peace to make up for it.' Truman offered no resistance, tugging the brim of his hat in Sarah's direction and heading for the stairs.

Nurse Haddon had glanced over her shoulder as she led Sarah back into the ward.

The woman who now sat on Sarah's bed did not look ill. It had been a long time since the colour of her hair was discernible, and since her cheeks had been smooth, though they were still pink. Her eyes required spectacles, and Sarah wondered if she would push them up her nose as Truman did. She sat upright with her hands folded over a lap that appeared to be generous beneath a plain but good-quality dark-blue dress. She was in animated conversation with Nell, who was sitting so straight that she needed to spread her legs to accommodate her belly, a posture for which Nurse Haddon would surely reprimand her.

But Nurse Haddon did nothing of the sort. Instead, she cleared her throat, then bobbed a curtsy to the older woman. It was such an awkward gesture that Sarah suspected it was one the nurse was unused to making. 'Mrs Thistle,' she said, 'how good of you to come.'

Mrs Thistle rose to embrace the nurse. 'Dear Georgina,' she said, 'I can always rely on you for strays.' She released Nurse Haddon, looking at Sarah and Nell. Her face, comfortable without expression, took on a certain hardness as she assessed Sarah. 'This is her, then.'

'Yes,' said Nurse Haddon. 'I believe there is no worthier recipient of your generosity.'

Mrs Thistle shook her head slightly, her lace cap shifting on top of her silver hair. She reached her hand up to roughly adjust a hairpin, and Sarah suspected that her glasses stayed in place out of fear. 'Why?' she asked. 'Because she survived what others did not? Tell me, did she do so out of bravery or virtue, or because she is the anointed of the Lord or the handmaid of Satan? Or was it due to more luck than most girls will ever see?'

Mrs Thistle had only spared Sarah one glance before discussing her as though she was a horse or a bale of hay. Nell, perhaps sensing Sarah's irritation, sidled over to her while the two older women were talking and squeezed her arm in a gesture of solidarity.

'Perhaps,' Sarah said, 'if you wish to know the answer to those questions, you should ask her.'

Nurse Haddon gasped, swatting Sarah on the arm. 'I do apologise, Mrs Thistle. Probably the shock.'

'No,' said the older woman. 'No, I don't think it is.' She spoke with an accent Sarah had heard in the mouths of some of those with whom she had walked to the mill each day; some of those who had died or been wounded in the massacre. Perhaps not from Manchester, but definitely Lancashire. A practical, unvarnished way of speaking, not given to unnecessary flourishes.

Mrs Thistle approached Sarah and reached out to tilt her chin up, examining her face.

Sarah knew she was risking permanent banishment from Nurse Haddon's protection, but she could not help herself. 'I am not livestock, madam. You will not be able to tell my age by looking at my teeth.'

Mrs Thistle let her hand drop, and Sarah earned another swat from the nurse. 'Mrs Thistle is kind enough to take in poor young women like you. Unless you fancy sleeping on streets you have never seen, I would urge you to greater politeness. Kindly apologise.'

Sarah looked at Mrs Thistle, whose eyebrows were raised.

'I mean no disrespect,' said Sarah, and felt Nurse Haddon exhale behind her. 'But I do not feel I owe you an apology. I simply spoke for myself, as there are no others to do so.'

Mrs Thistle stared at her in what was surely either outrage or fascination. But then, to Sarah's surprise, she shrugged. 'I wouldn't apologise either, I suppose. We've all had enough of being treated like livestock. But if I am to assist you, Miss Marin, this will be the very last time you speak so. And if I am to help you, I not only need to know how old you are, but everything else about you too.' She brushed back a strand of Sarah's hair. 'Including the story behind your family name. I do not think I have ever before heard a voice from Manchester in the mouth of someone with a French surname.'

CHAPTER 20

Nell was making a lot of noise. It was noise Sarah had heard before, of course, through the thin walls of the cottage in Manchester. Those low, elongated moans, rising shrieks and animal grunts had kept her awake occasionally in her childhood, but they had never had any more relevance to her than the sound of a brawl in the street.

This, though, was different. Nell was one of the only women she knew at this impossible distance from home, having a child torn from her body without a flimsy wall between them.

'Make yourself useful,' Nurse Haddon said, bustling into the ward with a pail of water, cloths draped over her shoulder. She positioned herself between Nell's legs.

Sarah glanced around anxiously. 'Make my . . . *how*?'

'Talk to her, for God's sake. Dip a cloth in the bucket, wipe her brow. Hold her hand. Let her squeeze yours until it feels like your bones will break.'

So Sarah stroked Nell's stringy hair, tried not to wince as the young woman's fingernails pressed into her palm, and told her that it would all be all right and that it was nearly over – assurances no one had any business giving to a woman in childbirth.

When the baby slid out of her mother into Nurse Haddon's hands, the nurse exhaled loudly, glanced at the roof, and nodded as though in thanks. Sarah stared at the scrunched purple creature, suffusing with pink as she opened her mouth to cry. There was a defiance to the sound, disrupting as it did the order and silence of the ward. Sarah felt a pull towards the little girl, an urgency to make sure she had no reason to cry.

'Poor little fatherless mite,' Nurse Haddon said, wiping her hands on a cloth.

'Amelia has a mother, though,' said Nell, reaching for her daughter and mimicking the scrunched face. 'That should be enough. And a father can do more harm than good.'

'It will have to be enough,' said Nurse Haddon. 'This town, it has been good to some. But I've seen it take, too. Do not let it swallow this one.'

⋆

When they walked out of the infirmary one week later, Sarah braced herself for another throng and was oddly disappointed to find the forecourt empty.

Mrs Thistle was walking between her and Nell, who was cradling Amelia and beaming at everyone they passed. The older woman must have noticed Sarah frown.

'Don't fret for them,' she said. 'They tried to nibble at you and didn't get any sustenance, so they have moved to other feeding grounds. And now you're one of mine, anyway.'

Sarah smiled as much to ease her discomfort as to acknowledge the nicety. Mrs Thistle had not mentioned her surname again, but that did not mean she was not making enquiries.

Nell was occasionally turning to smile at Mrs Thistle as though the woman had just showered her with riches, and was being ignored for her trouble.

Nurse Haddon had given Nell a week to recover from the routine violence of birth, a luxurious amount of time, bordering on indulgent. Many women at the mill had returned to their posts the day after giving birth, and Sarah had seen some stuff rags up under their skirts.

That morning Mrs Thistle had arrived, and Nell and Sarah had stood at the ends of their beds as she walked up and down in front of them. 'There is a boarding house,' she told them, 'run by a Mrs Vale, with paying customers. She needs maids to serve at table and work in the kitchen, and so forth. You'll both be equal to it, I've no doubt.'

'Oh, a boarding house,' Nell said, winking at Sarah.

Mrs Thistle pursed her lips. 'I know what kind of services are offered at some places that call themselves boarding houses, but I assure you this isn't one of them. It's a respectable establishment – visitors from Windsor and Parramatta, vicars, clerks, and so forth. The mariners from my ships stay there, and I assure you they know better than to misbehave. Mrs Vale ensures good behaviour and that guests don't take their leave without paying.'

'And what will we be paid?' asked Sarah.

Mrs Thistle glanced at her sharply. 'You will be fed and sheltered.'

Sarah clenched her jaw to stop herself scowling. Another one, at all this distance. Another who would take hours of labour and tell her to be grateful to work without pay. Another who had probably never been poor or known a stab of hunger that couldn't be alleviated. Another of those who had built the road her family walked to their graves.

✦

They walked through a town that looked, to Sarah, as though it hadn't quite made up its mind on what it wanted to be. A few handsome stone buildings with ornate trimmings quickly gave way to meaner structures: some well-built wooden cottages, some wattle and daub; others little more than sheds, just pieces of wood laid up against each other.

The streets lacked the mass of people she was used to, though people walked here and there. Women in plain clothes and cloth caps. Black-jacketed functionaries, heads down, stepping quickly towards whatever important business was calling them.

Sarah had been expecting to see others: the dark-skinned people who had inhabited this place before the British government had uncoiled across the sea and seeped onto the shore. She asked Mrs Thistle about it.

'Rarely see them in town,' the woman said. 'They've been moved on. Out. Only a little over thirty years since the first of us arrived, and it's as though they were never here. If you go out west you'll see them, in Blacks Town or Parramatta. Some are living in the bush a little south too. I know the governor was keen to bring them in, to civilise them. They seem to prefer their own ways, though.'

So, thought Sarah, *the government that cut off my brother's head after strangling him believes it has something to teach others about civilisation*. And Molly Thistle, the woman on whom she now had to rely, was speaking as though these people were an abstract idea or a fairy story. Or an exhibit one had to go to the trouble of travelling west to see.

Sarah had her hands clasped behind her back, and she squeezed one painfully with the other to stop herself screaming. She, too, was part of a faceless mass, toiling down in the basements of grand houses or begging on the streets. Yes, those on the upper levels knew people like her existed, but they didn't have to see or speak to her. They could conveniently ignore her humanity, as they were doing with the original inhabitants of this place.

She was unable to resist asking further questions. 'Why would they want to be civilised? Why would they trust any promises they get?'

Mrs Thistle shrugged. 'You hear stories of shootings and the like. Men and women and children marched off a cliff a few years ago. And the school at Parramatta, now. The Native Institute, they call it, set up to educate native children, although they forgot to inform the parents they would be keeping the children until they are fifteen. Of course there are those who think they're not worth educating, nor capable of learning. Although I did hear,' she lowered her voice conspiratorially, 'that one native girl came top in an examination, ahead of over one hundred settler children.'

None of the settlers in this part of town looked as though they had ever taken an examination. They passed a tavern that even at this early hour had dribbled customers outside, where they leaned against a wall and drank. Perhaps some were the husbands of the women who sat outside several of the small shacks that were increasingly interspersed between the stone cottages. Sarah thought that if the deterioration continued, by the time they arrived at the boarding house they would find they were staying in a tent.

But when they arrived a short time later, squinting into the low afternoon sun, the building looked as though it had been picked up from a different part of town and set down there. A sign swung out the front, THE ENGLISH

Rose in florid letters above a faded portrait of that flower. The front garden, neat and blooming with well-behaved gardenias, was on the other side of a little fence from scrubby bushland. There were shacks and a few wooden houses dotted around, none of which matched the two-storey grandeur of the guesthouse. Brick rendered with unchipped paint, it looked as though it wanted to lift its skirts to avoid the dirt road.

The promised chatelaine, Mrs Vale, opened the door. Her face was thin and square as though it had been baked in a bread pan. Her hair was severely scraped under her cloth cap, and her expression changed from neutral to annoyed when she saw baby Amelia.

Mrs Thistle bustled up, fully a head shorter than her companions, in her matronly lace and her plain blue gown. Sarah would not have thought of her as one to inspire deference. But the landlady clearly did not share this view, and curtsied as soon as Mrs Thistle reached them.

Then Mrs Vale stood aside and swept her arm in what she clearly thought was a grand gesture of invitation. Mrs Thistle walked through the door without acknowledging her.

They passed reception rooms with deep-red brocade chairs and green swagged curtains, then walked out through a door across a small courtyard and into an out-building kitchen. Mrs Vale invited Mrs Thistle to a seat; she made no similar invitation to the girls.

'Mrs Flaherty has just been delivered of a child, as you can see,' said Mrs Thistle, smoothing down her skirt as she sat.

Nell glanced at Sarah, presumably confused by being referred to as a married woman.

'Perhaps, Mrs Vale, you would care to offer her a seat?' Mrs Thistle said.

'Why of course.' The woman had a high, oddly baby-ish voice, strange from such a tall person, with a quaver in its tone. Sarah thought that surely Mrs Thistle was bound to be the kind of woman who did not appreciate displays of weakness.

'And of course it would be quite rude to leave only one standing,' Mrs Thistle said.

'Sit down, if you please,' Mrs Vale said to Sarah, the words rapped out like the commands Captain Watkins used to give.

'Such a walk,' said Mrs Thistle. 'I'm an old woman, you know. A cup of tea would be most welcome.'

'Naturally,' said Mrs Vale, whose posterior had already been halfway to her own seat. She straightened and went to the stove.

'I have been known to make tea,' said Sarah. 'Those who have tried it say I have some skill. Would you allow me, Mrs Vale?' She nearly choked on the words, on their willing servitude, but she knew her life would be easier if she won goodwill from the woman.

Mrs Thistle nodded and gave her a quick smile. 'If you would be kind enough, Sarah. I'm sure Mrs Vale is run off her feet.'

'Allow me to open the tea chest,' said Mrs Vale, glancing at Sarah with a frown that showed she did not believe the likes of her belonged anywhere near the tea. The small chest was of polished dark wood, the kind used by grand houses that favoured tea imported at impossible expense and guarded like gold. Mrs Vale took a tiny key from her pocket, opened the chest and watched as Sarah scooped out the leaves, before closing it, locking it and putting it away.

Mrs Thistle stood with far more speed and fluidity than one would expect from an exhausted old lady, went over to the pot, took a pinch of tea and sniffed it. 'Not mine,' she said, narrowing her eyes. 'This sort of muck would never come into the colony on a Thistle ship.'

'Well, I thought for the sake of economy ...' Mrs Vale said.

'You will remember our agreement, if you please,' said Mrs Thistle, sitting again. 'I know the trader who deals in these leaves, and he cares little for quality. On my next visit I look forward to a cup of my own tea. In the meantime, this will have to do.' She nodded to Sarah, who was placing the kettle on a small grille suspended over the fire. 'Now,' said Mrs Thistle, clapping her hands as though to bring a schoolroom to attention, 'it's very kind of you to offer these young ladies a place under your roof.'

'They are most welcome,' said Mrs Vale, not bothering to smile. Everyone in the room knew who owned the roof and had made the offer.

'Of course,' said Mrs Thistle. 'Your hospitality is legendary, particularly for the needy. And these girls will be earning their keep while helping you to run this enterprise. Perhaps greater efficiency will ensure you are not so late with the accounts.'

Mrs Vale drew her shoulders back as though she wanted to take offence, breathing deeply until the flush that had risen to her cheeks died down a little. She gestured at Nell. 'It might be difficult for this one to operate . . . efficiently . . . with a babe.'

Amelia clearly possessed some nascent social instincts, because she had fallen into an angelic sleep.

'Nell is not the first woman to work with a baby on her hip,' said Mrs Thistle. 'I managed it. Eight times.'

'And the father?'

'Awful business.'

Sarah stiffened, thinking she was about to reveal a truth about Nell that would prompt Mrs Vale to throw the young woman onto the street.

Instead, Mrs Thistle said, 'He fell into the harbour while unloading a ship of mine.'

Nell shrugged at Sarah. *Well, he might have.*

Sarah tried not to smile as she set steaming cups in front of Mrs Thistle and Mrs Vale.

Mrs Thistle lifted hers, sniffed it, and put it back on its saucer, perhaps a little too hard. 'Well, Sarah, you've done your best with what you had.' She glared at Mrs Vale. 'I look forward to better refreshment on my next visit,' she said, standing. 'In the meantime, I leave these young ladies in your tender care. Goodnight.' She nodded, opened the door onto the dusk that was drawing in, and swept out without bothering to close it behind her.

CHAPTER 21

Mrs Thistle's departure left an absence that Sarah was itching to fill. Mrs Vale was glaring at Nell and her child, while Nell smiled weakly back.

'You will be convicts, no doubt,' Mrs Vale said. 'She's partial to convicts.'

Probably because they're desperate enough to work for nothing, Sarah thought.

'Oh, I'm ticketed now,' said Nell. 'Seven years, I served. Got my ticket of leave last year. I was only fourteen, you see, when they loaded me on the ship.'

Mrs Vale looked to Sarah.

'No, madam, I arrived free,' she said. 'Although I don't remember my arrival. I was plucked off the rocks at the bottom of the cliff. The fortunate survivor of the *Serpent*.' She bowed her head, a gesture she would normally make when it suited her to seem compliant and demure. This time, though, she was ashamed; the bald description she had just given of the wreck was so inadequate, she feared it bordered on the disrespectful. She did not really believe in ghosts – still, she had no wish to be visited by an angry one.

'I see,' said Mrs Vale. 'We have a girl with some notoriety among us, it seems.'

'If I have any fame, it is unsought,' said Sarah. 'And too dearly bought as well.'

'Nevertheless, some of my guests might be diverted by your story when you serve them at table. Now, some rules.'

Amelia, who had been full like a tick from milk, was now gurgling and stirring in her mother's arms.

'Don't think Amelia understands rules,' said Nell quietly.

Sarah shot the young woman a glance. Mrs Vale was insufferable, but for now she was the only thing that prevented them from having to seek shelter in the local wooden shacks.

'You will share a room. On rising at five, you will make your way here and begin preparations for breakfast. I assume one of you, at least, knows how to make bread – get a start on that for the day. You will find chickens to the left of the house, so one of you will need to collect the eggs. Put them in that bowl of sand over there.' She nodded towards the sideboard. 'In this blasted climate, eggs go off quite quickly.' She stood up. 'I should not need to say this, but I will. Neither of you, for any reason, shall leave these premises without my consent. Now, follow me.' She led them to what was to be their bedroom, then left and closed the door behind her. Sarah half expected to hear a key in the lock.

The space was small, only the size of a storeroom – which it might once have been, given its location just off the kitchen. One tiny window let in a miserly ration of late afternoon light, helped by a candle in a holder on the sill. The door required jiggling to ease it past one of the cots, while the other prevented it from opening all the way.

Nell chose a cot and sat down, unbuttoning her dress and dragging it across to expose a nipple for a few seconds before Amelia began to suckle. Sarah sat on her own cot, but then, feeling restless, she stood up and made for the door, arching her body in order to squeeze between it and the bed.

'Where are you going?' asked Nell. 'Herself said not to go out!'

'I can't even pace in here! Herself can say what she likes. We are not prisoners, not of hers.'

'We might not be her prisoners, but she's the gaoler,' said Nell.

Sarah snorted but did not try to leave. She unknotted the cloth bundle Nurse Haddon had given her to find a plain nightdress meticulously folded on top of her old clothes. 'Gaoler or not,' she said, 'I can't be trapped here. I need to get out at some point.'

'Oh, so do I. Why do *you* need to leave, though? She seems to have warmed to you, that Mrs Vale.'

The woman didn't seem the type to warm to anyone, but Sarah didn't need her to. She needed to find the people Watkins had been dealing with, in the hope they were less venal than him. Her only connection to Sam was among those who believed in the ideals he had died for. But what could she say to Nell?

'I – I'm looking for someone.'

'Who? I didn't think you knew anyone here.'

Sarah opened her mouth. Nell would understand, surely; she wouldn't trust those in power. And telling the truth would allow Sarah to feel free in this small room, without having to guard her words. She had thought, though, that every man in the loft in London could be trusted. Her stomach clenched, and she closed her mouth again.

Nell frowned. 'Am I not your friend?'

'Yes. Yes, of course, but I . . . I doubt you'd understand.'

'I see. Because when a woman uses what's between her legs, her brains fall out.'

'No! No, I—'

'Keep your secret,' said Nell. 'Keep your secret and shut your eyes and sleep. You may need to be up well before dawn.'

✦

It took Sarah a moment to remember where she was. The last time she had been shaken awake, it was by Sam's hand, the morning of the uprising.

'You take a frightful long time to wake up,' Nell was saying as she drew back from Sarah's cot.

By the light of a candle, assisted by a weak sliver of moonlight, Sarah could see a lumpen form on Nell's bed. She sat up, alarmed, only to realise that Nell had arranged the bedclothes into a nest for Amelia.

'You'll watch her?' Nell was saying. 'I'll be back before dawn, all washed and ready for that cow in the kitchen.'

'What . . . wait, where are you going? You said yourself we're not to go out.'

'And *you* said we're not prisoners.' Nell bent over and kissed her daughter. 'We can't rely on the charity of Mrs Vale – or even Mrs Thistle. You'd think a ticket of leave would be the best thing that could happen here, but at least the King feeds you when you're a prisoner. There are no workhouses, no poorhouses. If you can't get work, you will starve.'

'But you surely can't be thinking of—'

'Why not?' said Nell.

'You have a child, Nell!'

'And how long will she live, do you think, when Mrs Vale gets rid of us? Oh, and she will, don't think otherwise. She doesn't want us here. She'll catch me looking at the tea chest the wrong way, or she'll say I stole something. I've seen them, Sarah. Women with babies in their arms, sitting against walls in town. Sometimes you can't tell if they're alive. I need something put by.' She tucked Amelia's makeshift nest around her.

Sarah closed her eyes and remembered stepping over the lifeless and insensible bodies in Manchester, trying to make herself believe they were broken barrels or pieces of lumber.

Nell said, 'She might be hungry if she wakes, but I hope I'll be back by then.'

'There must be another way,' Sarah said. 'You can't want to . . . Can you?'

A scowl twisted Nell's mouth. 'Want to? What a stupid question! Want the fumbling and the pain and the breath in my face? Oh, they think I want to, if they think about it at all. Because we're all whores, aren't we?' Nell walked over and looked down into Sarah's face, spittle flying out with her words. 'You're better, yes? More intelligent. More moral. You'll talk to me but not take me as a friend. You would never stoop, would never lift your skirts. But you know, really. You must do. The only difference between us is luck.'

Amelia started to stir and whimper, so Nell went to rub her back until she quieted.

'You can, at least, do this for me,' Nell said softly to Sarah. 'You can help me make sure she is never without a blanket.'

She opened the door carefully so it wouldn't creak, stepped around it, and was gone.

❖

Amelia had been mewling for about half an hour when Nell got back in. Her dress – grey, austere, baggy around her shoulders – had a slight rip in its collar. There seemed, in the watery dawn creeping over the bare stone floor, to be a fresh scarlet mark on her cheek.

Sarah was relieved to see her. She wanted to ask who had given Nell that mark, wanted to give the guilty party some marks of his own. But Nell looked exhausted. She gave Sarah a quick smile of thanks as she reached into her pocket and extracted some coins. She wrapped them in a handkerchief that she stowed under her mattress, then reached out to Amelia, whose face was beginning to scrunch and redden. She held the baby close for a moment, breathing in her scent, then sat on the cot and undid the buttons at the front of her dress with quick, thin fingers, letting the baby latch on. 'Hope she didn't make too much noise,' Nell said. She sounded close to tears. 'It was hard, harder than I thought. To leave her.'

Sarah shook her head. 'She only started complaining a little while before you got in.'

'Well, I'll get her sorted now. Mrs Vale does not strike me as the kind to be patient with a baby's complaints.'

'You're wrong, you know,' said Sarah.

'Am I? Is there a spark of charity in the woman that I didn't notice?'

'Not about Mrs Vale, you're most probably right about her. I meant about me thinking I'm better than you. I know where circumstances can take people. There are things, though, that can be done to help. Steps that, if we took them, would stop you needing to find rough men with money in their pockets.'

'Those are fairy stories,' Nell protested. 'Oh, I've heard the talk – everyone has. Every so often, somebody will decide to stand in the street and call for revolution against the governor, the King, whoever. Sometimes they get arrested, but for the most part they're ignored – by the constables, and by all and sundry.'

Sarah walked over to sit beside Nell. 'It's not a fantasy, or it needn't be ... We tried, in London. And we nearly succeeded.'

'We? Nearly – nearly did what?'

'Nearly started a revolution. But we were betrayed. My brother, the others, they were arrested. He was hanged.'

'Why would you do something so dangerous, though?'

'Because my parents died doing something that should not have been dangerous. They were killed for listening to a talk.'

'And when your brother was arrested, you ... you were set free?'

'I escaped on the *Serpent*, which nearly sentenced me to death in place of a judge.'

Nell was gaping at Sarah now, shaking her head. 'You're a criminal, then. The constables might arrest me if they felt like it, if they were bored. But you – if they knew, they'd hang you.'

'They don't know, though. Nor does anyone else, at least not here in Sydney. Except you, now.'

Nell was silent for a minute, thinking. 'I feel no need to say anything to anyone,' she said eventually, a resolute ring to her voice. 'Are you going to . . . ? You're not continuing with it, not here?'

'There is a man,' said Sarah.

Nell snorted. 'Isn't there always.'

'Not like that. I don't even know his name, just that he was supposed to be waiting at a tavern near the docks for an important delivery from the *Serpent*. He might know others who think as I do.'

'Not much to go on, a man in a tavern.'

'I know one other thing – he has a marking of some kind, maybe a tattoo.'

Nell was nodding slowly. 'I tend to see a few of those. Best draw it for me, in case it happens to pass before my eyes. Now, what would it look like?'

CHAPTER 22

Nell had fashioned a sling out of a bedsheet and tied it at a slant around her body, suspending little Amelia in its folds. Nell did not seem at all concerned about Mrs Vale's view of the household linens being used in such a manner.

The young woman had managed perhaps an hour's sleep before it was time to get to the kitchen. 'Can I collect the eggs?' she asked Sarah. 'If I have to stand still kneading dough I'll fall asleep.'

Sarah nodded, happy to mix the bread; she enjoyed the sensation of sinking her fingers into the dough.

When she had finished with the bread she was using the sugar nips, broad-leafed scissors, on the white dome of a sugar loaf when Mrs Vale entered the kitchen.

'Good morning, madam,' Sarah said with a polite smile.

Mrs Vale did not return the greeting, just walked over to her, squinting at the chunk of sugar loaf she had cut off to be broken up and used for tea. 'Do not give the guests sugar unless they ask for it,' the landlady said. 'If I see further evidence of wastefulness, Mrs Thistle will hear of it.'

Nell walked back in with the eggs, Amelia grizzling and squirming in her sling.

'Please keep your child under control,' Mrs Vale snapped.

'She's a baby, madam,' said Sarah. 'If Nell could control her, she would be the first in the world to do so.'

'Then I shall make doing so the responsibility of both of you.'

Nell feigned wide-eyed alertness whenever Mrs Vale's eyes passed over her, but more than once Sarah had to set a small spill to rights. At one point she caught a fork Nell had been cleaning, just before it clattered to the floor, which would no doubt have brought Mrs Vale bustling in with accusations of vandalism.

Sarah carried the food into the dining room, keeping her eyes down. She did not know if Mrs Vale had told the guests that the *Serpent*'s survivor would be serving them.

They sat around a large polished table. Some – she guessed Mrs Thistle's mariners – were having a lively conversation about the wind that was beginning to disturb the trees outside. Others sat awkwardly, trying to find space to read the newspaper. None of them paid Sarah any mind.

She and Nell must have done a decent job with breakfast, for Mrs Vale nodded to them and spoke no word of complaint. 'You had best be off, the two of you,' she said.

'Off to?'

The landlady shook her head and sighed. 'Did we serve beef last night? Yes. And do you see any cows here? Do you see any carrots or cauliflower? The only thing I can grow in this blasted soil is potatoes. So where, might I ask, do you think all the food comes from?'

'The market,' said Nell, adjusting Amelia in her sling and rubbing the baby's back.

'At least you have a few wits,' said Mrs Vale.

'And what might we use for money?' asked Sarah.

'You don't honestly think I would give you two money to trot off with. Be back at noon – you won't do a proper job in less time. Tell them to put their goods on the account of the English Rose, and mind you tell them to send the account to me, not to Mrs Thistle. And of course, ask for the best they have. Mrs Thistle expects certain standards to be met.'

✦

Nurse Haddon would have been appalled at the dust being kicked up by the girls' footsteps on their long walk to the market, staining their hems and threatening to reach the baskets Mrs Vale had given them. Their skirts, though, were purity itself compared with the clothes of those they passed on the road.

The men wore yellow canvas decorated with blotches left by ancient mud and perhaps blood. They shuffled along; they had no choice, chained at the ankles as they were.

One of them looked up, and Sarah braced herself for a leer that didn't come. There was no answering spark when she looked into his eyes. His was a far emptier face than those of the convicts aboard the *Serpent*.

Her parents had often worn desperation and anger on their faces, but they had never stopped being themselves. This man was lost to everyone.

'Chain gang,' Nell said. 'They'll be off to build a road or cut timber.'

Nell walked on. If Sarah had followed her, had not paused for a moment longer as the chain gang passed, she would never have seen him, and he might not have recognised her.

At first glance he was just another convict, although clearly new to the life. He was looking around rather than at his feet, perhaps still fascinated by the tall pale trees or searching for the sight of a kangaroo peering out of the forest. Then he looked towards Sarah. His eyes skimmed over her, wide and drinking in the strange light of this place. He began to turn away, then stopped. Perhaps he recognised a pattern of features. She certainly had.

He gaped at her before he began to smile. She felt almost dizzy from shocked joy, restrained only by her doubts about what she was really seeing. She started towards him, for some reason worried he would be annoyed she had lost the little leaden sailor.

Before she could reach him, an overseer appeared from the trees, cuffed him on the back of the head and pushed him on. Henry Landers shambled along behind the others, looking at her over his shoulder and nearly tripping on the unfamiliar ground.

⁂

As a child, Sarah had loved market day. It was a more cheerful gathering than each Sunday at church. Instead of sitting up and being told how she was irredeemably flawed and sinful and destined for hell, she could wander through the stalls, looking – but not too closely, in case she earned a glare from a stallholder – at the vegetables, pastries and meat. Eavesdropping on the adults as she wove around their legs, she had heard about what Mrs Figgis was up to with the butcher, and how Mr Cleary had come home drunk the second time that week, while his children were in a disgraceful state with no shoes.

But even if this market had been like the ones of her childhood, she would not have taken any of it in. Her joy at seeing Henry had been joined by less pleasant stable-mates. She felt ashamed for having imagined a sneer on his face and coins in his pocket; for picturing him tossing the little leaden soldier aside, as it was no longer needed for the ruse. She was ashamed, too, for being happy he was here. This Henry, bruised and chained up, with dried blood on his face, was a grotesque echo of the handsome lad in the Marylebone loft. Although if he was here, maybe Tourville was too; maybe they had not been informers. Her breathing eased at the thought – perhaps it was still possible to trust.

She had to find a way to help Henry. Perhaps she could appeal to Mrs Thistle to intercede. What if the old woman could request Henry as an assigned convict? If only Sarah could think of a way to explain how she knew him without any mention of rebellion.

For now, though, she and Nell had been given a list of items to buy. They were outside the market house, a plain building with an incongruous dome topped by a weather vane, like a servant wearing an ornate feathered hat. Carts churned up the dirt as they came and went, or stood by the outer wall as men in shirtsleeves carried goods in and out, while horses gave the occasional whicker from within their feedbags. Crates and barrels were piled up along the outer wall, seemingly unwatched, although Sarah heard a gruff man shooing away some children who had been showing an interest in his apples.

Inside the stallholders stood cross-armed behind their wares, staring unblinkingly at anyone who approached. Sarah presumed this was the price of setting out one's wares in a town full of criminals.

Nell, though, was delighted. Flitting from stall to stall, smiling at the merchants, she seemed without any expectation of a return greeting. Most of all, she seemed to like fronting up to a stall and demanding their best goods be put on the account of the English Rose. She did not, perhaps, receive the deference she was hoping for, but no one refused to serve her and Sarah. Items were wrapped in oilcloth or paper, or just plonked into the basket that Nell held out. And whenever Amelia cooed, a smile was extracted from a stallholder who would then add a misshapen carrot or scoop of beans.

Having made her last purchase, Nell was looking at the sky. 'Not close to midday yet,' she said. 'Herself must think us witless, to insist we take so much time on this. You should just leave it to me next time. Doesn't need both of us.'

'Does she think us witless?' said Sarah. 'Or does she just dislike our company?'

'Oh, she certainly dislikes our company. But maybe there's someone else whose company she prefers. Haven't seen no sign of a Mr Vale. Perhaps Mrs Vale entertains a particular friend on market day?'

It was a joke Sarah would have considered frivolous a year ago. Now, her laughter rose up before she had a chance to roll Nell's jest around in her head and condemn it as a vulgar distraction. She found she liked the idea that someone was still engaged in the business of life – she doubted, though, that the sour Mrs Vale was involved in any such activity.

'Do you know,' she said to Nell, 'I think next time I will do as you suggest and leave the market to you.

You are good at this, you and Amelia.' She stroked the baby's head.

'That we are. Never fails me, this girl.'

※

'You will turn the beds now,' said Mrs Vale, sweeping into the kitchen as Sarah and Nell were taking plates and cutlery out of the sideboard for dinner.

'But, missus, we only did that this morning!' said Nell.

'Clearly you did not do it to my satisfaction,' Mrs Vale said.

'This is going to take ages,' Nell said as she and Sarah climbed the stairs, after looking in on Amelia, who was asleep in her little basket.

Perhaps it didn't take as long as Nell had feared, but long enough so that by the time they returned to the kitchen, dinner had already been served.

As Sarah cleared the plates later, she noticed a lot of the food was uneaten. It was curious that the food they had brought back from the market could spoil so quickly. The beef, earlier glistening and covered in skeins of fat, was now tough and an odd grey colour. The cauliflowers had, in the space of an afternoon, developed black speckles.

Sarah did not, though, decide to tell Mrs Thistle. She was tempted to, certainly. But if Mrs Vale had replaced the market goods with lesser ones, Sarah did not know what had happened to the originals. And while Mrs

Thistle gave the impression of one who appreciated honesty, the rancour caused by a false accusation might see Sarah out on the street. And really, Sarah did not see why she should help this woman who was profiting off her labour.

Still, she wanted to know. Information was the only currency she had, even if she did not intend to spend it.

CHAPTER 23

After their next market trip, Mrs Vale had them lay their purchases out on the table. She lifted a head of cabbage and sniffed it. Prodded at a leg of lamb. Examined a carrot from every angle. 'Are you truly such simpletons? This is unacceptable! A waste of Mrs Thistle's money.'

'But that is exactly what you asked for!' said Sarah.

'I asked for beef.'

'No, madam, I fear you must be mistaken, but you requested lamb.'

'I know precisely what I requested,' Mrs Vale said. 'Go back, both of you. Prove to me you can tell the difference between a cow and a sheep.'

'She did ask for lamb,' Nell muttered as they left. 'I heard her.'

Sarah nodded and asked, 'I wonder, would you be able to manage this trip yourself?'

Over the past week or so, Nell had made several night-time excursions. Sometimes she returned to a contentedly sleeping Amelia, but more often than not to an exhausted Sarah rocking the baby back and forth as she tried to keep her from waking the household.

'I think I owe you that much,' Nell said.

Sarah squeezed her friend's shoulder and kissed the baby on the head as they departed. A part of her longed to go with them down the dusty road on the chance she might see Henry again, but she knew the chances of that were slim.

The fence at the side of the house was overshadowed by a large fig tree, behind which Sarah concealed herself. Half an hour passed, and Sarah was beginning to think the landlady had just put by the fresher food for later use, when a cart approached, driven by a man casting glances around when his eyes should have been on the rough road.

He pulled up outside the English Rose and clambered down from the cart. She expected him to knock, but the door opened and Mrs Vale stepped out.

The landlady lifted her chin up and slightly to the side, as though to avoid an unpleasant smell. The man wore no jacket, something Mrs Vale probably considered a crime in itself. His shirt was undone at the neck, its sleeves rolled up, and the white fabric had a yellow tinge with dark blotches down the front. His sweat-stained neckerchief had been tied carelessly so that one tail was shorter than the other. He had the mottled, sun-punished skin of a redhead, but it was impossible to know the colour of the hair that had once sprouted from his bullish head.

His nose was slightly crooked and had been shifted to the right, possibly by a blow.

When he smiled it was even more crooked than his nose, but Sarah was unsure if this was just the shape of his mouth or if he was smirking.

He spoke too quietly to be overheard, while Mrs Vale was growing agitated. 'I am simply not going to give you two crates! Not for the same price!'

The man leaned closer to her as he muttered something, his crooked smile widening.

Sarah could not see Mrs Vale's face but heard her exhale loudly. She went inside and came out with one small crate, then another. The man loaded them onto the cart before hauling out two sacks. He handed one to Mrs Vale and held open the other while she filled it with the items Sarah and Nell had bought. Then he pulled some crumpled notes from his trouser pocket and gave them to Mrs Vale, who pinched her thumb and forefinger around the money as though reluctant to touch it.

He took the reins, shook them and clicked his tongue, and the cart trundled off. Sarah waited an hour or so before she moved, skirting the house and keeping close to the scrub for a little way down the road, until she saw Nell approaching with Amelia in her sling and a basket over her arm.

She stepped out onto the road, and Nell gasped and then laughed. 'Thought you were a bushranger for a moment, out to steal my treasure,' she said, bending to kiss her daughter's head.

Sarah laughed too, and they walked together back to the house.

By the time they entered the kitchen, Mrs Vale had put away any evidence of her crime and was sitting at the table with a cup of tea. She jumped at the sound of the opening door. The basket's contents threatened to spill out, and when Nell adjusted Amelia, a turnip toppled to the floor and rolled before stopping near Mrs Vale's feet.

The landlady looked at the vegetable, then at Amelia. 'May I ask, how much has spilled onto the road on the way here?'

'None of it, I was only—'

'That child should not be here.'

'Where should she be, if not with her mother?' asked Nell.

Mrs Vale sniffed. 'There are orphanages.'

Sarah had heard of the orphanages in Manchester, and had seen children taken there when their parents couldn't support them, or were transported, or died. More each year. They never came out.

'Amelia is not an orphan,' Sarah said. 'She has a perfectly good mother.'

'Hm.' Mrs Vale walked towards Nell, stretching out her arms. 'Give her to me so you can do your work.'

Nell lurched back, clutching Amelia, the basket still on her arm. A small wheel of cheese hit the floor.

'Stupid girl, what do you think I intend to do? Take her to the orphanage?'

'How would I know?' asked Nell.

Mrs Vale tried to get her hands under Nell's sheltering arms to take Amelia.

'Let her go, witch!' Nell screamed into the woman's face.

Mrs Vale paused, then drew back her hand and cracked Nell across her face.

Sarah started forward to help Nell, although she felt her fist clenching and knew she would have to use every ounce of self-control to stop herself striking Mrs Vale.

Nell was panting. A droplet of blood ran from her split lip and splashed onto Amelia's head. Nell made no attempt to wipe it away, apparently unwilling to loosen her grip on her daughter as she stared at Mrs Vale through panic-widened eyes.

The landlady stepped away; perhaps even she was shocked by what she had just done.

'This is not what I would describe as a model of efficiency and decorum,' said a voice from the door.

✳

Mrs Thistle lowered herself into the chair at the head of the kitchen table and said, 'Tell me what has happened.'

Nell took in a shuddering breath. 'She—'

Mrs Thistle held up a hand to silence her. 'I will speak to Mrs Vale first, if you please. I'm sure the both of you can find some work that needs doing elsewhere.'

Nell gaped at her, and Sarah wanted to cry for her friend. She put her arm around Nell's shoulder and led her from the room. 'Come along,' she said gently, 'Amelia could do with feeding by now, I'm sure.' She looked over her shoulder as she left, unable to stop herself frowning at Mrs Thistle, who smiled at her serenely.

It was an hour before Mrs Vale came to find her, as she was dusting the mantelpiece in the drawing room, trying to navigate around the fussy little doilies and vases.

'She wishes to see you,' the landlady said, and swept out.

Mrs Thistle had helped herself to a cup of tea, or more likely had Mrs Vale make it for her. She gestured Sarah to a seat. 'Tell me, Miss Marin, do you believe Nell should be able to call Mrs Vale a witch with impunity?'

It was the kind of question Sarah expected: one that ignored the inciting offence and condemned the response. 'Mrs Vale was trying to take her baby.'

'Only so she could get some work done.'

'And after going on about orphanages! What was Nell to think? Do you believe someone should be able to hit a woman holding a baby with ... with impunity?' The word felt strange in her mouth; it was one of *their* words,

228

owned by those who decided the fates of thousands from a comfortable chair.

'I do not, as a matter of fact,' said Mrs Thistle. 'I will deny it should you tell anyone about this, but I'd have done the same.'

Sarah frowned. Was the woman trying to draw her out further, to coax her into stating her beliefs and then beat her with them?

'So Mrs Vale will be punished?' she asked.

'No.'

'But she will do it again, and the next time she strikes Nell she could hurt Amelia!'

'Oh, if she does it again, she will lose her position. I know she is not the most amiable person, Miss Marin. But it is hard for a widow here. Her husband was one of my carters – his wheel hit a hole, the cart overturned. I will not see her or anyone destitute if I can help it.'

'Would you be stricter with Mrs Vale if Nell wasn't a former convict?'

Mrs Thistle shook her head, chuckling. 'You think I care less for her because she came here in the belly of a ship?'

'Well, do you?'

'Miss Marin, there are those who think convicts – or former convicts – can't be trusted to tell you their own name. But do you really think this colony could afford armies of clerks and battalions of labourers? Surely you've seen the road gangs with their overseer. Well, that's the way of it. The guarded outnumber the guards, and not only breaking rocks. Private secretaries, even magistrates, came here because of a judge's sentence. And of course most of us stay here once our sentences are served. We value those with a criminal stain more than you might think.'

'We?' said Sarah.

'I've made no secret of it. Georgina Haddon, too – although she simply picked up a watch, enough to win her seven years. Whereas I,' Mrs Thistle said, drawing her shoulders back, 'stole a horse.' She paused, then, as if waiting for applause, and Sarah tried to resist the urge to give it. She ignored the slight flare of admiration she suddenly felt.

'You were lucky not to hang.'

'So I've been told – the first time by Georgina herself. We came here together, you see. That was . . . 1793? So I have been here for over half my life, and have been free for over half of it as well. It's an advantage here, sometimes, to have been a convict. Those who came free – those who came with the stamp of authority on their foreheads – have tried to remake the old world here, and the old world simply won't be remade. There are chinks for people like me to slip through. And then, well, once you get wealthy enough, everyone just seems to forget that you existed before you could afford to buy their houses.'

Sarah had never heard of a wealthy person who had not been born to it. Mrs Thistle shouldn't have existed, at least not according to the rules of the old world. She was probably wealthy enough to buy the cotton mill in which Sarah had worked. Although Sarah still mistrusted this wealth, seeing it as corrosive, she couldn't deny that Mrs Thistle's beginnings blunted her disapproval.

Sarah was not as sympathetic to Mrs Vale as Mrs Thistle was. She had very little faith in the landlady's promises not to inflict violence again. At the thought of Amelia lying broken on the floor, dashed from her mother's arms by a badly aimed slap, Sarah inhaled sharply. 'Mrs Thistle,' she said, 'I believe Mrs Vale is stealing from you.'

The old woman listened quietly. When Sarah finished, she frowned into her teacup. 'I thank you, but you will understand I need more certainty. I shall set my own watch.' She stood, smoothed down her dress, nodded to Sarah and stepped towards the door, leaving her teacup where it was.

The thought that Mrs Thistle might soon be having the house watched, perhaps even that night, was both comforting and terrifying. What if the spy saw Nell slipping out?

When they were alone in their tiny room, Sarah took Nell by the shoulders. 'If you must go, go around the back. It's darker there, without the light from the main house.'

Nell did not ask why, just nodded. This was clearly not the first time she had taken a warning from a friend on faith.

*

Over the following week Amelia seemed to grow used to her mother's absences, timing her sleep and wakefulness to accommodate them, so there was rarely more than twenty minutes between Amelia starting to grumble and Nell slipping through the narrow door. She would usually take the baby from Sarah, feed her, and lie down to claim whatever small ration of sleep was left between her return and their pre-dawn chores.

One morning, though, she did not immediately reach for Amelia, instead sitting on the bed opposite Sarah. Her cheeks were flushed, and she was smiling. 'I found him for you! At least, I may have.'

'What . . . who?'

'Him!' Nell said, as she went over to feed Amelia. 'Your man with the tattoo.'

'How did you—?'

'At a tavern near the docks. I was talking, you see, to a fellow. And this other man, he comes up, takes my fellow's shoulder, pulls him around and gives him a hearty thump on the back. And I saw that snake eating its tail, right there on his forearm.'

'And you've never seen anyone else with a tattoo like that?'

'Never. Oh, and I found a name for you. A young fellow was talking to your tattooed man and a few others, and when he left one of them said, "See you back at the docks, Keenan."'

Keenan. An unremarkable name, whose bearer might help her in a cause that had started out as a desire for freedom but had grown to include a yearning for liberty for one set of hunched shoulders, a slight, freckled girl, and a mewling mass of need too young to understand that her mother was as much a prisoner as she had ever been.

CHAPTER 24

While Mrs Vale had not wreathed herself in the Christian values of charity and honesty, she nevertheless seemed to enjoy attending church. She told Nell and Sarah, and probably anyone else who would listen, that she sat within feet of the governor, and closer still to Mrs Thistle.

To further bolster her credentials as a relentlessly moral and well-connected woman, each Saturday Mrs Vale attended a sewing circle that included the wife of the colonial secretary as well as the spouses of other functionaries, whose connections she would frequently mention to her guests at the English Rose.

That Saturday morning, once Mrs Value had departed with her sewing bag, Sarah went alone to the docks, covering the distance in less than half an hour. She brought a pencil sketch of the ouroboros symbol and could not stop fiddling with it in her pocket. As she walked down the hill towards the water, she could see bristling masts, and when she reached the bottom she could hear shouts and creaks while the vessels' contents were transferred into stocky, peak-roofed warehouses. By the time she plunged into the dockside mayhem, the paper was starting to tear at the edges.

Sarah kept an eye out for the silent men who saw more danger in conversations than in solitude. Those who refused to bow their heads in greeting to someone of a superior class, or who did not scuttle out of the way when the constables strode along the dockside, as they often did.

The problem was, of course, that this sort of man was unlikely to be forthcoming when a strange girl approached him asking for information. A couple of men were startled by the sight of her walking purposefully towards them, and disappeared into the crowd. Those willing to listen seemed surprised when Sarah, who surely looked unaccustomed to the docks, asked after a Mr Keenan, saying she needed to deliver a message from his sister; they just shook their heads. She gabbled her question more quickly each time, her desperation perhaps making them wonder why she was so interested.

She approached one knot of men who were waiting for goods to be lowered to them on a rope. They looked at her with interest and nudged each other. Nearby, an older man with crinkled grey hair sat on a crate, puffing streams of pipe smoke into the air. Their gaffer, perhaps, if longshoremen had such things.

'Know nothing about sisters,' he said when she asked, 'but Mr Keenan's over there.' He pointed to another ship being unloaded by longshoremen. 'The skinny one.'

She thanked the man and walked over. Keenan, thin and wiry, was taking a crate from one man and passing it to another. He was old enough to have a full brown beard although it had been unevenly trimmed, and he resembled most longshoremen she had seen, with his sweat-soiled neckerchief and sun-punished skin.

He carried his load inside a warehouse, and she waited near the entrance until he emerged again; she did not wish to march up to him and converse in the presence of a group of longshoremen.

When she unfolded the picture, he stared at it for a few seconds, then gave her a sharp glance. 'No time to look at some girl's silly scribblings,' he said, but did not move away. He spoke in an accent she had once heard in Angel Meadow, where many of the mill workers were Irish.

'Nor do I have time for liars,' she said.

He glanced at it again, and at her. 'The police use women, sometimes.'

'And if you thought I was a police informer, you would never have told me that.'

She gasped as he seized the paper, crumpled it and threw it into the ocean. 'I don't know what that symbol means,' he whispered harshly, 'and you should not be bothering a poor working man with such trifles.'

Sarah was a little startled by his anger, but also encouraged – the symbol must have some meaning to him, to evoke such a response. 'Of course you don't know what it means. But you might have seen it, somewhere.'

He ran his hands through his hair. 'All right, I might have,' he said. 'Perhaps not far from here. Above the door of a house, up beyond the stream.'

'Do you know who lives there?'

'I know very little. People go there most Sundays, when others are busy drinking themselves stupid.'

He paused. 'More are always welcome, if they're of the right mind.'

A man called out to Keenan, urging him back to the ship. He pressed his lips together, shook his head and walked back to his task, striding up the gang-board and onto the deck.

·✦·

As soon as Sarah had left the dockside crowds behind, she broke into a run. There was no time for her to search for the house before Mrs Vale returned.

By the time she was nearing the English Rose, her eyes were focused on the uneven road that seemed to enjoy tripping the unwary. She did not see the chain gang until she was almost upon them; they were a little way off the road below her as she came over a small hill. Judging by their axes and fallen trees around them, they had been cutting some timber. Their presence was brought to her attention by the shouts of an incipient fight. Two men, bare-backed and leg-ironed, had their heads down as they gripped one another, each trying to overbalance his opponent. The overseer was laughing and clapping, which was all of the encouragement most of the others needed to down tools and watch.

Henry was towards the edge of the group, glancing at the combatants but also looking around, frowning. She had seen that frown when he was reading Briardown's letters aloud to the others in the loft, instructions delivered when their leader was otherwise occupied. Henry had struggled to decipher the florid English, the filigree sentences. What was he trying to decipher now? Perhaps he was still making sense of his foreign surroundings. Of the tall, slender trees and the grey-furred creatures that clung to them. Of the alien seasons. Of the knowledge he would never return home.

As badly as she wanted Henry to see her, Sarah preferred not to draw any notice from the other men. She walked just behind the bushes that lined the opposite side of the track, picking her way carefully down until she was parallel to the group, hoping he would continue looking around.

He did, and when his eyes landed on her he smiled, showing a new gap in his lower row of teeth. He glanced back at the fight, which continued to consume the attention of the others, then walked towards her. His leg irons would no doubt be clanking, but she couldn't hear them above the shouts and the clanks of iron on the legs of the fighters.

She looked at Henry far more closely than she had on last seeing him, when the shock of his features among the scared faces and leering mouths of the gang had stopped her searching his face for strangeness among the familiar. It was there now, though. A yellowing bruise under one eye. A face of red and pink patches, where some parts of his skin had peeled off to present another layer to the sun for burning. Dry lips that cracked as he smiled. 'I can't linger,' he said. 'But you – you're safe! I had hoped—'

'As I continue to,' she said. 'There are others like us here. I don't know much about them, not yet, but perhaps they could help free you. I can't bear to think of you like this for – how long?'

'Well, I have a life sentence, although I might be able to get a ticket of leave after seven years. I'll never be able to leave the colony, though. Listen, Sarah, do not do this. Do not risk yourself again.'

'But they do not know who I am! I am safe.'

'No, you're not!' he said urgently. 'You never will be. You don't know—'

'Landers!'

The roar came from behind Henry, and Sarah realised that the sound of the fight had dimmed. The overseer was now strolling over towards them, a man whose face had been punished by fists as well as the sun. He grabbed Henry's shoulder and sent him sprawling.

The other men, including the two with bloodied lips and noses, were clearly delighted by this fresh entertainment, and laughed as Henry hit the ground.

He got to his feet, giving her a reassuring half-smile.

Sarah tensed, thinking the overseer might do the same to her. Instead his scowl transformed into a serious look of concern. 'Stay away from these men, miss. They're not the harmless kind who stole a bit of food. They have beaten people, sometimes almost to death. And that's not the worst of it. The one you were talking to is guilty of high treason.'

✦

Sarah was probably committing treason herself, for the second time, as she slunk out of the English Rose the next afternoon while Mrs Vale attended a charitable gathering after church, and made her way through town. She walked past a grooved rock funnelling water down to the open mouths of those who stopped to drink there, then she strode into the area known as The Rocks, on the western arm, far less hospitable with its jagged shoreline than other parts of the harbour.

Some of the buildings she had seen in Sydney, such as the courthouse where she'd participated in the inquest, were nearly as grand as those to be found in London, and clearly modelled on their counterparts. But here these buildings looked almost ridiculous, transplanted to a place of heat and dust and space.

In The Rocks, none of their kind were to be seen. A few wattle and daub cottages with fenced yards were interspersed with slab huts topped by roofs that had been patchworked out of any available materials and probably had no hope of keeping out even the most gentle rain. There were no roads, the only thorough-fares created by feet that had trod down grass until it refused to grow. The land rose up sharply enough that the upper row of huts was only accessible by a precari-ous track.

The house did not have any windows to speak of, simply shutters set into the daubed front wall on either side of a plain door. In the lintel above the door, some-one had scratched the crude shape of a serpent. A small veranda extended from the house, upon which people sat in chairs or on the wooden boards, drinking a substance that Sarah suspected was not tea.

She raised her hand to knock, and the door opened under her fist. A woman bustled up to her as stepped inside. Some of those lounging outside had not taken much care with their clothing; the expanse of flesh vis-ible would never have been tolerated in church. This woman, though – older, but not yet with as many years as Molly Thistle – would clearly never have allowed such a thing to happen to her. Even in the advancing heat of spring, a woollen shawl was crossed over her chest and tied at the back. Her skirts were so worn and faded that Sarah could not make out the design of the fabric, but they had been patched with some diligence. She had shown less care for the cooking pot she was holding, the base of which was covered in dents. 'This is a private residence,' she said.

Sarah tried not to laugh. 'I do apologise,' she said. 'I was given the impression I might find a particular kind of . . . conversation, here. Maybe I was mistaken.'

The woman narrowed her eyes and yelled, 'Mr Keenan!' She turned back to Sarah while they waited, staring at her as though fearful she might produce a phalanx of police from under her skirt. 'Mr Keenan!'

A door set in the rear wall of the cottage's front room opened, and the wiry young man stepped in.

'Another of your little mice, Mr Keenan,' the woman said. 'Why do you believe women can be trusted more than men?'

'I don't, not always,' he said, arching an eyebrow at Sarah. 'You get a feeling, sometimes.'

'Oh, a feeling! How odd that these feelings of yours are usually in relation to young women.'

'Mrs Addison, if she was a police spy, we would already be in chains,' Keenan said, with the weariness of someone who was constantly having to explain himself.

'Say nothing,' Mrs Addison told Sarah sternly. 'Not now, not afterwards. There are some here who don't share

Keenan's finer feelings.' She banged on the doorframe with the pot stop and called out, 'Time, you lot!'

'Well, as you're here, you might as well stay,' Keenan said to Sarah. 'If you're lucky, you might even hear something interesting.'

CHAPTER 25

The crowd at the front had swelled. Most of those who had been there when Sarah arrived looked as though they lived in The Rocks, that theirs was a world of bark and scrap. They had been joined by people who looked as though they lived in houses of brick. Nobody was rich, certainly, but some of the men were dressed as though they might work in Mrs Thistle's warehouses, some of the women appropriately attired for serving at Mrs Vale's table.

They all turned with the others at Mrs Addison's call, then filed slowly into the cottage. It was furnished with chairs of uncertain structural integrity, a seemingly impossible number jammed into the small room, while the empty, smutted fireplace had an upturned crate in front of it. Some shrank a little as they passed Mrs Addison, and she glared at each one, leaving them in no doubt that they were here at her pleasure, which was limited.

There seemed to be some common sense of propriety, with the better dressed of the men yielding seats to the most slovenly of the women. Keenan walked over to Sarah and gestured her to a seat near the centre, facing the fireplace and its crate podium.

'I have told you,' said Mrs Addison, standing in front of the audience once they were all seated. 'Again and again, I've told you. If you mill about the house out the front like that, every Sunday? Someone will report us, nothing surer. Pretend you're having a Sunday stroll. Come later – Mr Keenan doesn't mind being interrupted. But the next time I open the door to find a throng waiting for the loaves and bloody fishes, that'll be the last use you will have of this place. And I'll stop letting a room to Mr Keenan. Here he is.'

There was a smattering of applause, before those clapping remembered that nothing laudatory had been said as yet.

Taller than Mrs Addison by a head, Keenan stood on the crate that she had ignored. 'We are grateful, madam, for your indulgence,' he said with a little bow.

'Go to blazes,' Mrs Addison retorted, grinning as she swatted him on the arm.

Sarah's conversation with him at the docks had been in urgent whispers. She had not realised that his voice was quite so deep, nor that it carried so well.

'You will have heard, all of you, of the sentence handed down to those soldiers.'

A few nodded, while some glanced at each other in confusion.

Keenan smiled at Sarah. 'So our new friends can follow – soldiers killed that fellow on George Street. Beat him to death with palings from his own fence. And for what? He was trying to shelter a woman they wanted to get to.'

Some indignant murmuring, a few nodding heads.

'Now, none of us are likely to see the place of our birth again,' Keenan continued. 'And some of you did as little as stealing a scrap of food. These men, though. What did they get?' He paused, looking around the room.

He fancies himself a bit, thought Sarah.

After a moment, he pounded the fist of one hand into the palm of the other. 'A one shilling fine and six months in gaol!' he roared. 'Not banishment from everything they knew! Not exile! There is no clearer indication – if anyone needed any – of how the government sees us. The slaying of a working man is a lesser crime than stealing a head of cabbage!'

Was he happy with the response? The muttering in the room was louder, to be sure. But there was no standing, shouting, or thrusting of fists into the air.

He sighed, but kept going. 'We have no value to them! We are simply a means to greater profit. Oh, you'll hear them talk. Talk about how when they do well, everyone else does too – that they can hire more farmhands for the pastoral properties they barely set foot on, or obtain more servants for their houses. They say their good fortune washes down to the rest of us. Well, something washes down, but it is not fortune.'

'What do we do about it, though?' said a man dressed in a hessian waistcoat that looked as though it hadn't been hemmed, just a rough shape over a stained shirt. On his feet were leather sacks drawn closed by leather thongs. 'Take up arms? What good will that do, except to get us killed?'

'Thomas Spence wrote it was a pity that people did not perceive the immediate and inexpressible blessings that would infallibly result from a revolution. He said, "the good effects of such a charge would be more exhilarating and reviving to the hunger-bitten and despairing children of oppression, than a benign and sudden spring to the frost-bitten earth, after a long and severe winter." How are we to exercise any power? We are under the yoke of the King, but we aren't able to vote for members of his parliament. We have no recourse against the decisions of his governor, no means to influence the world being built around us. None, except arms.'

'A good way to hang!' a man called. 'A good way to die.'

Another man stood. Making no attempt to interject, he folded his arms and glared. He looked like a schoolmaster waiting for silence before settling on an appropriate punishment for rowdiness. He was old enough, too, to have been Keenan's schoolmaster. His bald head was fringed by grey hair, which he had made no attempt to tame so that it stuck out at the sides like the ears of the grey creatures in the trees. Hair also sprouted from his nose, and he had the florid, red-netted cheeks of a habitual drinker.

Keenan faltered as he returned the man's stare. 'Yes, Mr Baxendale,' he said, 'you wish to speak?'

Baxendale turned to the other man who had spoken. 'You think in shades of grey, if you think in terms of degree.'

'There are no degrees, Mr Keenan!' he continued. 'Either one is for the people, or one deserves death. And anyone not actively working for the overthrow of this corrupt system of government is a sympathiser.'

'What of those who are unable to join us in this effort? Those too poor, too frightened?' said Keenan. 'Are they to be put to the sword, in this world you wish to build?'

'If they are unwilling to fight for their freedom, they do not deserve it,' Baxendale said. 'Poor? Frightened? I have been both of those things, I still am. It has not stopped me, nor should it stop anyone else. But the poor are not the ones who should be most admonished.'

'I'm glad to hear you say that, Mr Baxendale,' said Keenan earnestly.

'It is the rich,' cried Baxendale, pounding his fist into the palm of his hand. 'Those who have the ability to bring pressure to bear in the administration, those with influence who choose to use it only on their own behalf. The McAllisters, with all of their land. Old Manning, with his trading and his public houses. And that Thistle woman – appalling creature she is. Those like her who came here as convicts the worst of all, for they know the cost of oppression and are willing to let others pay it.'

'Your passion is commendable, although while all the wealthy have a case to answer, we must not be distracted from the administration,' said Keenan. 'We lack the rights of even the most humble of our counterparts in Britain. They will not cede them to us if we simply ask nicely. The history of the world, my friends, is soaked in the blood of those who understood that the only way to gain their rights was to take them.'

✳

'And will you take your rights?' Sarah asked Keenan after the meeting had broken up. They were standing in front of the house as it slowly emptied, people nodding at Keenan or glancing cautiously at her as they passed.

'In course,' he said. 'We had been expecting some help. Help that sank before it could reach us.'

'Help?' Baxendale said. 'The only reliable source of help lies within you, boy!'

'Mr Keenan,' she said, 'would you care to introduce us?'

Baxendale glared at her, eyes wide and brows drawn as though she had just offended him beyond words.

'Miss Marin,' said Keenan. 'Noah Baxendale. One of our more . . . enthusiastic members.'

Baxendale bowed stiffly and shallowly.

'You speak as someone who has done more than talk in the past, Mr Baxendale,' Sarah said.

'And I speak with caution of the past. It holds its own dangers.'

'Even among friends?'

'And how can I be assured that I am? You heard of the conspiracy in London? Necks stretched over that, and all because they were betrayed.'

Memories of the arrests and hangings still assaulted her at odd times, gripping her without warning so that she needed to steady herself, catch her breath. Now they had been called forth so directly, she found herself swaying, swallowing, trying to see through glazed eyes.

Keenan reached out to steady her. Baxendale just stared.

'Perhaps, Mr Baxendale,' Keenan said, 'we should have a care for more delicate sensibilities.'

'Not at all,' Sarah said. 'I have no queasiness when it comes to rebellions.'

Baxendale raised an eyebrow at her. 'A kitchen uprising, was it?'

Sarah dug her nails into her palm in self-reproval. Even here, she could not tell anyone about her past. She would be adding to their danger with the weight of the knowledge, while adding to her own.

'General Ludd's men,' she said, and swallowed. 'They attacked the mill where I worked, when I was about twelve.'

So many horrors had arisen to replace the memory that she had not thought about it in a long time. She had watched with her mother from the window of the spinning mule room as they had arrived, a few at first and then a few dozen, and suddenly the space in front of the factory was thronged with people, a larger crowd than she had ever seen before. They were led by two men: one was carrying a straw figure, the other waving a red flag. The crowd was murmuring, in some cases talking or even laughing, but not shouting. Everyone stilled and fell silent, though, when the man holding the straw effigy handed it to another and stepped forward, looking up at the mill.

The Luddite leader may have been looking directly up at Hodgkins, the mill owner, or simply raising his gaze to where he thought a mill owner would stand.

'As a holder of those despicable power looms,' he yelled. 'General Ludd informed you he would detach a lieutenant and men to destroy them if you did not put them aside. This you have failed to do. Neither you nor Westminster has listened to our petitions. We have asked the House of Commons to pass an Act to put down all machinery hurtful to commonality, and repeal that to hang frame breakers. We have received no satisfaction. We petition no more. Now, we fight, and we start here.'

As soon as he had finished speaking, the crowd surged forward, shoving against the factory's main door. Judging by the tinkling sound below her, others were hurling rocks at the windows. She saw a boy, perhaps her age, being lifted through a window; the men lifting him were laughing, but he looked terrified.

Then she had heard the *crack-crack-crack* of what sounded like weapons firing. But she knew what it was – her father had told their family the previous night that the march of the Luddites had been expected, and some of the mill workers had been given guns loaded with blank rounds.

Perhaps the overseers were hoping that the sound itself would disperse the crowd, but it only slowed them for a few seconds. A few people slipped away, while others looked for the fallen around them and did not find any. Almost all at once, it seemed to occur to them that the weapons were just making noise.

She knew these people meant her no harm, that they only wanted the machines with which she worked. Still, their angry swarm frightened her.

She heard another bang, and another. The sounds did not worry the crowd, for now they believed they were in no danger. But Sarah, from her window, had seen red bloom over a man's chest as he fell back, spraying the people around him with blood. Then another bang, and a woman to the right of the crowd twirled and fell as though someone had grabbed her by the shoulder, twisted and pushed her. A third, and one of the men near the front – perhaps the one who had carried Ludd's effigy – was down.

The crowd panicked, running into each other, elbowing, scrambling past to get to the road that led away from the mill. They were met by a line of mounted Scots Greys, in tall hats and red coats with white straps across their chests, coming from the town.

Baxendale spoke with the same Yorkshire accent as the leader of the frame breakers. Now he was frowning at her. 'And what did you make of them, these Luddites?' he asked. 'Not everyone welcomed their actions.'

'Well,' she said, 'I suppose sometimes you need to burn a forest to the ground so it can grow again.'

Baxendale nodded. 'Perhaps you might explain that to him,' he said, gesturing towards Keenan. Then he jammed his broad-brimmed hat onto his bald head, nodded vaguely and walked away.

Keenan looked at Sarah, smiling and shaking his head, and she laughed. 'A charming man,' she said.

'What he lacks in manners, he makes up for in conviction,' Keenan said. 'Shall I see you home?'

They walked in silence until they came to the wharves that jutted into the harbour near The Rocks. Across the water were other wharves, leading to warehouses. One bore the name THISTLE in large black letters. Sarah winced. If she squinted, she could almost believe the sign said HODGKINS & SONS.

Keenan nervously cleared his throat. 'So, Manchester,' he said. 'Were you there, when the government slaughtered its own people for the crime of listening to a speech?'

Sarah was well aware her accent betrayed her origins, and she intended to hide in the truth, or a version of it.

'Most of Manchester was there that day,' she said.

'And did you lose anyone there?'

She could not disavow her parents by pretending they still breathed or that they had been taken by hunger or an illness. But she did not know whether the eyes searching for her could see this far, or what they knew of the circumstances that had led her to London.

'My – my last living relative died suddenly, sometime later,' she said. 'And now I work in a boarding house.'

'Oh yes,' he said, and spat on the ground. 'One of Mrs Thistle's, most probably.'

Sarah shrugged. 'Why do people hate her?'

'Not her. What she represents. The hoarding of resources. Those carriage wheels of hers that roll through the streets past people in rags. The bounty that goes into her warehouse, and only comes out again at a price. I've seen what she brings in – I've unloaded her ships.'

'But she's not the enemy. What of Lord Liverpool?'

'Do not call him that. Robert Jenkinson's his name. Even if he is prime minister, he should use the name he was born with, not an undeserved title bestowed by a fat, raddled Prince Regent.'

'King, now,' said Sarah.

'Hm, I'd forgotten. But it does not matter whose buttocks are on that throne, they will never move themselves onto a ship and come here. Jenkinson may be most at fault. But Mrs Thistle drinks from the same corrupt well. And she has an advantage over all of them – she's here.'

CHAPTER 26

Sarah did not let Keenan walk her all the way home, saying goodbye to him at Market Place.

When she reached the English Rose she stopped to let her breathing slow. She smoothed down her dress, tried to dust off the worst of the road's grime, fixed the hair coming loose from the black ribbon tied at the nape of her neck. She inhaled, darted around the side of the house and opened the kitchen door, bracing herself for a telling off.

Mrs Vale was not alone. And the way she was staring at Mrs Thistle told Sarah that she was not the cause of the landlady's distress.

Mrs Thistle was sitting calmly at the head of the table, a cup of tea in her hand. Perhaps it had been placed there by Nell, who was standing by the kitchen's other door with Amelia as though guarding the place against an invasion.

Mrs Thistle took a sip, slurping in a way that would have earned Sarah, or anyone else, a dressing-down from Mrs Vale, who was standing near the hearth, lifting the corner of her starched white apron to dab her eyes.

Mrs Thistle put her teacup into the saucer, the pieces of china rattling against each other. 'You see, this is what I mean,' she said. 'Honestly, the difference is so marked, I'm surprised you don't get complaints from the guests.' She got up, walked over to a cupboard and took out a head of cauliflower. After inspecting it closely, she threw it back in the cupboard without closing the door. 'But of course we *have* been getting complaints, my dear, haven't we? Just look at what happened after church.' She noticed Sarah standing in the doorway. 'Ah, Miss Marin! Marvellous, I am so glad that you are here. Won't you come in?'

Sarah stepped into the room, looking at Nell and hoping her friend would, by a raised eyebrow or a glare or a shake of the head, give her a signal as to what was going on.

'Sit down there, dear, next to me,' Mrs Thistle said, settling back into her own chair at the head of the table. Sarah pulled back a chair and lowered herself into it, watching Mrs Vale, who was glaring at her.

'We were just talking about a conversation outside church with a fellow visiting from Van Diemen's Land. Nice chap, I had a sherry with him last week. He marched up to us after the service this morning and told me he'd been served the worst rations he'd had since the army. Did you know, Sarah, that soldiers eat little better than convicts? Not really the reputation we want, is it?' She looked at Mrs Vale. 'I so appreciated your efficiency. Whenever I checked the accounts – well, I thought you were making food go a long way. We know why that is now, of course.'

Mrs Vale stared at her employer through reddened eyes. 'I have done nothing wrong.'

'I rather think you have. You've been seen selling my tea and provisions, exchanging them for far inferior counterparts.'

'It is not possible that I was seen,' said Mrs Vale, 'as I did no such thing.'

'Sarah,' said Mrs Thistle, 'Mrs Vale seems to believe you are a liar.'

'She has been plucked from the sea with no family, no money,' Mrs Vale said. 'She could be anyone, and you would believe her when she accuses me of such things?'

'When she told me, I was cautious. But then I sent my driver here. Been with me for years, he has. Was engaged by my late husband.' Mrs Thistle settled back in her chair, picked up the cup and saucer, took another sip and stared at Mrs Vale over the rim; the landlady was still gaping. 'Of course, you could be gaoled for this. Sent to the Female Factory out at Parramatta. I don't think you would like picking oakum. The girls who have to extract those fibres from the old rope, the pads of their fingers get bloodied and raw.'

Mrs Vale looked at the door, and Sarah tensed in case the woman tried to run at it, or at her.

'Fortunately for you, I have no intention of involving the police,' Mrs Thistle continued. 'Bad for my reputation, you see, and as the superintendent is a friend, I would rather our next conversation be a pleasant one. I will, however, accept your resignation.'

'This place – it will collapse, without me to run it,' said Mrs Vale.

'I rather think it won't. Miss Marin will do a fine job.' She smiled at Sarah. 'If you're willing to accept the post, of course, dear.'

'You can't be thinking of . . .' said Mrs Vale.

'Doing more than thinking of it. Really, my dear woman, I thought you had better taste than to consort with someone like Houlihan. How many times has he lost his ticket of leave now? Not even the thieves trust him. We're not short of our choice of criminals here, and you picked the most dishonest of the lot.'

'I have not—'

Mrs Thistle held up her hand. 'Please let us not waste each other's time.' To Sarah, she said, 'We'll get you and Mrs Flaherty some help. A girl from the Female Factory – I know a few. Of course you'll be sending the accounts for provisions straight to me, and you may expect certain friends of mine – friends whom you have not met – to call on this establishment as guests and then report to me on the standards you maintain. I do assure you, if there is an unhappy guest or a poorly cooked meal, I will know of it.' She glanced at Mrs Vale. 'Are you still here, dear woman? I should think you had best clear your personal belongings out of your bedroom. After all, by tonight it will have another occupant.'

✦

The bedroom was at the back of the main house. Its small window had heavy velvet drapes that trapped both heat and dust, and it still smelled a little of Mrs Vale's lavender water. It did, however, boast the best bed Sarah had ever slept in, with a decorative iron head, a downy mattress and a quilt that more often than not was kicked off by morning.

Nell and Sarah shared this bed, while Amelia slept in a straw basket beside her mother, unsettled at first by the change in circumstances. Nell still regularly snuck out at night. And the young blonde woman from the Female Factory, Lizzie, slept alone in their old room.

The guests had not taken much notice of the change in management. Those who arrived after Sarah had replaced Mrs Vale seemed to have no expectations as to who their host would be, and they were more than happy to have the dark-haired young woman as their landlady – especially when they found out that she had survived the wreck, as they invariably did. Someone would hear her name and remember reading of it, or they would be enlightened by a longer-standing guest who had seen her walk around with Mrs Thistle.

Their employer visited every week or so, and Sarah trailed her along with a tray of drinks as she greeted all the guests. She would pat Sarah's shoulder and say, 'Do you know how remarkable this young woman is? Not just for running an excellent guesthouse, of course, even though she is. But she also survived what no others did.'

Mrs Thistle delighted in focusing the general fascination with the *Serpent* and its rumoured treasure on the young woman standing beside her.

'I wonder, madam,' Sarah said once, 'whether you would consider not acquainting the guests with my past?'

'Nonsense, it's good for business,' Mrs Thistle replied. 'And my business includes you now, so I would go along with it if I were you.'

After a small flush of pride, Sarah felt ashamed. Had she betrayed her brother's memory by aligning with the woman? But aligned she was.

More than once she opened her mouth to ask Mrs Thistle if she would take on Henry as an assigned convict servant. That, though, would almost certainly lead to her employer learning of her involvement in the rebellion, as the reason for Henry's transportation was public knowledge. Nell and Amelia, Sarah told herself, would only be sure of a place under this roof if she was managing it. She tried to banish the images of a brutalised Henry that sometimes jeered at her when she closed her eyes.

CHAPTER 27

Someone had forgotten to inform the disreputable Houlihan of the change in circumstances. He arrived on a market day, as usual. Mrs Vale was long gone, and Sarah had taken Lizzie to show her what to buy, and from whom to buy it. Nell answered the door, Amelia at her hip, when Houlihan grew impatient and knocked.

She was laughing when she told Sarah about it later. 'Fellow nearly died when he saw me. He asked for Mrs Vale, and I told him she'd been sacked on account of dealing with undesirables. I asked him if he'd heard anything about that, and he spat on the ground, hurried back to his cart, flicked his reins and went off so fast I thought he'd lose a wheel.'

Sarah couldn't help laughing with her. 'It was the brave Amelia who scared him off,' she said, reaching over to stroke the baby's head. 'But, Nell, try to be as careful as you can. Someone like Houlihan, it's best if he has no reason to remember you.'

Nell insisted on coming with Sarah to one of the meetings in The Rocks, although Sarah warned her it was no place for a baby – she had been to several, now, and they often devolved into shouts as the participants battled each other to see who had the loudest voice or the most florid rhetoric.

'This entire colony is no place for a baby, at least for a poor one,' Nell said. 'They'll just be talking. And I'd like to listen.'

The two of them were in their plain brown dresses, their hair scraped back under caps, and no one seemed to notice them as they walked to the cottage marked with a serpent.

Mrs Addison bustled up as they entered. 'More of you each time,' she said. 'You think I have a larger house put by?'

Nell jiggled Amelia. 'I'll keep her quiet, I promise.'

Mrs Addison snorted. 'She'll be one of the better-behaved ones here.' She banged her pot on the door-frame again to call everyone inside.

Keenan took his place at the front of the room. 'Many of you will have heard of the latest death,' he said. 'Another girl bludgeoned late at night, this time behind the Gloucester Street shebeen. Apparently no one noticed anything suspicious. And why was she there?'

'I think we all know the answer to that one, son,' a man towards the back called.

There were some snickers at this, mostly from those sitting in his area. Sarah reached out to squeeze Nell's hand. She was aching to push Keenan aside so that she could speak. How many of the others here had heard Orator Hartford, or Delia for that matter? If she could get them to listen to her words and not the female voice in which they were delivered, she knew she could do a better job than Keenan.

He gave a heavy sigh, surely for effect. If they ever had a conversation beyond their exchange at the docks, Sarah would have to tell him that overemphasis never helped.

'She was there, Stephen, because she had no other means of feeding herself,' Keenan said. 'Don't be a fool – we don't welcome them here.'

Mrs Addison nodded. 'The lad's right. But if lack of idiocy was the price of entry, this room would be empty.'

Keenan ignored her, addressing the room again. 'She was there because this government, all governments, trade on patronage. You receive something only if you can give something in return. What can women like the one who was killed give, that the men who have gulped down vast acreages here can't buy? And what of help from their own sex? Why is Mrs Thistle not taking these women in, or giving them succour?'

Sarah inhaled sharply, her fists clenching. If it were not for Nell, she would have agreed with Keenan, to a point – although she noticed he wasn't asking rich men to provide similar help. She increasingly suspected Mrs

Thistle was not the problem; she was, after all, sheltering at least two women. If radicals like Keenan were willing to rail against Molly Thistle before the governor – if one woman was a more convenient target than the male administration creating the conditions that saw young women crushed in alleyways – they had already lost.

Sarah stood up, and a murmur ran through the gathering. She waited until it died down, clasping her hands in front of her to stop them from shaking. 'Please tell me,' she said, 'what it is that you *want*.'

Keenan stared at her, rocking back on his heels in surprise. 'Well,' he said eventually, 'isn't that obvious?'

'Certainly not to me. Perhaps you are directing your anger at Molly Thistle for having the gall to be a woman who can support herself without the assistance of a man.'

Baxendale got to his feet and said, 'If she acts as a man in business, perhaps she should be prepared to die like one.'

Sarah was shocked by a sudden surge of protectiveness, an impulse to tell this man that Mrs Thistle did not deserve to feel a blade. Others who'd been put to the sword across the seas had not deserved it either. Her father had not deserved it. And this woman's death would simply add to the pile of bodies, without improving the lot of those who remained.

Had Sarah sat in this room and listened to these words shortly after her arrival in Sydney, she would have nodded in agreement – she had, after all, participated in a plan to behead Cabinet ministers. She would have imagined a faceless rich woman, a blend of all those she had seen in carriages and walking through gardens, daintily holding handkerchiefs to their noses when they passed the unwashed.

Sarah knew Molly Thistle was shrewd, and the woman certainly did not seem to have any radical leanings. But Sarah was beginning to think she was not entirely self-interested. She certainly didn't deserve to be run through.

'You kill Molly Thistle, you kill the rest of them,' Sarah said, 'and then what changes? Do you think the King or the prime minister will say, "Oh, well, as you've shown yourselves to be so determined, we'd better hand the colony to you." What is your plan, beyond covering yourselves in the blood of the rich?'

'And what is your business, asking that?' Baxendale said, thrusting his chest out. 'You don't have the right.'

'She has every right, as does anyone else,' said Keenan, over the murmur of agreement that had started when Baxendale had finished speaking. Even some of the women were shaking their heads at Sarah. She remembered the insults from the crowd at St Peter's Field, female voices calling Delia Burns a whore and urging her to mind her business.

'Mr Baxendale, murdering people will only enrich the peddlers at your hanging. What you need, what we all need, is a way to make the government fear us – one that they can't hang us for. If we had the ability to vote—'

Baxendale laughed, percussive and mirthless. 'Something that cannot even be had in England, unless you own land. They will not hand us the keys to the colony for bloodshed? Neither will they hand men a vote for sitting silently and waiting to die.'

'Not just men,' said Sarah.

'You think *women* should vote?' Baxendale started laughing again, and a few others joined in.

One man said, 'What on earth would be the point? You would only vote as your father or husband told you to!'

'If we are good enough to bear your children,' Sarah said, 'then surely we are good enough to have some influence over the world in which we raise them.'

'Whose children are you bearing?' Baxendale asked, glaring at Nell. He walked over to her, bending so his nose almost touched hers. 'I see you,' he said. 'Whoring for the constables. You'll go off with anyone in a uniform. Did they send you here?'

'What? No! I—'

Baxendale straightened up. 'Oh, she drinks with constables but it's a coincidence she shows up to discussions of rebellion,' he said in a mocking singsong. 'Well, if you think they can protect you from righteous anger, you may be disappointed. If you are giving them information, there may yet be another harlot dead in an alleyway.'

Nell clutched Amelia, who started to cry.

'I remind you, Mr Baxendale,' said Keenan, 'that we are here to find a better way, not a different one that is just as bad or worse. Watch your words or I will ask you to leave.'

Sarah took her friend's hand and pulled her to her feet. 'I had believed you all valued liberty – everyone's liberty.' She put her arm around Nell and walked to the door. Once they had reached the street, she asked Nell, 'You know him?'

'Seen him at that tavern. The man with the snake on his arm? That was him.'

'Have you . . . ?'

'God, no. He's so joyless. Sits by himself, drinks, occasionally tries to pick a fight, leaves with great huff and bother if too many constables or soldiers walk in. Why were you arguing, though? You wanted to kill people in London.'

'I wanted change,' she said, 'and that seemed the only way to achieve it – the only way presented to me, anyway. Now, if you see Baxendale again, be careful of him.'

'He's harmless,' said Nell, but she was still frowning in the direction he had gone, while clutching her daughter.

CHAPTER 28

'I don't mind not going – been getting sick of the sight of you, to be honest,' said Nell, smiling and rocking Amelia as she sat on the bed.

A thick envelope had been hand-delivered by a servant to the English Rose earlier that day. It contained a stiff card on which someone with far better handwriting than Sarah would ever possess had inscribed the details of a garden party to be held at Mrs Thistle's home, and informed her that her presence had been requested.

'You should have been invited too, though,' said Sarah. 'Should I ask?'

'Absolutely not. I shall stay here and make sure everyone is fed and no one leaves without paying. *You* may have the boring conversations, and endure the stares and the sneers. Do bring me back a honey cake, though.'

Mrs Thistle had sent a coach for Sarah. She had never been on horseback, and until she had come to Sydney the only real conveyance in which she'd ridden had been the rickety cart that had taken her and Sam, and some other human flotsam sundered by the events on that Manchester field, to London.

She had not thought about it as a child, not even when a carriage wheel had splashed her with mud, or a horse whose rider assumed the right to move without impediment had forced her to scramble to the roadside. She must have assumed that those able to travel this way were somehow more deserving of such comforts, otherwise why would God have bestowed them? As she had grown, she had begun to ask herself not what their virtues were, but what they had done to earn their place on the padded seat or in the saddle. Whose suffering they had ignored or augmented, and from whom they had held back succour. Whom they had refused to feed, and whose cries they had refused to answer. Whom had they cut down on a peaceful field.

The seat that she sat on now, the coachman and the horses, had been paid for by Molly Thistle. Had the woman blocked her ears to cries for help, or even been the cause of them?

Sarah felt the weight of what she had heard at Mrs Addison's. Perhaps she should warn Mrs Thistle of the potential danger, but such a warning would mean telling her employer about where she had been. That might be enough to send noses sniffing in Sarah's direction. And she had seen no indication that the group planned to do any more than talk – it was all bluster, she told herself.

No sword would actually come down on Mrs Thistle's neck; no gun would send a bullet towards her.

Was it cowardly to stay silent, though? *You have asked me to be brave too often*, Sarah thought, although she wasn't sure whom she was addressing.

✦

The coach drew up to a house on the bend of a river. Its square turret overlooked the water, a two-storey building extending from its flank, with broad verandas and many windows hinting at the vast space inside.

Sarah could see the gathering from quite a distance. The brightly coloured clothes of the women were threaded through the jackets of the men – mostly black, but occasionally blue along with one or two red coats belonging to soldiers. These guests were ambling around an extensive lawn that sloped down from Mrs Thistle's house towards the river.

The old woman must have seen the carriage pull up and recognised it as one of her own. She strode over the grass to the door, which she hauled open before the coachman had a chance to dismount from his little seat. As always, she was wearing a dark-blue dress; this one, though, had a broad lace collar of such a startling white that it must have been new.

'Don't stare, my dear,' Mrs Thistle said, following Sarah's eyes over to her guests. 'Quite rude – wouldn't

273

want to embarrass yourself. Or me, of course.' She cupped Sarah's elbow and propelled her into the party.

As they passed by, almost everyone stopped talking and stared, then whispered to their companions. It was as though Sarah was there to provide relief from the monotony of the music being scraped out by a lady violinist sitting on a stool near the river.

Mrs Thistle nodded towards the musician. 'One of my daughters,' she said. 'She cannot resist performing. Confident lass. I just wish she had any interest in the business.'

Sarah and Mrs Thistle came to a stop near a knot of men, all facing each other, all nodding earnestly as one of them spoke. Mrs Thistle reached out an age-spotted hand to tap him on the shoulder, in a way that to Sarah seemed every bit as rude as staring. He was smiling, though, not scowling at a perceived insult.

'Here is the lady with whom you wished to speak,' Mrs Thistle said, smiling brightly as befitted the host of a party trying to jolly everyone along. 'Miss Marin, may I present Mr Nicholas Greenwich, superintendent of police.'

He bowed briefly to Sarah and nodded to Mrs Thistle. 'Miss Marin and I are acquainted. We met at the inquest into the wreck of the *Serpent*.' He turned to Sarah. 'It is a pleasure to see you under happier circumstances. Would you walk with me?'

She looked over her shoulder at Mrs Thistle, making no attempt to keep the anger off her face, the rage at being presented like a neatly wrapped package to a man with unknown intentions. But Mrs Thistle just gave her a broad smile, waggled her fingers, then walked towards her other guests.

The man's hand was on the small of Sarah's back, guiding her towards the edge of the garden party. She stepped forward to put some air between them, and he laughed softly. 'You need have no concern of me. In fact, you could not be safer.'

'Could I not?' she said. 'Are superintendents always above reproach?'

'Of course not. But in this case, I assure you I have the purest motive in seeking you out. That of maintaining public order.'

'I am a threat, then? Men quake at my approach?'

'I couldn't say. Would they have reason to?'

'Well, look at me! I am hardly imposing.'

'How you look is irrelevant,' he said. 'I have seen a man filleted by a wife who stood barely to my shoulder. What you say is of far more interest to me than how you look – and I am very interested in what you've been say-ing of late.'

'Asking people if they would care for marmalade with their breakfast bread? Things must be very slow in Sydney, if I am the focus of the leading protector of the peace.'

They were nearly at the river's edge, and he stopped, staring across from the precisely clipped lawn to the unruly pale trees and scrub on the other side. He expected, perhaps, to see a face peering back at him, that of a fugitive who had eluded capture.

He looked at her abruptly, all pretence of banter gone, and she had an uncomfortable feeling that if he was hunting for a fugitive, perhaps he had found one. 'Please be assured, I am concerned for your welfare. I am told, well – many things. Among them, that a young woman has been asking for information. About certain societies with certain views that do not sit well with me, and that are hardly conducive to peace here.'

Sarah felt a surge of fear. She tried to slow her breathing, as she suspected that Greenwich would interpret anything but calm as an admission of guilt. Perhaps one of those at the meeting had recognised her as the survivor of the wreck and was secretly in police employ; perhaps they had also reported Nell's presence. Sarah did not know what happened to babies whose mothers went to prison, but from what she had seen of the colony, she suspected the courts did not exert themselves in finding them homes.

'I would very much like to know, superintendent, of what I am being accused.'

'Nothing. This is more in the way of a warning,' he said, his face serious. 'You should seize the opportunities of this new town, and if you're not willing to work towards its success, at least don't undermine it. I am not actively pursuing this matter, but I do assure you that if more reports reach my ears, my approach will change with alarming speed.'

'I thank you,' said Sarah. 'However, I am not in a position to cease an activity in which I haven't been engaged.'

'Of course not. And I haven't acquainted Mrs Thistle with my concerns – as yet. You may, after all, be as innocent as you claim.'

CHAPTER 29

Nell grinned as Sarah undid the bundle Mrs Thistle's maid had given her. The woman had been silent while she wrapped the treats in a piece of cloth, slanting glances towards Sarah; she had clearly been unused to requests for honey cakes from Mrs Thistle's guests.

Nell picked up the small square, smelled it and closed her eyes. 'All right then, was it?' she said after a moment. 'The party?'

'Well, no, not really. I had an odd conversation.'

'You can tell me about it,' said Nell, 'but don't expect me to answer for a little while.'

She began nibbling at the cake as Sarah told her about Superintendent Greenwich.

'You think he knows what we've been up to?' Nell asked. 'Or even what you did in London?'

'I worry that he might know everything. But surely if he did, I'd be in prison. Or already dead.'

'Unless he wishes to investigate Keenan and the like.'

'Well, there is that, I suppose. Perhaps that's why he hasn't told Mrs Thistle.'

Nell swallowed and put her hand on Sarah's. 'But you must tell her. About everything. If she knows what happened to you in England, she'll understand.'

Every time Sarah saw Mrs Thistle, she felt the urge to tell her. But the police superintendent had eaten her food and drunk her wine, and Sarah knew it was more important than ever to stay silent.

'Oh, must I? Why do you believe she will not hand me to Greenwich?'

'Because she's jealous, that one, of everything she owns. And she believes she owns us. That may be enough to make her protect you – but if she learns the truth from Greenwich, or anyone else, she will have a fit. She'll buy a prime vantage point at your hanging, and her face will be the last you see before they lower the hood.'

✦

Sarah was used to awakening before the rest of the boarding house. Once her mind knew what time it was expected to come to consciousness and reanimate her body, it did so with remarkable punctuality.

The morning after the garden party, though, she was awoken by Amelia fidgeting and mewling in her tiny straw basket. Sarah expected to hear Nell shushing and soothing, the sound of fabric moving as she undid her collar to feed the child. The little girl, though, received no such attention; her tiny, questing noises strengthened into a tentative cry, then another, then a series of staccato sobs.

Sarah rolled over, intending to shake Nell awake and tell her to attend to her child for God's sake, but no one was there.

Nell had never returned this late before.

Sarah snatched the baby up from the cot and strode in her nightdress into the lightening kitchen where Lizzie was setting out the breakfast things. Thrusting Amelia at her, Sarah took a breath to steady her voice. 'Have you seen Nell?'

'No, miss.'

Sarah had tried to get Lizzie to call her by her first name, but the girl was too cowed by her experiences in other households to comply.

'Do you think you can take care of the little one? I hope I'll be back in time to help you with breakfast. Perhaps you can use Nell's sling – it's up in our room.'

Sarah was asking a lot, she knew, but Lizzie nodded and gave her a concerned look. 'Is Mrs Flaherty all right?'

'I hope so. I certainly hope so.'

❖

As Sarah ran towards the docks, she passed a chain gang. Was Henry among them? It didn't seem that any of them recognised her, because a few made lewd comments as she sped by.

By the time she got to the tavern Nell visited most often, her thin leather shoes were worn through. The detritus of the docks was nestled against the walls, crates and baskets and ropes slowly decaying, a moat of rot that no one cared to remove. She rattled the front door, but the sun was still a little too low to bring out even the morning drinkers.

Sarah went to the side of the building where she found an alleyway and tentatively began to walk in. 'Hello?' she called. 'Nell?'

The sun had no interest in illuminating this slice of the earth. Sarah heard a crunch, then winced as a shard of broken glass punctured her foot through the worn sole.

The crates in the alley were not collapsing quite as much as the ones at the front of the building, which had surely felt the weight of staggering drinkers as they passed. Some bore the name THISTLE, the type in which tea was imported. Nell loved breathing in the fragrance of leaves from the tea chest.

It was the shoe Sarah saw first, dangling off the tip of a still toe. She walked, slowly, towards where the leg disappeared behind a barrel.

She stopped just before she could see what was lying there. As long as she did not see it, there was a chance it wasn't real. That Nell was sleeping, perhaps, or that this was some other woman.

Nell did not need a friend now, though. Nell needed a witness.

So Sarah crossed herself, gesturing to a God she believed was either uninterested or non-existent, and stepped forward.

Nell's head was a little to the side, as though she herself was silently questioning the truth of her own death. Her eyes were slightly open, her cheek bruised. A wet red bloom had spread out from several knife wounds in the centre of her chest, soaking into the flowers on the fabric. Her skirt had been hauled up and now lay underneath her hips. The fabric at the front covered enough to spare her a final indignity, although Sarah doubted that had been the design of the killer. She knelt, pulled Nell's skirt down and moved her legs together. Tried and failed to close her arms over her chest, as they were already stiffening. Bent down, kissed her forehead. Then stood, and ran.

☀

Amelia was asleep in Lizzie's arms, still clutching the moistened cloth the young woman had given her to suck on, a poor substitute for her mother.

One of the boarding-house guests had agreed to carry an urgent message to Mrs Thistle. When she burst into the kitchen, she went straight to the sideboard and extracted a cut glass decanter, unstopped it, splashed rum into a teacup almost to the brim, and handed it to Sarah, who pushed the cup away. She remembered how the liquid had scoured her throat when Briardown had occasionally offered it around at a meeting.

Mrs Thistle sat down and pushed it back to her. 'Drink.' This was clearly an order.

Sarah nodded, lifted the cup as daintily as she could, drank, choked a little, and drank again. 'She was . . . she had some acquaintances who could be dangerous.'

'I know what she did, Miss Marin.' Mrs Thistle sighed, putting her hand on Sarah's shoulder. 'You know the constables – they are supposed to treat all murders alike, but this . . . I doubt they will exert themselves.'

Sarah set her cup down so hard that rum splashed onto Mrs Thistle's sleeve. 'So what is it to them? An accident? The wages of sin? Because of what she did, she is worth no more than a dockside rat?'

Mrs Thistle squeezed Sarah's hand almost painfully. 'I am in a reasonable position to exert influence over those who would once have seen me as expendable. And I will do so on Nell's behalf.'

Sarah inhaled slowly and rubbed her eyes. 'Thank you.'

'I regret her death. And you should also know this – no one can be permitted to do as they please to someone under my protection. This cannot go unpunished. If it does, the next man will feel as though he can encroach, and the next, and they will start nibbling around the edges of me until I am back in rags.'

⁕

Mrs Thistle's influence was as broad as she had claimed. That night, the constables descended on the tavern in which they usually drank. Heads were likely knocked and necks stood on, and in the end several men told them they had seen Nell leaving the tavern with Houlihan, the man who had been Mrs Vale's fence.

Throughout the hearings over the next few weeks, Sarah stood next to Mrs Thistle as Houlihan stood in the dock, wearing his yellowed neckerchief, and claimed he'd been nowhere near the tavern. And as witness after witness – the tavern keeper who relied on the goodwill of the constables, some of whom drank there, and a variety of dock workers, many of whom were employed by Mrs Thistle – said they had seen him at various points that night: unsteadily climbing into his cart, driving it over someone's dog, picking fights.

Many people dribbled in and out of the courtroom. Some were court officials, others simply members of the pubic seeking entertainment.

When it came time for Sarah to testify, the crowd was swelling out the courtroom doors, standing on their toes and craning to see her. There was still a widespread fascination with this woman who had cheated the ocean.

'You know what to say,' Mrs Thistle had told her. 'Provide the best version of the truth.'

Houlihan spat on the ground when the judge intoned the death sentence. The man who had left Nell with her life leaking onto the ground would be punished, and no one else would die because of him.

Sarah realised that for all of the talk in the Marylebone loft, and the equally fine visions woven by Keenan and Baxendale in The Rocks, Mrs Thistle was the only person she had met who had achieved something beyond words. She had caused a judge to hear of Nell. She had made the superintendent exert himself on Nell's behalf. She had caused a tiny crack in the thick wall that had always stood between Nell and just treatment. She had forced a tacit acknowledgement, through the sentence of the court, that without Nell the world was diminished.

CHAPTER 30

Mrs Thistle's carriage was waiting for them outside the courthouse, but she waved the driver away, asking him to return in an hour. She took Sarah's arm and started walking towards the harbour. 'I need to smell the sea,' she said. 'Just for a minute.' Her voice sounded strangely thick, and she was staring straight ahead, her lips firmly pressed together.

They walked in silence for a little while. When Mrs Thistle brought them to a stop, they were outside the tavern where Sarah had found Nell's body. Mrs Thistle nodded down the path they were walking on. 'Look,' she said. Sarah followed her gaze to the brown-grey warehouses that lined the harbour, again noticing the sign that read THISTLE.

'It wasn't as though I couldn't afford to pay her,' Mrs Thistle admitted, 'and you. In something more than food and board. But people are always hanging off me like leeches, you see, trying to extract more. So I've always given as little as possible, to everyone. You are no leech, and neither was Nell. If I had paid her, she might not have …' Molly Thistle inhaled. 'She died in sight of the name of someone who could have saved her.'

Sarah looked from the warehouse to the woman. Until now she had seen one as an extension of the other; she had not, she realised, believed Mrs Thistle any more capable of regret than the building named after her. 'You do not like those who take what isn't theirs, so you should not either,' she said. 'Houlihan deserves the full weight of Nell's death. Do not lighten his burden.'

'If I'd been a little more generous—'

'You cannot know what would have happened. Ask for penance for the sins you have committed, not for the ones you haven't earned a right to.'

'You are right, of course,' Mrs Thistle said. 'I have not sought anything from God for a long time, but my penance will be measured in the coins that flow to others. Including to you, Miss Marin.' She patted Sarah's hand before moving off. She clearly expected Sarah to stay in step with her, so Sarah nearly stumbled into her back when she stopped abruptly. 'I suspect you have sought penance of your own. I hope you will tell me, one day, what for. Perhaps even your real name.'

Sarah did not trust herself to move. Any attempt to deny it would be clumsy and easily seen through.

Mrs Thistle gave her a small smile. 'I am from Lancashire too. Never met a Marin. I did, though, listen in when my girls were having French lessons. It means "sailor", yes? Odd that a woman with such a name should be the only one to survive a shipwreck.' She straightened. 'I can forgive anything but dishonesty. I assure you, I grant absolution far more easily than a priest. But if sins go unatoned for, I am less yielding than the worst of them.'

✦

A few days later, Sarah was invited for afternoon tea at Mrs Thistle's home. Lizzie was more than capable of running the boarding house for an afternoon, and Mrs Thistle had arranged for another Female Factory convict, Caroline, recently delivered of a baby, to feed Amelia.

Every morning Sarah set out eggs, cheese, bread and marmalade for the wet nurse. Lizzie would hold Caroline's baby as she quickly ate, while Sarah went to get Amelia from her basket, used less now as Sarah tucked the little girl in with her each night. Caroline would then unlace her shirt and sit with a baby in each arm as they fed.

Sarah tried not to resent Caroline – the girl was doing nothing, after all, but giving Amelia nourishment. But Sarah had trouble forgiving her for not being Nell.

When Sarah arrived for tea at Mrs Thistle's house, a young woman around her age, but far better fed than the Female Factory girls, opened the door, stood aside and beckoned her into an entrance hall, before gesturing her to a brocaded seat. As she sat there, the indoor silence weighed on her, seeming to carry an expectation of an answering quiet, a disapproval of any activity that might lead to the scuff of a shoe on the floor tiles, at least those unprotected by the large ornate rug.

Unable to remain seated for long, she walked quietly around the room. It was darker than it could have been, painted in a rust-red, with a large mirror on one side reflecting the stern colour back to itself. Apart from the couch and a small side table on which a blue-and-white pot sprouted roses, there was only one other object.

The picture was framed in gold-painted wood: a man whose lower face was obscured by a precisely clipped beard. His eyes, glancing off to the side, squinted slightly in irritation, and the remaining hair that adorned the back part of his head was severely swept back. She had seen this kind of portrait before; usually the subject was dressed in a uniform and festooned with medals, or at least in clothes embellished by the painter to seem far richer than they were in reality. This man, though, wore a simple black waistcoat and jacket, a white shirt and a cravat.

'The number of visitors I catch staring at that picture,' said a voice from the top of the stairs. Mrs Thistle was descending, her gait slightly uneven and so quick that Sarah feared she might trip. The woman clearly knew every board, though, and was beside her within a few moments. 'He would have loved it here. A creature of the water, was William.'

'Your late husband.'

'Yes. He would have loved my warehouse too. The only ones he saw were those we had along the Hawkesbury. A lot better behaved than the harbour, most of the time, but the vessels aren't as big, can't carry as much. I need, you see, to be the one with everything, spices and silk and skins. If I don't have it, they go somewhere else and tend to stay there – most would prefer not to do business with a woman.' She called over her shoulder, 'Lilith!'

Sarah had heard similarly open-throated shouts on the dock.

'Lilith! The tea things!' Mrs Thistle walked towards the door near the side table, opened it and gestured Sarah through.

At the centre of the room a small table was surrounded by armchairs, all facing a window looking out to the front gardens. Mrs Thistle gestured Sarah to a chair and slumped into the one opposite. 'You and I, you know, we are the only ones who are mourning Nell.'

Sarah hadn't known what to expect from Mrs Thistle in her own home. Naturally she'd expected Nell to be mentioned, but she had assumed it would be more in the way of nice words: Nell was a grand girl, a good friend, a good worker. Not this genuine grief.

'Amelia will, in time,' Sarah said.

'Probably not. She won't remember her mother, not really. Would have been off to the orphan school with her, but I have arranged for her to be placed with a family

I know, out in Windsor. They have seven children, they'll barely notice one more, and the older ones look after the younger anyway. She will be safe and fed.'

It took Sarah a moment to understand what Mrs Thistle was saying. She had assumed Amelia would stay with her, that she would be the one responsible for guiding this fragment of her friend through the colony's dangers. 'She – she cannot be one among many. I won't allow it!'

Mrs Thistle arched an eyebrow. 'It is not up to you.'

'She is happy with me, though. She knows me. She will be so frightened with strangers.'

'No one is a stranger for long, to a child of that age,' Mrs Thistle said gently. 'Amelia will be treated kindly. She will have brothers and sisters and as fair a chance of happiness as anyone. Don't let your fondness rob her of that.'

Sarah closed her eyes, trying not to cry. 'She will be told about her mother, though?'

'Well, that's really up to the family. The father's a half-decent pastoralist, sells wool through me. We will consign Nell to our own memories, with great regret. You mustn't think me unmoved. I just believe we can do better for her than simply wail at her passing.'

Sarah thought of the many times she had cradled and nuzzled Amelia. She had walked around their small room singing and humming, and rocking from one heel to the other. The sweet smell of Amelia's head would be lost to her, while the baby's morning chirps might be unappreciated by her new family, her cries unanswered for an instant more than necessary. This was a child whose mother could have put her in an orphanage, as many did. This was a child for whom that mother had risked her body to attain the means to fend off starvation, should it come to that – Sarah still had the money Nell had earned, and would give it to Mrs Thistle to send with the girl. This child, and her mother, deserved remembrance.

'If we cannot see that her daughter remembers her,' said Sarah, 'what can we possibly do?'

'Try to make sure she's the last one to die in an alleyway,' said Mrs Thistle.

CHAPTER 31

'I need a helper,' Mrs Thistle told Sarah. 'Nell's murderer would not have paid for his crime unless I was able to get to the superintendent. But I'm an old woman. My children are not interested in following me into trade, although they will own everything after I die. I want to make sure there are those who know how things ought to be run.'

Once a week, at least, Mrs Thistle took Sarah to the docks where they watched crates being handed down and barrels being rolled along planks, and Mrs Thistle would yell up to the men who were moving them. If they knew what was good for them, they stopped. If they had dealt with her before, they opened the crate or the barrel straight away, and Mrs Thistle would pull out sawdust-packed china or extract a handful of tea leaves and let them run through her fingers, rubbing them between her forefinger and thumb while smelling them, the same gesture she used to test the bolts of cloth that came off the ships.

By this time, the captain would have appeared at the rails, having heard she was there. She would look up at him. 'How many crates of this? Four? And you do realise that this finest tea, as it says on this crate, has grass clippings in it?' Or, 'It was wine I asked for, not rum. Good Lord, this whole city is awash with rum – I would make no money if I imported it.'

Sarah was unable to spot the grass clippings or any of the other deficiencies over which Mrs Thistle berated the captains. 'They have to know you're looking,' she said once, as they walked away. 'They have to know it's not good enough, whatever it is.'

Sarah found herself enjoying the older woman's company, and she was more interested than she had expected to be in the workings of the business. And if she gained Mrs Thistle's trust, she might be able to convince the woman to put her in charge of the convicts assigned to the enterprise. She could get Henry assigned to one of the Thistle properties, without revealing his background.

Another part of running things was the collection of rents.

At first Sarah was alarmed when Mrs Thistle invited her for what she called 'a spot of debt collecting'. When her parents' piecework had stopped coming, but before they started at the mill, she had hidden behind her ma's skirts whenever there was a pounding on the door, and she had heard her pa trying to sound strong while he pleaded for more time.

'I can't be part of putting a family on the street,' she said.

Mrs Thistle snorted. 'Is that what you think of me? Well, I suppose it's a reasonable assumption given the behaviour of most landlords. Believe me, dear, my properties are not the sort in which those on the verge of penury live. They're businesses, mostly, and the occasional private residence. I have forgiven more rent than you realise for those who have lost their positions or been recently widowed. But sometimes people are just taking advantage, and those are the ones who deserve a little reminder.'

Sarah had to admit to a creeping affection for the woman: an admiration for what she had built, and an appreciation for her odd mix of kindness and practicality. She certainly did not deserve to be run through, whatever Baxendale said.

※

On their first day collecting rents, the streets they walked were close to the heart of the town, the houses huddled together as though seeking protection from some of the rougher inhabitants. They were followed by a large, silent man with the strap of a leather satchel across his chest, whom Mrs Thistle had introduced to Sarah as Mr Ash. He walked several feet behind them so that no one who glanced at the two women would guess they had any association with him.

'They never expect it, you see,' said Mrs Thistle. 'They know what's coming, of course – yank open the door, all ready to snarl, and there I am. Well, I'm not a threatening hulk of muscle.'

Mrs Thistle barely came up to Sarah's shoulder, and her lace cap, faded hair and little half-moon spectacles were the best disguise she could ever have adopted.

'Of course, the surprise doesn't work for long,' Mrs Thistle said. 'It's why I always bring a friend.' She gestured to her with her head back towards Ash.

They had approached a two-storey sandstone building, a rarity even for this part of the settlement. Mrs Thistle knocked, more gently than usual. 'This could get a little delicate,' she whispered to Sarah, then seemed surprised when a young man opened the door. His shirt would probably have been considered quite fine had it not been stained in places and undone. His skin had not been troubled by a razor for some time, and the substance on his head was more knot than hair. He did not greet them, simply leaning against the doorframe and staring at them.

Mrs Thistle said, 'I was looking for—'

'Not here,' said the young man, starting to close the door again.

Mrs Thistle gestured Ash over. He strode forward and placed a palm on the door just as the latch was about to snick home. He pushed, and it slowly opened.

'Where is he, then?' asked Mrs Thistle.

'Moved to his house upriver. Says it smells here. You know where to find him – still drives the trap in every day.'

'And you are?'

'Michael. His nephew.' The man bowed, almost overbalancing. 'He said I could stay here.'

'Hm. And did he happen to mention anything about the rent?' When Michael shrugged, Mrs Thistle moved to peer down the edge of the house. 'Shame you let the gardenias wilt, he was proud of . . . ah! Now, what is that?'

Sarah followed her and saw the side of some sort of contraption, shiny and well cared for in this house that was being allowed to crumble.

Mrs Thistle strode down the side of the house before Michael knew what was happening. When he did, he darted out the door at a speed of which Sarah would have thought him incapable, but Ash stopped him with one hand against his chest.

Mrs Thistle was smiling back at Sarah. 'Do you know what this is?'

Sarah looked at the large copper pot resting on a grate over a fire pit; a pipe ran from it into a wooden barrel. She shook her head.

'It's knowledge,' Mrs Thistle said. 'It's advantage. And it may prove very useful indeed. Come on.' She strode back to the front of the house.

'I'll dismantle it!' said Michael. 'Just don't tell—'

Mrs Thistle held up her hand. 'I've no intention of telling your uncle. Best he doesn't know I was here, actually. And I only saw a cooking pot, nothing that needs dismantling. Are we agreed?'

Michael gaped, nodding.

'Do not break this agreement,' said Mrs Thistle. 'I would hate to have to come back.' She wrinkled her nose, nodded to him, and swept out between the gateposts. 'Just one more errand,' she said to Sarah as they walked away, Ash a few yards behind them.

* * *

The errand required a long walk. Sarah wondered why Mrs Thistle had not used her carriage, until it became clear where they were going when the more genteel buildings gave way to the familiar wattle and daub homes and slab huts of The Rocks.

Had Mrs Thistle been dishonest with her? Sometimes she worried herself to the point of nausea about whether to reveal her past; it would be unbearable if Mrs Thistle had lied to her as easily as breathing.

'I thought you did not rent to those on the verge of penury,' Sarah said.

'Nor do I,' said Mrs Thistle. She opened the paling gate of a small but neat cottage, and they walked through a scrubby, bald yard to a door, Ash following them far more closely than at the last house.

A woman opened the door. She wore her cloth cap tight against her skull and had a cautious blankness to her face with which Sarah was familiar. She was absent-mindedly jiggling a baby, and a little boy peered out from behind her skirts.

Her eyes widened when she saw Ash, and Sarah feared she was about to slam the door until her mouth spread into a smile. 'Why did you bring the lummox, missus?'

'I have to keep him occupied, Annie, you know that. May we come in?'

They walked into the kitchen, Ash loping as the small boy was now sitting on his foot, arms around the calf, and giggling. Two other lads, a little older, were also there, and waved at Ash when they saw him. Care had been taken over the kitchen, and the small, rough table at its centre was scrubbed clean.

'Tea, I think,' Mrs Thistle said, settling onto a stool without invitation.

'I'm sorry,' said Annie. 'I have none.'

Mrs Thistle smiled and nodded to Ash, who began to unpack his satchel. He extracted an oilcloth bundle and handed it to Annie, who opened it carefully on the table, bent over and inhaled the scent of the leaves it contained. 'Nothing finer than Thistle tea,' she said. 'Archibald wouldn't drink anything else.'

'A man of discernment, he was,' said Mrs Thistle softly. 'Now, your lads – how do they fare?'

Sarah sat silently as the women chatted, while Ash pulled more bounty from his satchel: cured meat and pickled vegetables, and a small paper packet that he handed to Annie, who secreted it inside her skirts.

Afterwards, as they were walking back towards the main part of town, Mrs Thistle said to Ash, 'Thank you for having her fence replaced.'

He nodded. 'You were right, the one new paling on the old fence stood out – I caught her staring at it.'

'Archibald worked in one of my warehouses,' Mrs Thistle told Sarah. 'He came home one day to find two soldiers in his yard. They were after a young woman who had run up to the house a little while earlier, begging Annie for shelter. When Annie had let her in and slammed the door on the soldiers, they'd remained outside shouting suggestions about the sport they would have with both women. Then they'd tried to break down the door. When Archibald told them to get about their business, they pulled palings from the fence and beat him to death with them.'

Sarah covered her mouth. Those little boys had just farewelled them on the front yard that had once contained the bloodied form of their dying father. But the story, for all its horror, sounded familiar, and she realised Keenan had spoken of it at the first meeting.

'What happened to the killers?' she asked.

Ash snorted. 'They found a surgeon to say Archibald died of an excess of passion. The soldiers got a fine and a few months in gaol, then went back to their lives as though it had never happened.'

'There are several like Annie in the colony,' said Mrs Thistle. 'Women whose husbands died while in my service. You remember what I told Mrs Vale about Nell's husband falling into the harbour and drowning when unloading a ship of mine? I didn't imagine it. Those women will be looked after until they die – and you must make sure that continues, should I follow their husbands to the afterlife too soon. So no, I don't rent to the poor, because you cannot rent a property if you don't charge anything.'

CHAPTER 32

In the week since Sarah had met Annie, something had settled in the pit of her stomach. A lumpen, pulsing creature that would not shift, and that became more agitated when she thought of all Mrs Thistle didn't know. All she might find out.

Had Sarah left it too long to come forward with the truth? Questions rolled around in the back of her mind like sparring scuttlers outside a beer house. They were her only night-time companions now, although the echoes of Amelia's presence still woke her before dawn, even after the increasingly common nights when sleep was driven away by her arguments with herself.

She knew that in failing to decide, she was making a decision. She knew she only allowed the wrestlers to keep at it because they distracted her from her commitment to dishonesty. She knew she would stay silent.

❋

Sarah was walking to the market, a task she had come to dread as it was another part of her day defined by Nell's absence. Sometimes when she passed someone on the road – a pinch-faced matron or a red-cheeked function- ary – she would catch herself turning to nudge Nell so that they could indulge in some salving criticism. Or she would point to a dollop of grey fur in the trees, realising after an instant that she was not doing so for anyone's benefit.

She also, of course, raked her eyes over any road gangs she passed, looking out for Henry's red hair, but she had not seen him since the awful moment she had stood by helplessly as his overseer knocked him to the ground.

Abraded by all her disappointments, she told herself that today she would look only at the road. She barely glanced up as the road gang approached, and had nearly passed them before she caught the flash of red.

She waited for them to get some way into the dis- tance, and then followed.

They eventually settled near a stand of pale trees that gave Sarah a means of concealment. She watched as the overseer removed the chains connecting the men's leg irons together, as he shoved each of them towards a tree to cut down.

Behind the trees, she made her way to where Henry stood. He started when he saw her, but he did not slow his axe's harassment of the trunk. He inched sideways until he was close enough to murmur to her as he worked. 'I've been looking for you. I thought they might have found you. I have been dreading news of your hanging.'

'Why? I don't even know whether they're still looking.'

'They surely are.' His words came out in small bursts between whacks of the axe. 'They must not like being outrun by a woman. And you, to them, are a she-devil. Tourville will have told them all about you.'

The little group in the Marylebone stable had felt like a family, of sorts. Sarah would not have chosen Tourville as a companion, but the group had stopped the ground from shifting beneath her when her parents died. She'd had a place, a purpose, something to do besides keening. The certainty that this had been a chimera was almost too much to bear.

'There's no question Tourville was a spy, then,' she said, in a voice that quavered more than she would have liked. 'We did not accidentally give ourselves away.'

One side of Henry's mouth twitched upward. 'I was worried you would suspect me. Do not, though, think yourself safe.' He glanced at the overseer, who was scolding another convict several yards away, and set the axe down. 'Is there . . . anyone to protect you?'

'A man, you mean? No, and nor would I require his protection if there was.'

Henry smiled. 'I had hoped – but feared, as well, to be honest – that you might have found someone with sufficient influence to shield you. Tourville will have written to whoever he can think of, anywhere he thinks you might have gone, to tell them about you. You have to assume that one of those letters has arrived here. And if you are exposed, you will need more than your own strength to survive.'

'There is someone – not a man,' Sarah added quickly, when Henry's face fell.

He picked up his axe again, before the overseer could notice the lack of movement. 'I do not need to know who this woman is. But does she know the truth?'

'No. I wanted to tell her, but I didn't know how, not without risking both our lives.'

'But surely she won't help you if she first learns of your past from a newspaper or the police.' He took a few more swings at the trunk, nudging her aside so that if it chose this moment to fall, it would not crush her. Then he laid down the axe again, and brushed a strand of hair from her face. He looked at her, silently, perhaps trying to commit her features to memory, fearful he might not see her again. She wished she had done the same with her mother as they had marched to St Peter's Field.

Eventually she said, her voice low, 'They made corpses out of my parents and my brother, and they made a liar of me.'

'The government?'

'Of course! Who else?'

'Briardown,' said Henry, and looked away from her. His jaw was tight, and he was clenching and unclench- ing his fists. 'That man showed us his murderous path to liberty, told us it was the only one, that all we needed to do was to believe, keep faith. I do not want to take any culpability from the King and his bloated ministers, but Briardown put me here too. He helped put that rope around your brother's neck, and may yet put one around yours.' Henry drew in a jagged breath. 'Do you know, I always believed – still do – that you were the bravest of us.'

'How can you say that? I escaped! I ran away and then disguised myself to watch my brother die with more courage than a battalion of soldiers.'

'You did not hang your brother, and as for your escape – what good would it have done to stay? When I was in Newgate, I thought you'd also been arrested. Every night when I closed my eyes, I imagined you doing the same in the women's prison. I was convinced I would hang. I thought about it all the time, rolled it around in my head. Tried to prepare, so I wouldn't embarrass myself on the gallows. But I knew all of that would be useless if I climbed the platform to find you there.' He pressed his hand over his face, rubbing eyes inflamed by dust and incipient tears. 'It's a journey I never want you to make,' he said. 'Which is why you must tell this woman the truth.'

'If she tells others, I will certainly hang!'

'But there's no other way! Your only choice is between taking a risk on this woman's mercy, or waiting to be arrested.' He took her hands. 'Remember that you're a rightful inheritor of the earth. You have survived worse, and you will survive this. You must.'

In the distance, the overseer began shouting for the men to gather. Henry squeezed her hands and kissed her cheek, then picked up his axe and walked into the trees.

*

As Sarah crept away from the road gang, rain started to fall – one drop, then a few, and in the next moment thick sheets of water forced her to wipe her eyes with her sleeve every few minutes. This would not be a good day for the market. Anyway, she now faced a far more difficult task than buying cauliflower in a downpour.

She began walking to the docks with the hope of finding Mrs Thistle, who was often there at this time. But would the woman make the journey on a day like this?

Sarah should, of course, have known better than to think rain would keep Mrs Thistle from doing what she pleased. There she was in a hooded cloak, standing with a ship's captain under a canvas cloth held up by Ash and another large man as she inspected crates. She was feeling some cloth between her fingers. 'If this silk is from China,' she said, 'then so am I.'

Sarah went up to her. 'Begging your pardon, madam,' she said, as calmly and deferentially as she could manage.

Mrs Thistle looked at her, then back to the captain standing next to her. 'That's all. And don't forget to close that crate up before the men take the canvas away.' She smiled at Sarah. 'Well, Miss Marin, I suggest we leg it.'

They were thoroughly drenched when they threw themselves into Mrs Thistle's covered coach, but the old woman showed no concern for the upholstery. She took off her shawl. 'It will be humid tomorrow, and I detest humidity.'

Sarah inhaled deeply. 'You once told me that you believe in freely given honesty.'

'I do.'

'I need to tell you a story. One that began on a field in Manchester.'

By the time they reached the stately house by the river bend, Sarah had told Mrs Thistle everything, from the deaths of her parents to her headlong escape in the *Serpent* to the meetings in The Rocks, and that there were those who wished the woman harm. Finally, Sarah spoke of the young man who currently laboured on the chain gang.

After she had finished, Sarah waited for Mrs Thistle's reaction. But for a few minutes the woman just stared straight ahead. Perhaps her jaw was a little more set than usual.

Sarah was on the verge of saying more, when they arrived at the turreted house. The sight of it seemed to restore Mrs Thistle's will to speak. Her voice was thick, strained. 'My driver will take you back to the English Rose. He will return tomorrow morning to take you wherever you wish to go. He may well return during the night, to ensure you are still there. Do not make any attempt to come near me.' She turned to Sarah. 'Ever. Again.' Then she stared straight ahead again, her chin lifted. 'I will be inspecting the English Rose shortly after you leave, to make sure nothing has been taken.'

'I would not steal from you,' Sarah said. She was stung by the suggestion, even though she had just admitted to actions that many would view as far worse. 'You may not understand why I acted as I did, but I have never taken what isn't mine. I simply tried to take what is.'

'I would not know of what you are capable, for I don't know who you are.'

This, more than anything else Mrs Thistle had said, threatened to crush the breath out of Sarah. The only person who really did know her, she realised, had probably not yet put down the axe he had taken up as she left.

'Will you . . . ?' Sarah swallowed, her mouth dry. 'You will not tell the superintendent?'

'He can do his own work.'

'And will you promise me to tell Mr Ash there are those who mean you harm? Have him with you at all times. Be careful.'

Mrs Thistle laughed joylessly. 'Please do not concern yourself about that. Your friends are not the first men to fantasise about assisting me towards my eternal reward. If anyone is talking loudly about it, you can be assured they will not actually do it.'

'I wanted to make sure they didn't, and I had hoped . . . You said that you would forgive almost anything for honesty.'

How have I let this happen? Sarah thought. She had handed Mrs Thistle the power to hurt her, to decide what kind of person she was, to sit in judgement. Only now did she realise how badly she wanted the woman's approval, and how badly its withdrawal would ache.

'And I would have forgiven you,' Mrs Thistle said. 'But this, now – this is not honesty. It is desperation.'

'Please, Mrs Thistle—'

The woman whipped her head around to stare at Sarah. 'Damn you to eternal hell for this,' she said coldly. 'Do you know how rare it is to find someone with any sort of facility for business here? Someone whose company you enjoy – someone you are beginning almost to regard as family. Another daughter. And that could have continued, if you had told me at the first opportunity.'

Sarah was beginning to cry, even though she knew Mrs Thistle despised signs of weakness. 'Perhaps if I had told you straight away, we would never have reached this point together. Even if you had not organised my arrest, you surely would never have trusted me with the English Rose or brought me to the docks. You would not have been able to see beyond what I did in London – and if you would like to know, Mrs Thistle, what desperation truly is, you need only look there.'

The old woman's mouth was puckered now, her chest rising and falling. 'I will never forgive you. For the lie, and because it has cost us each other.' She rapped on the coach's wall. A servant opened the door, and she stepped out and closed it behind her.

As the coach started moving again, Sarah looked out the window towards Molly Thistle, who was walking slowly up the path to her door, staring resolutely ahead with a stiffness that suggested she was trying to prevent herself from glancing back.

✦

That evening, Sarah's mind could not latch on to anything. Still, the business of the boarding house was soothing as it left no room for thought. She and Lizzie were now practised at moving around each other in the small kitchen, cooking and cleaning.

It was not until everything had been set right, put away, smoothed over, that Sarah allowed herself to acknowledge that this was her last night at the English Rose. She could, she supposed, have left the evening's service to Lizzie. She probably should have – she was likely in danger of arrest at the English Rose, but she wanted to prove to Mrs Thistle that she was not a thief, of time or anything else.

Lizzie had gone to bed, and the fire was dying. Sarah had not told the girl about the change in management, and although she felt a dull ache of guilt, she could not bear all the questions the revelation would bring.

Sitting at the kitchen table and staring at the wall, Sarah did not attempt to stir the embers. She almost welcomed the dark as it slowly erased the corners of the room. If the kitchen was no longer real, then her removal from it, perhaps, would not be as painful.

Her entire world was populated by ghosts now. Even the living were so lost to her, they might as well be dead. She doubted she would see Henry again, even as she heard his chains in the rattle of the kettle when she replaced it on its hook above the fire. She hoped Mrs Thistle was not feeling vengeful enough to punish him for Sarah's dishonesty. The old woman had a spectral form too, one who sat beside her and berated her for destroying what could have been the best of friendships.

When the fire had died down to a pile of glowing embers, Sarah stood, took her cap from a peg by the kitchen door, hung her apron in its place, and walked out.

She had lived at both ends of the earth. With Henry serving his brutal sentence, there was no one free left for her at either of them. Except, perhaps, one person. This person might just be prevailed upon to help her. To hide her. Perhaps even to find her a place in the bowels of another ship.

✦

Sarah had never seen Mrs Addison in a good temper in daylight, so she certainly didn't expect the woman to be in a better mood when roused by a knocking at the door at such an unreasonable hour.

Sarah was not disappointed. Mrs Addison, her hair untied and the colour of a musket barrel, violently pulled open the door as though she was trying to punish it for committing the crime of being knocked on. She said nothing, just stared at Sarah, her stance demanding explanation. Sarah found herself oddly in the grip of an impulse to curtsy, which she squashed. But she supposed a bit of politeness could not hurt. 'I am sorry to bother you, Mrs Addison. I know this isn't a convenient time, but is Keenan in?'

'I thought you were too sensible a girl to get entangled in this business.'

Sarah was not sure to which business she was referring, but Mrs Addison was already gesturing her inside. The room looked oddly cavernous without the jumbled collection of chairs and people. The only chairs visible now were at a corner table, occupied by Keenan and Baxendale.

The younger man rose politely when Sarah entered, while Baxendale leaned back in his chair, folded his arms over the top of his belly, and glared. 'You surely don't mean to involve her,' he said to Keenan.

'If she has any sense, she won't let you,' said Mrs Addison. 'Come to that, I just remembered I'm not entirely sure what all this is about. I'll leave you to it.' She went through the door at the back of the room, slamming it behind her.

'I did not involve her,' said Keenan to Baxendale. Then to Sarah, 'Are you in need of assistance?'

'I am, as it happens. But I don't wish to disturb your work, whatever it may be.' She looked at the table between the men. It bore a map of the docks, and on top lay a stub of graphite that had been used to circle the part of the dock nearest the Thistle warehouse.

The part where Mrs Thistle liked to inspect her cargo most mornings at dawn. Where she could be expected to do so tomorrow.

Poor, brave, stupid Keenan.

CHAPTER 33

Sarah was about to leave without a word and try to warn Mrs Thistle. But if lies had brought her here, she thought, perhaps the truth could help her head this plan off. And it would not be her fault if Baxendale and Keenan interpreted the truth in their own way.

'I am to be out on the street,' she said, 'after an argument with my employer.'

Keenan fetched another chair and insisted on helping her into it, with what seemed to be his approximation of a courtly gesture. She noticed he was blushing. 'I'm sorry to hear that,' he said. 'This sort of thing – it is why, you must see, all your thoughts of persuasion, of suffrage – noble as they are, I'm not saying otherwise – will not work. Stronger action is needed. Something emphatic.'

Baxendale leaned forward. 'And remind me, who is your employer?' he asked curtly.

'Molly Thistle,' said Sarah.

Keenan slapped an open hand down on the table. 'There you are, then!'

'There you are, indeed,' said Baxendale. 'And very convenient it is too, for one of Thistle's people to show up just when we are discussing certain arrangements.'

There was little Sarah could rely on, but she was confident in Baxendale's disdain for women. 'Mr Baxendale, I did not come here to discuss Mrs Thistle. I am in desperate need of help and thought I might find some here. Are you the sort who likes to talk about helping society, but takes no action?'

Baxendale leaned back a bit, seeming slightly mollified.

'I am not quite sure what is being discussed here,' she continued. 'It is best I leave. I hadn't thought to catch you in the middle of important business, and am sorry to disturb you.' She stood up and headed towards the door.

'I thought you'd been put out,' said Baxendale. He reached behind his seat to lift up a rifle that he laid across his lap.

'I will be. She has given me until tomorrow.'

'Why wait for tomorrow?' he asked. 'I do believe that you should stay here.'

'There's really no need for compulsion, Mr Baxendale,' said Keenan, in a wheedling tone. Although he was young, Sarah had assumed his authority with the group had been conferred by Mrs Addison. Now it seemed he only had as much as Baxendale allowed him.

'No? You don't think she will go straight to the police? Or to Mrs Thistle?'

'Well, I suppose—'

'Mrs Addison!' Baxendale called.

The woman opened the room's rear door almost immediately; she had probably been eavesdropping.

'Make up a bed for Miss Marin. She will stay here tonight. That will be all, both of you. And, Mrs Addison? See that she doesn't leave.'

Keenan gave Sarah a weak smile. Maybe it was his way of telling her he would take the matter up with Baxendale, but she did not feel hopeful.

Baxendale returned his gaze to the chart on the table, so he didn't see the mocking curtsy Mrs Addison dropped him. She put a hand on Sarah's arm and guided her through the rear door. 'You would think *please* was coin, the way he refuses to spend it,' she said quietly to Sarah when they stepped into another room. This one seemed to be Mrs Addison's domain: a small fire was going, with a single wooden rocking chair pulled up to it. The ceiling was crisscrossed with laundry lines, empty for the moment.

'Baxendale is a bully,' said Mrs Addison. 'Keenan, irritating as he can be, isn't a bad young lad. Someone's neck will stretch for this, and Baxendale will make sure it isn't his. Are you able, do you think, to put a stop to this nonsense in a way that doesn't get Keenan arrested?'

'I don't know, in all honesty. I am certainly willing to try, though.'

'It's a shame, then,' said Mrs Addison, 'that my back was turned. You took the opportunity to bolt out that unlocked door over there.' She pointed to the opposite end of the hallway.

Sarah smiled and squeezed the woman's arm. 'Thank you,' she whispered.

'Do not thank me, just save him. And hurry – Baxendale will surely haul his rear end through that door to check on us.'

Sarah nodded, then moved as quickly and quietly as she could towards the door.

✦

It was already after midnight. She was thankful for the full moon, as these streets presented enough opportunities to stumble in full daylight. She felt like a nervous horse, shying at the dark shape of a branch in the light breeze, or the movement of a pig or goat tied in someone's yard. Most of the houses she passed were shuttered and eyeless. It was not until she got close to the docks, close to the tavern where Nell had died, that any light created by man was visible. She knew better, though, than to get too close to that particular building.

An hour had passed, perhaps more, when she found her way back to the English Rose. The naked dirt of the road that devolved into track was at least light enough to enable her to follow it, although with a new moon and no lantern she would have been helpless.

Dim light was coming from the English Rose's top floor – perhaps those unable to sleep were soothing themselves with books. The lower floor, though, was in darkness. She paused, looking for the outline of the coach and not finding one. She exhaled in relief; hopefully Mrs Thistle had not sent her driver to make sure she hadn't left.

Ten minutes later, Sarah was in her bedroom. She supposed she should pack, although she owned very little. She stripped the bedsheets hoping that whoever made her room ready for its next occupant – Lizzie, probably – would have one less thing to do.

Sarah could not risk sleeping past dawn and missing her opportunity to get to the docks in time to warn Mrs Thistle. In any case, she doubted her jumbled mind would admit the possibility of rest. Mornings usually came far too quickly, before she was ready to meet them; this one was dragging, as though it had gathered up her wishes for more time and was granting them all at once.

She thought about what she might do after warning Mrs Thistle. Walk into the bush, perhaps, towards the smaller outlying settlements. Try to get a job as someone's cook. Or beg passage aboard a ship in exchange for work.

None of those eventualities seemed desirable, or even plausible. The only prospect that brought her close to anything resembling peace was the idea of walking straight to the superintendent, laying her story before him, and waiting for the trial at which she would be found guilty of high treason. There would be some pain, and some fear, and then – well, that depended on who you listened to. But the possibility of a reunion with her parents and Sam, and with Maisie, Coombes and Nell. Or, failing that, oblivion.

She sat down at the room's small desk, and reached for the pen and ink pot. Only a few weeks ago she had used it to write orders for supplies and keep the accounts up to date, usually while trying to ignore Amelia's fidgeting when Nell was working downstairs.

Now Sarah opened the drawer, drew out a piece of paper and placed it on the desk's inlaid leather surface. She was less careful with the ink than usual, and the page was soon festooned with blotches, some nearly obscuring words. She hoped that if Molly Thistle ever read this, it would be legible enough.

What would Sarah do with this letter? She doubted Mrs Thistle would take it from her hand, and she had no means of getting it to the woman's house. Perhaps she would leave it in the drawer, then, in the hope that whoever was next in this room might find the package addressed to the landlady.

Dear Mrs Thistle,

I do not seek forgiveness, as you have made it clear that none will be forthcoming. I ask only that you read this, for in it I attempt to explain my actions. You will no doubt still find them inexcusable, but perhaps a little more understandable.

I mentioned my mother, when we last spoke. Her name was Emily. I believe you would have enjoyed her company. Sadly that opportunity will never arise, as she was trampled to death by a horse while my father, Jack, lay near her with his chest slashed open, both murdered for listening to a man talk about suffrage.

I believe you would have also liked my brother, Sam, although he may have frustrated you at times. He did me — a young man of extremes, either paralysed by despair or rushing to action.

I think that Aidan Briardown, the man who led us in London, liked that in him. He could wave a perfumed handkerchief in front of Sam's nose and watch my brother bound off, following the scent.

I loved Sam, of course. And I saw him hanged for a crime that was not actually committed. My brother's biggest mistake was putting too much faith in one man and the vision he created that could never come into being.

I have asked myself many times whether I wish we had succeeded. In truth, I wish we had not tried. But we could not see any other way. You have been where we were. You and I share something that people like Superintendent Greenwich will never know: the memory of an empty belly, with the knowledge that there is no prospect of it being filled. The action my group planned was, we believed, the only possibility of relief.

325

You will say, of course, that I am making excuses – I do know how you hate that. But I am not. I have done what I have done, and I have lost what I have lost.

There are only two people left for me in this world. One is the man I told you about. If you are able to let him know what has happened to me, I would be grateful.

The other, I lost to my own dishonesty.

I wish you long life and health.

Yours in regret,

Sarah McCaffrey

Sarah blotted the mess of the page and folded it into a small packet, writing Mrs Thistle's name on the front and secreting it in the drawer.

Then she walked slowly down the stairs to the kitchen. She would have left a note for Lizzie, but the girl did not have her letters. Sarah would just try to make the morning as easy as possible for her.

In the kitchen she took out the ingredients and tools to make bread. She had always been fascinated with the transformation of water and flour into a new substance, and she loved sinking her fingers into the dough, pushing her palms down as she kneaded, the repetition unclenching her jaw and sending her into a blank state where no feelings existed.

When she had finished she put a muslin cloth over the bowl of dough, leaving it in the middle of the table where Lizzie would find it.

✦

By the time Sarah was halfway to the docks, the sky was lightening so much that she feared she would miss Molly Thistle.

She could see the mast of a ship rising over the low building in front of it, next to the Thistle warehouse. If its captain was not already getting an earful, he was probably bracing for one.

Sarah walked down one side of the warehouse, peering around the corner. She knew that if Mrs Thistle saw her coming, the woman would simply turn her back and walk away.

The door was open while supplies were being carried in, under the eye of Ash. Sarah wondered what would happen if she approached him – would he refuse to listen, perhaps even restrain her?

Then he saw her. He strode towards her, while signalling to someone beyond her. She started turning to see who it was, but she stopped when her eyes passed a stack of crates piled up about ten feet from the warehouse. Crouching there, hidden from anyone on the wharf, was Keenan. The barrel of his musket rested on top of a crate.

Sarah ran towards the wharf, but Ash thundered up and grabbed her by the shoulders. She tried to squirm around him and saw Mrs Thistle standing by some tea crates.

'Watch out!' Sarah yelled at the top of her voice. 'Watch out, he has a gun!'

It was the work of an instant. For the constables who had been approaching from behind to pinion her arms. For Keenan, taking advantage of the momentary confusion, to pull the trigger. And for Molly Thistle, who had been staring towards her, to fall to the ground.

CHAPTER 34

Sarah now found it almost laughable that she had spent so much time thinking about what she would do after warning Molly Thistle. The decision, of course, was made for her.

In the prison, a warden took her past a few cells in which several women were jammed. Some of them leered or called out, and she thought she would be taken to another such cell, to sit on a bench, and to be befriended or beaten depending on the mood of her cellmates.

Instead she was shoved into her own tiny stone room. A bucket in the corner still smelled of the excretions of the previous occupant. She wanted to avoid sitting on the dirty floor, a small patch of which was covered by straw. She smiled a little when she saw that; at least she had experience sleeping on straw.

The smile did not last. She had achieved precisely nothing at the docks, except giving Keenan enough time to shoot Molly Thistle.

She told herself the injury might not have been fatal. Perhaps Keenan had ultimately left Mrs Thistle with nothing worse than a scar and a story.

But Sarah had seen the way the woman had fallen. Molly Thistle had not put her arms out to protect herself and had not scrabbled at the air on her way down, showing no sign at all that she was sensible of her journey to the timbers of the dock.

Sarah recalled what Henry had said of his time in Newgate. All she wanted, now, was to be granted enough time to prepare herself so that she would not be remembered as the woman who cried and howled on her way to the gallows. She had heard talk about 'making a good end', but she had never understood it until now.

After a time she sat on the straw, hugging her knees and resting her forehead on them, while keeping her eyes closed and watching small pinpricks of colour swirl in the darkness behind her eyelids. They might well be the last colourful things she would ever see.

The door opened. She did not bother to look up, expecting it to be a warden with some feeble sustenance.

'So sunk in despair already, Miss McCaffrey?'

It took a second or two for her to register that Superintendent Greenwich had used her real name.

She gathered the strength to look up. He was standing there in his black coat with its silver buttons, so like the ones the Bow Street Runners had worn. He was holding a piece of paper in one hand, and he kept himself a little away from the muck-coated stone wall.

'Mrs Thistle,' said Sarah, 'is she . . . ?'

'Dead? You wish to know if your plan succeeded?'

'It was not my plan!'

'It brings me no joy to see you here,' he said. 'I tried to warn you.'

'Warn me, or get information from me?'

'Truly the former, if you can believe it. At the time I wasn't sure who you were, although the thought had occurred to me. I recently received a very interesting letter.' He waved the papers he was holding. 'You remember Albert Tourville, I presume.'

She nodded.

'He wrote to the governor, who passed the letter on to me. Tourville has described you in detail – long dark hair, Northern accent, et cetera, et cetera. He thought you might have found your way onto a ship, and I dare say my counterparts in South Africa and Bombay have received similar letters. I didn't pay much attention to it at first, even though I am not in the habit of receiving correspondence from the aristocracy.'

'Tourville is not an aristocrat!'

'Well, he would have been, if history had taken a different course. He fled France as a child, you see.'

'Yes, with a cousin, he said.'

'No, with his nanny. His parents had been imprisoned, you see, and ultimately beheaded. Tell me, was it his suggestion to behead the Cabinet? In any case, he writes that, let's see . . .' Greenwich unfolded the letter, shaking the pages a few times. 'Ah, yes – he writes that he will, until his last breath, *cut down those willing to shed blood in the name of their misguided ideals.*' He refolded the letter. 'I am greatly disappointed. Mrs Thistle was kind to you, in her way. I know she can be vexing, but she did not have to take you in as she did. She did not even have to glance in your direction.'

He sounded like a schoolmaster mildly rebuking a child, and like a man who would forget her as soon as he left the cell.

'I was just trying to warn her!' Even as Sarah said the words, she knew she came across like any other lag claiming innocence – but she found it unbearable to be asked to atone for a crime she had tried to prevent.

Greenwich shook his head. 'After we spoke at the garden party, I convinced myself that you had been caught up against your better judgement in ridiculous, treasonous plans with no chance of success. That you were just a young, foolish woman with nowhere else to go, so I should let you be. I even felt sympathetic towards you. But you kept meeting with those people, and you involved yourself with no coercion in a plan to assassinate Mrs Thistle. And then, of course, I opened the letter from Tourville.'

'I only discovered their plan the night before. I was trying to save her!'

'Was this plan not discussed at a meeting sometime prior? And would that not have been an opportune time to warn Mrs Thistle?'

'It was mentioned, but I didn't believe they were serious. And I did tell her, that there were those who wished her harm. She didn't seem concerned in the slightest.' Sarah paused to think. 'You were having me followed?'

'Tourville is not the only police informant to infiltrate a rebel group,' Greenwich said.

'If you had someone at that meeting, you must know I argued for peace.'

'Yes, I would have, too, if I had already been betrayed by one person and feared a similar betrayal by another. It would be a convenient story to tell, should a time like this arrive. Mr Baxendale has an exceptional memory. His wife was killed, you see, in a convict uprising some time ago. So he, like Tourville, takes this sort of thing quite seriously.'

'But he was the one who drew Keenan into this. And you were willing to let him, at the risk of Mrs Thistle's life.'

'Do not think Mr Keenan is an innocent who was unduly influenced. He has been a concern to us for quite some time. And he is still at large, as he managed to slip away while the constables were arresting you. But I assure you, he will be captured, tried and hanged.'

'As will I,' said Sarah.

'That is yet to be determined. We will send you to the Female Factory for the present, and I shall be writing to Tourville and awaiting further instructions – he intimated that Her Majesty's Government would prefer such a crime, and such a criminal, to be dealt with on their own shores, as visibly as possible.'

She might, then, be hanged on the same gallows as her brother had been. Oddly, she found herself wishing they would hurry up and do it.

CHAPTER 35

What if she survived a violent shipwreck, only to drown in calm waters?

Unlike the other women in the sloop pushing its way upriver, Sarah had her hands manacled. Some of the others aboard were laughing as they boisterously shoved each other, and Sarah was terrified of being tipped into the water.

Most of these women were being sent to the Female Factory for minor infractions. Perhaps they had not displayed the required decorum while in service, or been caught weaving drunkenly down a street. Some were new arrivals to the colony being sent west until they could be farmed out as assigned servants or indifferent brides to unknown men. Most here, though, had been given a trial.

No charge had been laid against Sarah. Her presence on the boat had been a surprise to its master; the constable had simply appeared as the boatman was readying to cast off, asked if the man in charge could fit another, and left Sarah there without awaiting a response.

She could tell that no one quite knew what to make of her. She did not sleep when they stopped for the night, and she spent her time silently staring at the water, wincing whenever the boat rocked. If she looked long enough into the blank face of the river, perhaps she could dissolve herself, leaving behind an animated corpse with no memory of names like Sam, Henry and Nell.

After the sloop arrived at their destination, the women were led in a gaggle from the river to an expansive scrappy lawn encircled by a high wall, over which loomed a two-storey sandstone building. An overseer came out of a smaller building to the side of the yard and started separating them into groups, reeling off their names. When he reached the bottom of his list, he looked up at the only woman wearing irons. 'Heard from the superintendent about you.' He beckoned over a man with wiry grey hair and bushy eyebrows, whispered in his ear and nodded to Sarah.

The man, who had to be a turnkey, gripped her painfully by the elbow, propelling her under a low archway and towards a building that seemed hewn all of a piece from one of the cliffs. Appended to its side was a patch of yard where women broke rocks beneath a canvas awning, and some of them looked up as Sarah passed.

'Back to work, you lot!' the turnkey yelled as he led Sarah through a door into the stone building.

Once she had been forced up the set of rickety stairs, the rooms she passed had bare floors, broken windows, and the smell of excrement. Some contained several cots, but the room the turnkey unlocked had just one. The only light came from a tiny window set high in the wall, and apart from the cot, the only furnishing was a bucket in the corner. The cell was small enough for Sarah to cross in one pace; she suspected that if she did not have her wrists constrained, she could stretch out her arms to touch both walls at once.

She was gripped by an irrational conviction that once the door closed, it would never open again. 'How long am I to stay here?'

'Not sure,' he said. 'Until you hang, I suppose.'

'Am I not even to get a trial?'

'Ah yes, but the magistrates, they don't look kindly on high treason.' He scratched his pock-marked cheek. 'Makes an interesting change, having you in here. Most of the crimes them out there have committed are far less imaginative.'

Sarah's mind began clouding with panic, and she feared she might get to a point where thought was impossible, where wailing and gibbering was all that was left. She took a few breaths and steadied herself. 'Can I have some paper? I want to write a letter, you see.'

'To some of your treacherous friends?'

She allowed herself only a moment's thought. Any significant pause might make him suspicious. 'No,' she said, 'to my aunt.'

Although the light in the doorway was dim, she could see that this man had recently been chained himself. He had a bent back, and around his wrists, closed but not healed, were livid marks, the kind made by manacles that had stayed on for a long time.

'I don't want to cause any trouble,' she said, 'but my aunt doesn't know where I am. Or what I am. Likely I'll never see her again, and I want to tell her myself. I want to explain, to say goodbye.'

The man was frowning, confused now as he stared at her.

'I think I can be at peace with my fate,' she said, 'if I've made my peace with her. It would be unbearable, thinking of her not knowing.'

He paused, rubbing at his eyebrows. 'We read it, you know. Whatever goes out of here.'

'I wouldn't write anything to give you concern. I just wish to soothe the fretting of an old lady who's been kind to me.'

He nodded slowly. 'Paper costs money. Don't suppose you have anything to pay with?'

Sarah found herself backing against the wall. It occurred to her how vulnerable she was. How she could scream and fight and kick and it would make no difference. How she was more isolated now than she had been in the middle of the ocean on the *Serpent*.

He was shaking his head. 'Not that,' he said gruffly. 'Look, I can't promise you anything. I'll see, though, and that's the best I can say.'

Before she finished thanking him, he had shut and locked the door.

✦

Sarah soon lost track of time, as she only saw another person when the hatch to her cell opened and food was pushed in.

One day, the door opened fully. She could tell it was daytime because she could see the turnkey's extravagant eyebrows and permanent purple bracelets. He handed her a piece of paper, along with a small stick of charcoal, and said, 'You have an hour.'

Sarah stared at the paper and charcoal. It seemed almost impossible to believe there was a world in which such things still existed.

'Thank you,' she said, 'I am so—'

'You can show your thanks by being finished by the time I come back. And I'll be checking it, don't think I won't.' He started towards the door, then paused. 'My daughter,' he said. 'In London. I had no letters, you see, when I first was freed, and couldn't get anyone to write for me. She didn't know what had become of me, so I learned my letters. I wrote to say I'd been sorry to leave her, and I hoped to make my way back to her.'

'Perhaps you will,' said Sarah.

The turnkey shook his head. 'A man wrote back, said they'd been married and a fever took her.' She thought he might say something more, but he just sighed and left.

For a moment she held the charcoal above the paper. She had no way of knowing what had happened after Keenan had fired his rifle; she might be seeking aid from a corpse.

Eventually, she touched the charcoal to the paper.

My dearest aunt Georgina,

I am very sad to tell you that I have been imprisoned in the Female Factory for a crime for which I do not hold out much hope for acquittal. I regret the disappointment and grief this news must cause you. Please rest in the knowledge that you have my highest regard, and my gratitude for your many past kindnesses.

This may well be the last you hear of me in this life, so I wish to ask a very small favour. I still owe a debt to your sailing companion Mrs Rose, who visited me in the infirmary. She lives, as you know, to the north-west of the town. Would you be kind enough to call on her and tell her I regret I may be unable to repay her kindness, but that I will think of her in whatever time remains to me with great affection, as indeed I think of you.

Sarah recalled Mrs Thistle's reaction to Nell's murder.

Mrs Rose is an upright woman. I ask her forgiveness for the wrongs I have done her, but will not own the sins to which I have not earned a right. I ask her for

absolution, which I have known her to give more easily
than a priest.
   Your loving niece
   Sarah

She folded the letter. The address she wrote on the outside was that of the building in which she had first opened her eyes after the wreck.

Mrs Georgina Haddon, Sydney Infirmary

CHAPTER 36

Sometimes on waking, Sarah could not tell where she ended and the stones of the cell began. The part of her body that had been lying on the floor was cold, felt foreign when she touched it, and had as little feeling as a rock.

She had tried asking the men who brought her meals what was to happen to her, or if they knew anything of Mrs Thistle's fate. They never answered. Perhaps those in power had decided to dispense with the trial altogether, and had already condemned her to a slow, voiceless death in this cell.

Although she had no clear grasp of time, she suspected she had been there at least a month, because the stifling heat had started to dissipate, and she caught the occasional tang of wood smoke on the rare breeze.

She wondered if Henry knew what had happened to her. She imagined him hopefully looking up from his labour, waiting for a visit that wouldn't come.

Either Nurse Haddon had not passed on her message, or it had been ignored. Or Mrs Thistle had not survived.

Sarah had been arrested in the brown woollen gown that Nurse Haddon had given her. She had kept it pristine when such things had seemed important, but now it was frayed and stained. Her fingernails were chipped and ragged because she passed time scratching pictures in the muck on the floor whenever a small amount of light penetrated the cell. When she was in darkness, she sang half-remembered hymns to a God she no longer believed in. She had long since stopped caring about the deterioration in her voice, which had come to resemble the call of the crows that would sit in the trees outside the English Rose. She wished that she had spent more time appreciating their glossy black feathers and thanking them for producing what song they could.

For a while she had felt a flare of hope whenever the door opened, but now the key seemed to mock her each time it entered the lock. She did not look up anymore.

'Hardly the greeting I would have expected,' said a familiar voice when the door opened one morning. 'I would have thought that gratitude was in order.'

Sarah, who had been on her knees staring at the far wall, got up as quickly as she could – a process far slower than it had once been, driven by muscles that had rarely moved since the cell door had closed for the first time.

Molly Thistle seemed a little thinner. She had a black cane, and when she stepped into the cell there was a catch to her gait. Her eyes fell on Sarah's privy bucket, and she winced; the guard had not yet emptied it that day. 'I had visions of a tearful embrace, but just now I'll thank you to keep your distance.'

Sarah began to smile, the skin on her lips cracking. Then she stopped. Her dreams had brought her back to London, to the yard at Newgate where Sam was hanged, to the field where her parents had died. Had they now brought the phantom of Mrs Thistle, a smoky wisp of hope that would be snatched away by the next breeze?

'Well?' said the old woman sharply. 'Are you coming?'

'Am I ... where?'

'To see the superintendent. Now, do not hope too much just yet. You may be coming back here. It all depends.'

'On what?' said Sarah, still bewildered.

'On how I acquit myself, and whether Superintendent Greenwich slept well last night or fought with his wife, and on how much he cares about his reputation. He's removed himself to a house near here, having grown tired of living in the bustle of Sydney. If we call on him now, we may gain an audience before he leaves. That meeting may end with your freedom – or it may end with me in a cell next to yours.'

✦

Sarah was certain that she stank, though she could not smell it after being surrounded by her stench for so long. Molly Thistle did not mention it, and had probably smelled as bad herself when she was a convict, but she left the carriage window open. A more delicate woman would not have allowed Sarah to make any contact whatsoever with the fine upholstery, but Mrs Thistle did not seem to mind, smiling warmly at her from the opposite seat.

The carriage's upholstery was the first soft surface on which Sarah had sat since her arrest, and its windows admitted more light than she had seen since her cell door had closed.

She had thought so often of Mrs Thistle that she wondered if she had finally descended into madness. Was she actually grinning at the wall of her cell? If she were living in a fantasy, though, she would surely not have imagined the occasional jolt the carriage gave her, or the slightly too-cool breeze flowing in through the partially open window. And surely she would have made herself less fragrant.

As her sense of reality began to return, she warned herself not to hold it too tightly – there was no guarantee this trip would not end with her back in her cell.

'I . . . I am glad you're alive,' she said. 'I was not part of the plot, no matter what the superintendent says.'

'I am alive, very possibly, because you shouted and I looked up. The shot went into my shoulder. Bit feverish for a while, and it knocked me down so hard that my ankle still hasn't forgiven me.' Mrs Thistle put a gentle hand on Sarah's. 'I received your letters. And while I am still angry, still hurt, I did miss you. It certainly is not easy to find someone who is congenial company, who understands business, whom one can trust – despite certain information being withheld.' She smiled again, then shook her head as if to clear it. 'Anyway, it takes a while to train somebody to do things just so, and then you disappeared.'

'Hardly by choice,' said Sarah.

'Well, now you have another choice in front of you – or a necessity, if you prefer. And what you decide, by the time this coach stops moving, will determine what I say to the superintendent.'

'I wasn't aware I had the ability to decide anything right now.'

'Oh yes,' said Mrs Thistle, 'one of the most important of your life. Are you, or are you not, planning to consort with your revolutionary friends if you regain your freedom?'

'But it's not freedom, not really. Nell wasn't free. Even after her sentence, she was not free to choose.'

'Would you like to change things for others like Nell Flaherty?'

'Of course,' said Sarah.

'Let me explain, then,' said Mrs Thistle, leaning forward and patting Sarah's knee. 'When I was your age, suppose I had decided to involve myself in a group pushing for revolution. Suppose I'd been arrested, as you were, and put into a solitary cell. Never met William, never married him. Never made the business I have made, or accumulated the influence that comes with it. I would be in my grave, and you would soon be joining me.'

'I am grateful for your intervention—'

'One day, someone might be grateful for yours – unless you squander this opportunity. I need your word, Sarah, that you will lay this aside.'

'And instead concentrate on helping you accumulate more wealth?'

'Why not?' Mrs Thistle smiled. 'Because you, my dear girl, will be accumulating it too. Enough, perhaps, to make changes in the lives of those around you, rather than wasting your breath in hushed conversations in dingy rooms.'

Sarah turned to the window. The scrub they were passing looked so different from the hedges she and Sam had passed on their way from Manchester to London. She realised that it must now have been a year or more since he was hanged, and she swallowed, trying not to release the gathering tears. Sam was beyond her help; Henry was not.

'One condition,' Sarah said. 'Two, actually.'

'I don't really think you're in a position to negotiate.'

'Am I in a position to request?'

Molly Thistle sighed. 'Very well.'

'It concerns two people,' said Sarah. 'One dead, and one very much alive.'

❖

348

The superintendent's whitewashed house crouched amid broad lawns. They were dotted with willow trees transplanted from the place of his birth, and trellises that trained flowers to grow according to their master's wishes.

'Perhaps I should wait in the carriage,' said Sarah, indicating her filthy state. The skin on her hands had a yellowish tinge, and her arms sagged where what little fat there was had melted away. When she pushed her tongue against her teeth, they felt not quite as securely moored as they had been. Her lips were as rough as a sun-dried mud path.

But Mrs Thistle said, 'Nonsense. Do the man no harm to see what damage more than a month in a solitary cell can wreak.'

The superintendent's maid clearly agreed with Sarah and did not believe such a creature deserved admittance. 'Your . . . your servant will wait outside,' she said after Molly Thistle had stated her business and demanded an audience.

'My *associate* will not. She is a party to the matter to be discussed.'

The maid paused, but Mrs Thistle looked at her with such intensity that she clearly decided it was preferable to announce this strange visit to her master than stand and endure the woman's gaze. After a few minutes she returned to show Mrs Thistle and Sarah into the superintendent's study. They walked through a drawing room that was far less welcoming than Mrs Thistle's. Its utilitarian chairs were clustered around a small polished table beside a fireplace that did not seem to have been called upon for warmth in quite some time, its cold metal grate looking out onto a room unadorned by pictures, ornaments or anything else to indicate the nature of its owner.

Superintendent Greenwich's study was even more sparse. His plain desk was neatly stacked with papers next to a wooden ink pot that would have been at home on the desk of the humblest clerk. There were two chairs, one in front of the desk and one behind, both of plain, upholstered wood. The only item in the room approaching the decorative was a magnifying glass on the desk with a mother-of-pearl handle.

'He will be with you shortly,' said the maid, offering the chair in front of the desk to Mrs Thistle, who sat regally without responding.

Moments later, Greenwich opened the door and walked in. He glanced at Sarah with a frown, bowed to Mrs Thistle, who nodded serenely, and took his own seat behind the desk. 'How did you secure the release of this prisoner, madam?' he asked.

'Dear Charlie. Remember him? You and he shared a game of whist at one of my parties. Anyway, he is rather an admirer of some of the wines I import, and his taste for them has only sharpened since he ascended to the bench. He's told me that Miss McCaffrey can have a day out with me. Which, of course, can be extended if the police decide that they do not wish to pursue charges.

If, for example, there is insufficient proof of the allegations against her. If, come to that, there are any official allegations at all.'

'As charming as you are, madam, I have already written to England of her capture. I cannot simply release a woman who has been involved in treason.'

'Nor would I expect you to. But there is no such woman in this room. Miss McCaffrey has kept regrettable company over the past year, it is true. The young, they are so easily led astray, but with my influence she has seen the danger of her actions and wishes to take no further part in such meetings.'

'She was directly involved in a conspiracy to murder Cabinet members!'

'So that Frenchman says,' said Mrs Thistle. 'Can you believe him, though? If somebody is duplicitous enough to betray their comrades, are they also wily enough to present themselves to the police as something other than they are?'

'I will not be discussing this matter with you, madam. And Miss McCaffrey must be returned to the Female Factory. I will be happy to accompany you there to make sure that nothing goes amiss.'

Sarah felt a sudden thump in her chest. She would not survive a return; her mind's moorings would snap.

But Mrs Thistle shrugged. 'As you wish, superintendent. I know, of course, that you're a gentleman of the highest integrity. One who clings to the last letter of the law.'

Superintendent Greenwich didn't answer but drew his shoulders back, clearly believing the compliment was justified.

'So you'll have no objection, I'm sure, to me alerting Charlie to the still on your premises in Sydney.'

'What on earth are you talking about, woman?' Greenwich said, all politeness disappearing. 'If you attempt to spread false rumours about me—'

'Nothing false about them. Your nephew – Michael, is it? He seemed a dissolute lad when I called to collect the rent that he – or rather you – haven't paid. Well, when someone like that answers the door, reeking of drink, I have to inspect the premises. He may well be making a nice little allowance out of supplying the shebeens. His business will have to be shut down, of course, when it becomes public. He will likely go to prison. If you could kindly attend to the matter of the overdue rent – four months, now, I believe, it would be most appreciated. Expeditiously, if you will, as I believe your employment circumstances may change when this business becomes public.'

Sarah thought back to the odd contraption she had seen that day. Mrs Thistle had not called it a still; she had called it leverage, and now she was using it on Sarah's behalf.

Sarah tried to quash her sudden joy – nothing was certain. She could not, though, and she would pay for this hope when she was back in her cell. But perhaps it would be worth the price, as she would never again feel hope if Mrs Thistle's plan did not work.

'I had no idea!' Greenwich insisted.

'Oh, I'm sure. But the thing is, you see, this still is at your residence, officially anyway. Now, as pleasant as it is to be away from that town, you really must take more of an interest. Things grow when you're not looking, and they are not always pleasant.' Mrs Thistle stood. 'Well, if you're to escort us back to the prison, you had best be quick about it. I'll be happy to take you into Sydney in my coach. And then we shall go on to Charlie – I think he'll find this conversation quite enlightening.' She motioned Sarah towards the door. 'I regret that your freedom was so brief, dear girl. And that the superintendent's nephew's freedom is also coming to an end.' Mrs Thistle put her hand on the doorknob.

'You are the most infuriating woman I have ever met,' said Greenwich.

She smiled. 'Thank you, superintendent.'

'Miss McCaffrey will warrant that she shall have no further conversation with those of revolutionary sensibility.'

'She's given me her word,' said Mrs Thistle.

'And you will be responsible for her behaviour henceforth. I assure you, if I have reason to arrest her again, I will find a way to extend her wrongdoing to include you as well.'

'Quite understandable, but I am certain that such a situation won't eventuate. Now, may I offer you a seat in my carriage?'

'No, thank you,' Greenwich said firmly, his nose wrinkling as he looked at Sarah. 'I have important matters to attend to here.'

'Of course, we mustn't detain you,' said Molly Thistle, still smiling. 'Sarah and I must return to the English Rose in haste – it has rather fallen down without her. And of course you must now write a letter to your colleagues in England. Perhaps about mistaken identity, or with the news of Prisoner McCaffrey's untimely death.'

Mrs Thistle opened the door and gestured to Sarah, who shook her head. 'I believe, madam, you had one more request of the superintendent,' she said, her voice quavering a little at the thought that this man could still change his mind, that she might be throwing away her freedom.

'Ah, yes. Might I ask for an assigned convict servant for one of my properties. I need a young man with a bit of strength to him, and I'm given to understand that such a one might currently be labouring on a road gang near the English Rose.'

EPILOGUE
Sydney Cove, August 1823

Sarah knew they whispered when they saw her coming. At first, the whispers had been amused, patronising, sometimes profane. What would this small woman do if things were not to her liking, after all? Use the weapon of womanly tears? Stamp off in a funk to Mrs Thistle? Some of them, resting their elbows on the gunwales of their ships and staring, speculated that such a creature could be put to better use behind a dockside tavern than she was examining wares about which she was surely ignorant.

Since then, the tone of the whispers had changed. Now, when captains and sailors saw the slight figure in her well-made day gown with a lace collar and her expensive silk bonnet, they whispered to those around them to make ready and to ensure that the highest quality goods were brought out for her examination.

Silence was the best response they could hope for; a quirked eyebrow or a grimace was concerning. But the dread of those whose livelihoods depended on being paid for their cargo was that this woman would find nothing redeeming in the crates and barrels that had been brought forward.

Mrs Thistle had handed the docks to Sarah a year earlier. All matters of import were discussed in the old woman's comfortable drawing room, on the pale-yellow upholstery of her chairs and couch, and over tea presented by Lilith.

That day, Mrs Thistle had said, 'In all honesty, I'll miss it. But I need everyone to see you as an extension of me. Otherwise you will be of no more use than a messenger.' She fell silent, sipping at her tea and peering through her half-moon spectacles at Sarah over the rim of her cup.

'You do not want me to seek permission, then, should I wish to send something back where it came from?'

Mrs Thistle shook her head. 'I trust your judgement. And, just as importantly, they must know that. If you hesitate, if you seek permission from me or anyone else, you are done for. They'd take it from a man, of course, but from you? Not unless it is the way with you from the beginning.'

So now, with Mr Ash trailing her, Sarah reached into the sawdust of a crate and pulled out a saucer nestled there as part of a tea set. She held it up to the light, moved it backwards and forwards, and scratched a fingernail on one of its floral decorations. She nodded at Ash and moved on to the next item while he was organising for the crate of porcelain to be taken to the warehouse.

Next were bolts of finely woven woollen cloth. She rubbed one between her fingers and looked at the captain. 'Ireland?'

'Exeter, madam.'

She lifted one of the bolts to check the ones beneath. The black gave way to grey, and then to blue. She reached down and pulled out one of the lighter shades; the smear of an unidentifiable substance marred the pale-blue fabric.

The captain frowned. 'It must have been like that already. Surely you can't think I would allow harm to come to the cargo once it is in my care.'

'I would have thought, captain, that you would thoroughly check everything before departing. By the time it gets back to Exeter, this fabric will have travelled further than most do in a lifetime.' She shook her head at Ash and moved on to the next crate, with the captain scurrying after her.

When she was finished, with one shipment of tea, another of skins and the bolts of cloth to be sent back to their destination, Ash said with a broad smile, 'I imagine you want to inspect the warehouse now, miss.'

She smiled back. 'No harm in it, I suppose.'

✦

The tall brick warehouse sat on the harbour's edge, its small windows under a peaked roof, THISTLE painted in large black letters between the first and second storeys.

Inside, crates were neatly stacked on top of one another, and shelves held tea, cloth and cutlery.

The light was dim, and there was no fire – Mrs Thistle would never countenance it. She had once told Sarah she had nightmares about flames licking upwards along the shelves, curling the edges of papers, spreading the fragrance of burning tea.

It was not so dim, though, that Sarah could not see the man towards the back, supervising the unpacking of a crate while he marked items off with a pencil stub on a piece of paper. He looked up and gave her a smile every bit as broad as Ash's had been.

It had taken a long time for Henry to smile as he did now. He was self-conscious about the front tooth that was missing, a gap visible whenever he stretched his lips. And for a while, too, he had not trusted his circumstances and felt that showing any faith in his good fortune would tempt fate to snatch it from him.

It would be another four years before he received his ticket of leave, and even then his sentence meant that he would never be able to leave the colony. Now, though, he did not look like a man who wanted to. Nor did he look like the young man she had seen on the chain gang. His back had straightened, and his skin no longer had a greyish cast.

Some in England might have been shocked to see a man still serving his sentence in such a position of mercantile authority. They would never have allowed a convict to work at a warehouse. But here, where a tiny fraction had arrived free, such arrangements were common, and the colony would have been unable to function without convict clerks and magistrates, along with convict labour.

Henry set his papers on a shelf, then strode towards her. He looked as though he was about to open his arms. Then he glanced at Ash, and took her hands instead.

'You realise the wedding's tomorrow,' Ash said to him. 'A visit to the barber might be in order. You do want to look pretty, after all.'

'I'll never be as pretty as you, Mr Ash,' Henry said, and the larger man chuckled.

He had taken a liking to Henry when the lad had first been assigned to Molly Thistle as a dockworker. Ash had taught Henry to box, and how to dangle a line into the harbour during quiet times on the docks in the hopes of pulling out a fish, and probably a great many other things that Sarah did not wish to know about in the taverns dotted around the foreshore.

Now, Ash turned away with a theatrical wink. 'Just be waiting outside . . . for those crates from the dock.'

After he had gone, Henry kissed Sarah's forehead. She found herself wishing, more frequently, that he was not so self-consciously chaste. But he had decided he could not afford to give anyone in the colony reason to doubt his propriety – least of all Mrs Thistle.

'Are you sure,' he whispered, 'that you want to marry a convict? You could meet ten better than me in an afternoon at one of Mrs Thistle's garden parties.'

It was a question he had asked many times before.

'I'm marrying a man of principle,' said Sarah. 'And joyful to be doing so.'

'And this man of principle is fortunate to be alive.'

Keenan had lost his life in the same manner as Sam. The swift trial and well-attended public hanging had happened while she was in the Female Factory.

'I had always thought Sam would be at my wedding,' she said.

'I thought, you know, about marrying you when I had become a member of the provisional government.'

'Do you still feel it?' she asked. 'The tug towards rebellion?'

He shook his head. 'I feel that Briardown found a young man into whose ear he could pour the ideas that would shape him. But no, I don't.'

'I do,' she said, and he frowned.

'You mustn't talk like that! Superintendent Greenwich hasn't forgotten.'

'I don't mean storming government house and holding up the governor's head in front of a screaming crowd. You know as well as I do that there is more than one way to start a revolution.'

He shook his head, and she grinned and stood on her toes to kiss his cheek.

'I beg you to find a way that preserves your life and liberty,' he said. 'I think we have both had quite enough of prisons.'

✦

Every Wednesday, Mrs Thistle insisted on a visit from Sarah after she had done her rounds of the docks. That day, the chair she always sat in was pulled up to the window to catch the last of the afternoon sun. Lilith had told Sarah that Mrs Thistle forbade anyone else to sit in it.

The spectacles on the woman's nose had grown a little thicker in the past months, and it took a few seconds longer for her to lower herself into her chair. Her eyes, though, were still sharp and darting blue, and she had lost none of her ability to cajole, intimidate and negotiate her way through a settlement that had never been kind to those of her gender and class. 'So,' she asked, 'what got sent back today?'

'Cloth, tea. Some skins, as well – the hide had been scraped to the point where I could see light through it.'

Mrs Thistle nodded. 'Good. You must send something back each time. Even if you can't find a problem with any of it.'

'Always flaws to be found, if you look hard enough,' said Sarah. 'I was walking past Greenwich's old house yesterday, and it might make a good location for the home.'

Mrs Thistle put her teacup down. 'That, dear girl, is a very lucrative property,' she said. 'Perhaps we can find something more suitable for your destitutes.'

'My *destitutes*, as you call them, are in circumstances that you and I could easily have found ourselves in, had our fates taken even the smallest step to one side or another. And you often tell me that honesty and consistency are crucial to maintaining this business.'

'And you're about to point out that I did promise,' said Mrs Thistle.

Sarah smiled, practised copying the old woman's usual expression of alert serenity as she sipped her tea.

'Oh, very well. I will make it over to you, and you may open its doors to the most unfortunate women in the colony. And you will, I hope, remember that thanks to me, you are not among their number.'

Sarah put a hand on Mrs Thistle's knee. 'Always,' she said, hearing a catch in her voice. Mrs Thistle smiled, and Sarah fancied she caught a shine in her eyes beyond her spectacles. She realised she had never seen the woman shed tears.

'Well, I am about to give you something else to be grateful for,' Mrs Thistle said. As she was not a woman given to tender moments, whenever one arose she deployed her most businesslike voice and her briskest manner.

She took a wooden box from the side table. Sarah had not noticed it, but now she could not stop looking at its intricate inlay: amid flower petals of light wood, an S was twined around an H.

Mrs Thistle moved the box so that its little brass catch was facing Sarah, and opened it. Inside was a fine gold chain, from which hung a circular charm in the shape of a serpent eating its own tail. The work was very fine, with the scales of the snake picked out along the circumference of the circle, its eyes set with tiny chips of ruby, its fangs sharp and precise.

Sarah looked up to Mrs Thistle and beamed. 'I never thought that you would be presenting me with such a thing. Surely it would be provocative if Superintendent Greenwich saw me wearing it.'

Molly Thistle shrugged. 'Then don't wear it in front of him,' she said. 'It's just a symbol. But one way or another, that snake got you here.'

She handed the box to Sarah, who traced her index finger around the little snake before she looked up at her friend and smiled, taking the necklace out of the box and fastening it around her neck. 'You're right, it is just a symbol. And symbols only have the power we give them.'

ACKNOWLEDGEMENTS

There are a great many people without whom I couldn't have written this book.

Stirling Smith, senior maritime archaeology officer at Heritage NSW in the Department of Premier and Cabinet, was extraordinarily helpful and patient with my questions.

While doing an Australian Institute for Maritime Archaeology course, I was lucky enough to meet Renee Malliaros and Paul Hundley from the Silentworld Foundation, and Kieran Hosty from the National Maritime Museum, all of whom were very generous with their time and information. Particular thanks to Renee for taking me through the Institute's collection.

Thanks also to Tony Curtis, one of the few people in the world who has sailed a tall ship, for reviewing the manuscript.

I don't believe editors get the credit they deserve. They can have a profoundly positive impact on a book, and in this case I owe so much to Angela Meyer, the publisher who believed in this story, Tegan Morrison, who took it on, and editor Kate Goldsworthy. They all left this book far better than they found it. I'm also hugely indebted to my agent, Fiona Inglis.

Finally and as always to my parents, Tom and Judy, my husband, Craig, and my wonderful and supportive children, Rory and Alex – I love you all, and thanks for putting up with this process.

AUTHOR'S NOTE

With the exception of the Peterloo Massacre depicted in the first chapter, nothing in this book is closely based on real people or events. But some characters were loosely inspired by historical figures, and some parts of the plot share contours with historical events.

The Peterloo Massacre

The incident in which Emily and Jack McCaffrey die is closely based on a massacre that occurred during a peaceful protest in Manchester. In August 1819, sixty to a hundred thousand people gathered in St Peter's Field to hear Henry Hunt talk about parliamentary reform. His speeches were so well known that he was widely referred to as Orator Hunt.

Many of those attending would have been hungry. The Corn Laws that protected British merchants from competition with foreign grain also brought about a chronic shortage of affordable food. One of Hunt's platforms was a call for the Prince Regent to select ministers who would repeal the Corn Laws.

In the months before the St Peter's Field meeting, authorities were growing increasingly nervous about the public mood. The French Revolution of 1789 to 1799 was still within living memory, serving as a warning to some and an incitement to others. A month earlier, local magistrates had written to the home secretary, Lord Sidmouth, saying they feared an uprising. The notice Sarah sees, declaring the meeting illegal, has the same wording as one that appeared in the lead-up to the event.

As magistrates watched the gathering from the window, they became alarmed at its size. They read the Riot Act, a law that gave them the right to call on large crowds to disperse or face punishment. It's unlikely many heard them, and those who did perhaps chose to ignore the direction. So the Yeomanry, mounted and armed with swords and clubs, were ordered in to arrest the speakers. This force was made up of local worthies, business owners and the like, known to many of those attending. When members of the crowd linked arms to prevent the arrests, the Yeomanry began slashing indiscriminately and were soon joined by the Hussars.

By the end of the day, up to twenty people had been killed and hundreds injured. The event became known as the Peterloo Massacre to contrast the behaviour of the armed men with that of the British soldiers of the famous Battle of Waterloo, who were considered heroes.

The role of the Female Reform Societies in this event has not, perhaps, received the attention it deserves. Delia Burns is an amalgam of Alice Kitchen of the Blackburn Female Reform Society, and Mary Fildes of its Manchester counterpart. Fildes was on stage with Hunt, as Delia is with Hartford, and carried the banner that Delia carries. Female reformers of the period were parodied in cartoons, often portrayed as whores.

The excoriating poem *The Mask of Anarchy* by Percy Bysshe Shelley, quoted at the beginning of the novel, was written in 1819 after word of the Peterloo Massacre reached Shelley in Italy. It expressed what he called 'the torrent of my indignation'. It was not published during his lifetime, eventually appearing in 1832.

The Cato Street Conspiracy

The failed rebellion in which Sarah takes part is broadly based on the Cato Street Conspiracy. The conspirators, led by Arthur Thistlewood, were Spencean Philanthropists: followers of the radical writer Thomas Spence. They met in the loft of a disused stable in Cato Street, near Edgware Road, overlooked by a public house called the Horse & Groom.

When news reached them of a Cabinet dinner to be held at the Grosvenor Square home of Lord Harrowby, the group hatched a plan to storm this event, behead the Cabinet members, and form a provisional government.

The dinner, though, was a fiction fed to the conspirators by one of their number, George Edwards, a police spy. From the vantage point of the public house, the Bow Street Runners watched the conspirators assemble before moving in to arrest them. Briardown's statement just before the group is arrested uses the words of Thistlewood.

Five of the conspirators, including Thistlewood, were hanged then decapitated, and a further five were transported for life. The hangings described in this book are drawn from reports of the executions.

The radicals with whom Sarah makes contact in Sydney are completely fictional, and I'm not aware of the historical use of the ouroboros (serpent) symbol in any of the contexts described in this book.

Mary Reibey

Molly Thistle isn't a fictional stand-in for Mary Reibey, but she does owe something to the woman depicted on the Australian twenty-dollar note.

In 1791, fourteen-year-old Mary Haydock was convicted of stealing a horse in Lancashire and sentenced to transportation. She was dressed as a boy and went under the name James Burrow. A few years after arriving in Sydney, at age seventeen she married Thomas Reibey, a former East India Company man who owned farms and other property, and traded in corn, wheat and cedar.

Thomas's business interests frequently took him away from Sydney, and Mary ran the business in his absence. Among other roles, she was a hotel keeper. When Thomas died in 1811, leaving her with seven children, she took over the business and expanded it dramatically, amassing property, buying ships and trading. At one point she held 405 hectares of land and was one of the richest people in the colony.

Mary Reibey has always fascinated me. In particular, I can't help wondering what it must have taken to run such a successful business as a woman and former convict in the society in which she lived, so I suppose it was inevitable that she would provide inspiration for one of my characters.

The Wreck of the Dunbar

The wreck of the *Serpent* is fictional, but it does share some characteristics with an actual wreck that occurred some decades later.

On the night of 20 August 1857, in heavy seas and thick rain, the *Dunbar* was driven into the cliff face a little south of the entrance to Sydney Harbour. The impact would have been tremendous – at the National Maritime Museum I held thick bolts, which once kept the hull together, that had been bent into 's' shapes by its force. One hundred and twenty-one people lost their lives that night; only one, a sailor named James Johnson, survived. He was thrown far enough up the cliff to grab hold of a ledge, and two days later was winched to safety. The wreck of the *Dunbar* remains New South Wales' deadliest maritime disaster.

We'll never know exactly why the *Dunbar* collided with the cliff during that storm. It's possible that Captain James Green mistook The Gap for the entrance to the harbour, or that he believed he had overshot it and made a sharp turn. Perhaps one factor was the positioning of Macquarie Lighthouse, some distance from the tip of South Head. Today, if you stand on North Head, you can look across the harbour mouth to the red-and-white striped Hornby Light on South Head's northernmost extremity, built as a direct result of the wreck of the *Dunbar* and that of the *Catherine Adamson* nine weeks later.

The description of the wreck of the *Serpent* draws on contemporary accounts of the aftermath of the *Dunbar* wreck, especially *A Narrative of the Melancholy Wreck of the 'Dunbar'*, a pamphlet published soon afterwards.

The idea for this story grew out of my interest in the *Dunbar*. I hope you enjoyed it.

Meg Keneally
Sydney, May 2020

FURTHER READING

Some of books and documents I relied on in writing this story include:

'Manchester Political Meeting', *The Manchester Observer*, 21 August 1819

'Female Reformers', *The Black Dwarf*, 24 November 1819

The Women at Peterloo: The Impact of Female Reform on the Manchester Meeting of 16 August 1819, M.L. Bush, *History*, vol. 89, no. 2 (294), 2004, pp. 209–232

The Peterloo Massacre, Robert Reid, Windmill Books, 2017

Peterloo: The Story of the Manchester Massacre, Jacqueline Riding, Apollo Books, 2018

Peterloo: The English Uprising, Robert Poole, Oxford University Press, 2019

Writings of the Luddites, edited by Kevin Binfield, Johns Hopkins University Press, 2004

The Struggle for the Breeches: Gender and the Making of the British Working Class, Anna Clark, University of California Press, 1995

Enemies of the State: The Cato Street Conspiracy, M.J. Trow, Wharncliffe Books, 2011

The Cato Street Conspiracy, John Stanhope, Jonathan Cape, 1962

The Political Works of Thomas Spence, edited by H.T. Dickinson, Avero (Eighteenth-Century) Publications, 1982

Narrative of the Cato-Street Conspiracy, Anonymous, Published by John Fairburn, 1820

The Cato Street Conspirators in New South Wales, George Parsons, *Labour History*, no. 8 (May 1965), pp. 3–5, Liverpool University Press

A Narrative of the Melancholy Wreck of the 'Dunbar,' Merchant Ship, on the South Head of Port Jackson, August 20th, 1857, Anonymous, Published for the Proprietors by James Fryer, 1857

Mary Reibey – Molly Incognita: A Biography of Mary Reibey 1777 to 1855, and Her World, Nance Irvine, Library of Australian History, 1982

Dear Cousin – The Reibey Letters: Twenty-two Letters of Mary Reibey, Her Children and Their Descendants, 1792–1901, edited and with a commentary by Nance Irvine, Hale and Iremonger, 1992

Minding Her Own Business: Colonial Businesswomen in Sydney, Catherine Bishop, NewSouth, 2015

Aboriginal Australians: A History Since 1788, Richard Broome, Allen & Unwin, 2010

The Rocks: Life in Early Sydney, Grace Karskens, Melbourne University Publishing, 1997

So Much Hard Work: Women and Prostitution in Australian History, edited by Kay Daniels, Fontana, 1984

Depraved and Disorderly: Female Convicts, Sexuality and Gender in Colonial Australia, Joy Damousi, Cambridge University Press, 1997

Macquarie, Grantlee Kieza, ABC Books, 2019

Archaeology in The Rocks, Sydney, 1979–1993: from Old Sydney Gaol to Mrs Lewis' Boarding-house, Jane Lydon, Australian Historical Archaeology, 1993

READING GROUP QUESTIONS

1. Why do you think Sarah chooses to be a revolutionary at the start?
2. Why do you think Sarah changes her opinion about the best way to change the world?
3. What did you think of the depiction of the colony in New South Wales at the start of the 19th century? What do you imagine life was like at that time?
4. How does the novel explore gender and the position of women in the early 19th century?
5. In what ways do Briardown and Molly Thistle represent different ways of changing society?
6. Who was your favourite minor character?
7. How do you think Sarah's life would have been different if she had remained in Britain?
8. How does the novel explore secrecy and betrayal?
9. In what ways are the themes of *The Wreck* relevant to the modern day?
10. What do you see as the significance of the book's title? To what extent can wrecks be both physical and metaphorical?